ONE MORE PAGE BEFORE I KISS YOU

VICTORIA CONNELLY

Cover design by Jane Dixon Smith
Author photo © Roy Connelly

ISBN: 978-1-910522-25-7
Published by Cuthland Press.

To Cindy and Jules with love

FOREWORD

I can hardly believe that it's been six years since the last Book Lovers novel was published. Thank you for being so patient waiting for the next instalment! My beloved characters have never been far from my thoughts and I've been longing to return to them and find out what they've all been up to.

This novel picks up where we left everybody and there are plenty of gentle reminders of past storylines. However, you don't need to have read the previous books to enjoy this one, although I'd be very happy if you did because I loved writing them and you might have fun reading them.

So, welcome back to Castle Clare, Suffolk! Come and catch up with all the Nightingale regulars and meet cousin Megan – at long last. She has quite a story to tell you!

Victoria x

CHAPTER ONE

Megan Nightingale might have been biased but, to her, the library at Castle Clare was the loveliest in the world. Perhaps it was because of its size which was small, cosy and welcoming. Maybe it was because of its setting – tucked behind the main square of the little market town. But mostly it was because it felt like home and she simply couldn't imagine working anywhere else. To her, it was a peaceful sanctuary – a book-lined palace in miniature where she could serve the needs of the beloved town she'd grown up in.

It amused her how the whole of the Nightingale family worked with the written word in one form or another. It had all begun with Megan's Grandpa Joe and Grandma Nell. They'd opened the very first bookshop in Castle Clare and Megan's father and uncle had been raised in the rooms above the shop where her cousin Sam was now living. While her uncle and aunt had taken over the running of the bookshop, Megan's father had become a university lecturer, teaching English Literature and Theatre Studies. Ralph Nightingale had specialised in Arthurian legends and Megan's older brother had thus been named Tristan. Megan adored him. He was a freelance editor and also organised Castle Clare's literary festival each summer which Megan loved to help him with whenever she could.

Then there was her younger brother Luke. He was a journalist but had aspirations to write a novel one day. Only 'one day' always seemed to be some vague sort of date in the future. Perhaps, Megan thought, he should talk to Castle Clare's local author, Callie Logan. Megan was always getting requests to order more of the famous author's books and they had pride of place on a stand in the children's corner.

Since the opening of that first bookshop in Castle Clare, the Nightingale family had bought the shop next door and then one across the street. All three were now run by her cousins Sam, Josh and Bryony. Polly also helped out on a part-time basis, covering for her siblings in between school runs. It was safe to say that books and the written word were pivotal in the lives of the Nightingales.

Depending how quiet business was in their bookshops, Megan's cousins visited her regularly. She loved how close they all were. In fact, Megan had shared a house with Bryony until recently, but life had evolved and both Megan and Bryony had felt it was time to get places of their own. Still, she missed those late-night chats on the sofa over mugs of hot chocolate, discussing the latest film adaptation of a beloved book or bemoaning the lack of decent men in Castle Clare.

But that was before Ben had returned, Megan mused, thinking of Bryony's first and only true love. The couple had had a lot to forgive and forget after Ben's abrupt departure six years ago, but Megan had no doubt that they were together forever now.

As the door of the library opened that July morning, Megan glanced up from the shelf in fiction where half the books seemed to be in the wrong order. She smiled politely. It was one of her regulars and she'd given him the nickname The Loner because he never interacted with anyone and he didn't return her smile now – he simply nodded. Occasionally, she'd catch him looking at her and wonder if he needed help, but he never asked. He just came and sat at one of the computers for an hour or so.

The next customer to enter the library that morning was Winston Kneller. Dear Winston. He came in almost every day to read the newspapers and to chat. He rarely got a book out even though he belonged to Sam and Polly's book club. He said he liked to support the bookshops when he was able to. Winston was never any trouble, but there had been that incident when Megan had let him bring his old dog, Delilah, in out of the rain. The resulting smell when Delilah had passed wind under the communal table had forced Megan to ask them both to leave. Luckily, it had stopped raining by then.

Hortense Digger – or Honey as she preferred to be known – was the next to arrive. She was wearing a cerise-coloured dress with a yellow jacket and a slash of red lipstick. She could always be found browsing the romantic novels while her arch enemy, Antonia Jessop, turned her nose up whenever she noticed such books in the library. It was her mission in life to rid such books from the shelves and replace them with titles that had been nominated for prestigious literary awards.

'But nobody wants to read *those* sorts of books!' Honey would tease.

Megan had long learned never to judge her customer's tastes and to leave people alone in her library. She always smiled and offered a friendly hello – just to let them know that she was there if they needed assistance. But many people just came in to sit or to browse, or simply to warm up or keep dry. It really wasn't any of her business as long as they were reasonably quiet.

But there was one customer she had a particular soft spot for – Flo Lohman. She often came into the library after picking up her great-nephew, Sonny, from school. It had been lovely for Megan to watch the developing relationship between Flo and Sonny. The young boy had grown so much in confidence and was now able to come up to the desk and request a book all on his own – a once terrifying prospect for him. Of course, there'd been that awful episode with his father's recent arrest and prosecution for stealing artefacts from a local church. It had been in all the local papers, but the people of Castle Clare had done their best to shield Sonny from the news. That was one of the things Megan loved most about living in a small town: everyone looked out for each other.

As the door to the library opened once again, Megan noticed that a poster had caught in the breeze and fallen from the notice board. She went to replace it. It was for Sam and Polly's book club, inviting new members to join for the September meeting when they would be reading *84 Charing Cross Road* by Helene Hanff. Being a bookworm herself, Megan had read it a couple of times already and knew that it would be a big hit. She smiled as she remembered it was written completely in letter form, recording a twenty-year correspondence between an American bookworm and an English bookseller. It was full of wonderful discussions about secondhand books. What was that passage she particularly adored? Something about Helene Hanff loving the way that secondhand books fell open to the pages a reader has read the most.

Oh, dear, Megan thought. She was going to have to search for it now. That was the trouble when you were a bookworm – words, phrases and sentences got a hold of you sometimes and you simply had to give in to them.

If she wasn't mistaken, there was a copy of the book on the shelves right now. She scanned them quickly. Ah, yes! There it was. She pulled the paperback out from its home and flipped through the creamy white pages, wondering how well she remembered it. It was probably due a reread, she decided. She could even attend Sam's book club to discuss it. She hadn't been to a meeting yet and felt terrible about not supporting her cousins, but life just seemed so full sometimes and her evenings were a precious time for her own personal reading.

She took the book back to her desk and checked it out. For a moment, she wondered if she was doing the right thing in monopolising it when it was the next book club choice, but she knew that – like Winston – the members liked to support Josh's shop when they could and buy new copies from him.

It was approaching midday when she had a visitor. Megan loved to wear colour, frequently choosing blossom pinks and turquoise blues, yet she always felt drab whenever she saw her cousin Bryony, who not only swirled through life in full colour but dazzled with the patterns she chose and her billowing scarves, bright hair bands and ropes of beads. Today, she had her long dark hair tied back with a shiny green hair clip that looked like an exotic butterfly. Megan always wished she had the courage to wear her hair more adventurously. It was long and dark like her cousin's, but she usually just wore it loose or – if she was feeling very daring – tied back in a simple ponytail.

She smiled as she admired Bryony's clothes today. Her cream blouse was both lacy and frilly and her long skirt danced around her legs in peacock hues. Silver bangles shone at her wrists and a pair of silver and green bead earrings knocked against her neck when she moved.

'Polly's holding the fort for me so I thought I'd get this back to you,' Bryony said as she approached Megan, holding out a beautiful old copy of *Walden* by Henry David Thoreau. It was from Megan's personal collection and Bryony had monopolised it for a good long time, but cousins didn't mind about that sort of thing, did they?

'What did you think?' Megan asked, taking the book and surreptitiously checking it for creases, stains and dog-eared pages as she was wont to do.

'Well, I can see how it's a classic and ahead of its time and everything – that need to get away from society and just *be*. I love all that. But the prose is so dense – and *all* those classical allusions!'

'I know. It's not an easy read,' Megan agreed.

'I think it's probably best to just stick to all the quotes from the book on social media site. *Much* more palatable!'

'So, outside of the North American wilderness, how's everything?'

'Good! I can't believe Ben's moving in this week.'

'Wow! That's come round quickly.'

'He can't stay at his sister's forever, though. And it's time, isn't it?'

Megan noticed the slight hesitancy in her cousin's question. 'I think it might be.'

'I know he probably won't be as tidy or as quiet as you.'

'Nobody's *ever* as quiet as me!' Megan said with a grin.

'But he does have a certain... *something*, doesn't he?' Bryony gave a girlish giggle. 'I sometimes worry, though.'

Megan frowned. 'What about?'

'That he'll get itchy feet and want to go travelling again.'

'You think he will? I thought you said he was happy to be back here and ready to settle down.'

'Yes, he's said that – countless times. Probably to appease me.'

'I think you're worrying too much.'

'I know. I just... I can't bear the thought of losing him again.'

Megan saw the look of fear in Bryony's eyes and her heart ached for her. She wondered what it must be like to love someone so intensely. She'd yet to have that experience. She'd been in a few relationships, but they'd never lasted more than a couple of months or so. Maybe she was destined never to meet anyone. The thought didn't really perturb her.

As if reading her mind, Bryony asked, 'Any interesting men in your life?'

Megan grimaced. 'Only safely tucked between the covers of a book.'

'Oh, Megan! You've got to get out more. You're a real catch, you know that, don't you? You're smart, cultured, beautiful–'

'Happily single!'

Bryony snorted. 'That's what Josh said until April Channing came to town and just look at him now all loved up!'

Megan nodded. She'd witnessed the transformation in her cousin, but she really didn't see that in her own future.

'I'm married to my books,' she told Bryony.

'That's *exactly* what Josh used to say!' Bryony leaned forward and kissed Megan. 'I'd better scoot back before Polly eats all the pastries.'

'Is Colin the Baker still wooing you with sweet treats?'

'Oh, no! We have to pay for them these days. Outrageous, isn't it?'

They both laughed and Megan watched as Bryony left the library in a swirl of colour and a jangle of bangles.

She was just about to tidy up the mess left in the children's corner after a harassed mother had had to leave in a hurry with her screaming toddler, when her mobile pinged. She usually turned it off during working hours and, if she was truthful, didn't like having it on at all. Not lately at least. Not since the messages had started arriving. But she'd been waiting to hear back from her mother to see if she needed anything from the Co-op in town which Megan could drop off after work.

She bit her lip, feeling a flurry of nerves as she picked up her phone.

Sure enough, it was another of those messages.

She quickly switched her phone off and plunged it into the depths of her handbag, placing *Walden* on top of it for good measure.

When a customer approached the desk a moment later, she greeted him with a warm smile. He would never have guessed the anxiety she was feeling.

CHAPTER TWO

Rick Wildman was born with a restless soul. He was always in search of adventure. He'd spent his childhood growing up in the idyllic Suffolk countryside with his older brother Leo, scraping his knees, falling out of trees and generally having a brilliant time. After a gap year that went on for three years and five months, in which he'd worked his way around the globe, he studied for a combined degree in history, geography and literature because he couldn't bear to choose just one subject when he loved absolutely everything. And then he surprised everyone by taking a job as a builder's assistant, taking further courses and learning all the skills required to become a builder himself.

'Why didn't you just do that to begin with?' his mother asked, perplexed as to why he'd put himself through three years of expensive education.

Rick had simply shrugged. 'It seemed like a good idea at the time.'

And that, in essence, was Rick. He lived very much in the moment, pursuing each new passion with every fibre of his being.

Now, after years of doing up other people's houses, he felt the need to find a place to call home. A proper place – not some dreadful rented property where he couldn't so much as hang a picture on the wall, let alone knock the wall down. He wanted to find a project. The trouble was that even projects cost money. The most run-down old barn in a plot of neglected land still cost hundreds of thousands of pounds.

So Rick felt almost guilty when fate seemed to intervene because, along with his older brother, Leo, he was left a sizeable inheritance from a great uncle they'd only met once. It seemed a little odd to be left so much when the two brothers had given so little to the relationship. There'd been no phone calls over the years, no Christmas gifts or birthday cards, and Rick had felt absolutely awful in case his ardent desire for enough money to buy a place of his own had somehow caused the old man's demise. But he quickly put the ridiculous thought out of his mind.

Leo used his half to pay off the mortgage on his small Victorian cottage. He'd also paid Rick to do a few repairs and then he'd rented it out while he took off travelling. Rick had been surprised as Leo had seemed so settled in his life in rural Suffolk, but a longing to see more exotic places once again hit him hard and Rick had a feeling it might have something to do with his heart being broken a couple of times in recent years. New horizons could often heal old wounds.

Of course, Leo's departure meant that Truffle and Blewit the cocker spaniels would now live with their Uncle Rick. But he didn't mind. He'd always doted on the mother and son with their glossy chocolate brown colouring, their long silky ears and their eager noses which were always ready to sniff out a new adventure.

And then the search had begun. Rick was renting a damp pokey town house and knew that, with money in the bank, this was his chance to do something wonderful. Driving Leo's Land Rover, which he'd also inherited for however long his brother was away, he had scoured the Suffolk countryside – discovering villages and hamlets that he'd never known existed. It was fun, but it was also frustrating because, the longer it took, the more he began to believe that the place he was looking for didn't actually exist.

And then, one winter morning when a sharp frost sparkled across the land, he drove out to Melton Green. The village homes were well detached – all set on a large grazing common. The cottage he was looking for was down one of the unmade tracks. The estate agent had warned him it was tricky to find as the village didn't allow for sale boards on the common. But he'd found it.

Oak Farm Cottage.

Dating back to the sixteenth century, the thatched timber-framed building had been part of Oak Farm for generations. It had been lived in by tenants but – latterly – had fallen into disrepair and was now being sold along with a good plot of land that included a section of ancient moat, a meadow, a small wood and several old barns. It was a little piece of heaven – a rural retreat – and Rick knew he could pick it up for a song, but that he'd spend his inheritance on materials to do the place up because the fact was Oak Farm Cottage was practically a ruin. Rick, however, didn't see that as a negative. It was more of an opportunity to work with the right natural, breathable materials to bring this old house to life again, and to make it truly his. It would be the greatest undertaking of his life so far and he couldn't wait to get started.

Rather wonderfully, the estate agent rang to say he was running late which gave Rick the chance to wander around on his own. He'd already done his research on the property. It had previously been two cottages but was now one house. Two brick chimneys rose above the rotten thatch which hung in tatters like hair that hadn't been brushed for a decade. The plaster was flaking off, revealing the timbers behind, like an emaciated body revealing the skeleton beneath.

Rick pressed his nose up to a dirty window, peering through the hammocks of cobweb, knowing what he'd see. There were birds nesting in the old place now. It was their home and there were feathers, scraps of nest and other detritus strewn across the room. There were even weeds sprouting up between the gaps in the brick floor. Rick was amused that the house had been left like this. A quick sweep and de-cobweb might have added a few thousand pounds, but the owner obviously didn't have the time or inclination. It was what it was.

Rick followed the path around the cottage. An overgrown lawn studded with the dead stalks of ragwort, frozen with frost, led down to a stretch of moat as long as the house itself. Rick peered into its dark depths, wondering just how deep it was. And how cold. On this winter day, it was hard to imagine ever swimming in it, but he wondered if it might provide welcome relief on a hot summer's day.

High hedges, many of them evergreen, gave the garden a sheltered feel. It truly was a little world of its own. Then the space opened out into the meadow. Again, Rick tried to imagine it on a summer's day, maybe just after being mowed. No – not mowed – *scythed*. If he was feeling energetic.

There were so many details that captured his imagination, but it was the trees that really took his breath away. Even in the heart of winter with their bare limbs revealed, he could imagine the shade and beauty they'd provide throughout the warmer months and the habitats for wildlife.

The peace of the place enveloped him. He could feel that it had been loved once. He found a storm-smashed greenhouse and the rotten timbers of raised beds, and knew that the garden would have grown produce for the household. He tried to imagine the generations of families who would have lived here. And now him – because he was quite certain that this was the place he'd been looking for even before the estate agent arrived to show him around indoors.

Rick knew that Oak Farm Cottage was the project of a lifetime. He now had quite a bit of experience working on old buildings, but this house was going to use so many skill sets he didn't have. Of course, you could learn anything you needed from YouTube these days, couldn't you? And old-fashioned books too. He'd already made a list of books he was going to look up – big costly tomes, they were. Perhaps he should see if he could get them from the library before splashing out on them. He'd need every penny he had for the building work.

But, even if it cost him all of his inheritance as well as the meagre sum he'd managed to save after years of hard graft and paying off his student loans, it would be worth it for this was a place where he could grow and, one day, maybe even raise a family. He grinned. He was getting ahead of himself. *Way* ahead. But there was something about the place that was weaving some kind of romantic spell over him. It was as if he could see the past, present and future all at once and that was a very heady feeling indeed.

CHAPTER THREE

The interesting thing about a library collection, Megan thought – and not for the first time – was that it was ever changing with books being borrowed and returned, others being reserved by other libraries and her customers ordering titles she didn't have from the county's collection. There was also the almost constant job of 'weeding'. Megan always enjoyed that. She'd patrol the shelves looking for old books that looked ready for retirement – either from lack of love and interest or from too much. She was always surprised by how much life a book could hold – there were cracked spines and creased covers, pen and pencil marks, coffee rings and food stains, dog-eared corners, pages trying to escape their confines and – in a couple of cases – that concertinaed look when a book had got wet and had doubled in size. Megan would often shake her head, wondering just how her poor books became so battle-worn. Sometimes, a book would go on to be sold to raise much-needed funds for the library, but some just had to be discarded. They had served their time.

Megan had just weeded out a beloved beach read which smelled distinctly of factor 50 when she caught sight of a man entering the library. He was standing at the entrance looking at the posters and she saw his eyes rove over the one advertising the upcoming Castle Clare Literary Festival as well as the Knit and Natter group, but she doubted very much if that would be his sort of thing. Still, you should never judge, she told herself. If he wanted to choose one of the colourful balls of wool from her stock cupboard and join in with the regular circle of knitters, she was sure they'd welcome him. Actually she couldn't help thinking that there wouldn't be raised eyebrows within the group so much as flirtatious eyelashes because he was certainly handsome. Tall with broad shoulders and a mop of dark hair that fell across a tanned face and curled over the frayed collar of his checked shirt, she knew that he definitely wasn't a library regular because she would have remembered him.

As he came inside and approached the desk, Megan joined him, placing the beach-worn paperback on a shelf to deal with later.

'Hello,' she said with a smile. 'Can I help you?'

'I'm not actually sure,' he said, his voice deep and melodious. 'Do you have any old maps of the area?'

'I'm afraid not. It's years since we've kept maps in the smaller branches. You'd have to go into Ipswich or Bury St Edmunds for those. But you could try your local church too. They often keep a few.'

'Oh, great. Thanks.' He smiled and she noticed how lovely his eyes were – a sort of chestnut flecked with amber, she thought, bright against his suntanned face.

She cleared her throat in an attempt to sweep clean her mind. 'Is there anything else I can help you with?'

'Yes,' he said quickly. 'I was hoping you had some books. I've got a list here.' He presented her with a small piece of lined paper torn from a notebook. It looked like it had been shoved in and out of pockets a number of times, but the handwriting on it was beautiful. Scanning the titles, she sighed.

'I don't think we have any of these here, but let me check the system for you.' She sat down at the computer and, a few minutes later, she had her answer.

'You can order three of them from other libraries. I can do that for you now if you like. But we don't have this one,' she said, pointing to one of the titles, 'and it's out of print, I'm afraid.'

'Yes. I thought it might be.'

'And this one isn't available in Suffolk at all. I can order it through the Norfolk library service. But there'll be a charge.' She told him how much and he nodded.

'Cheaper than buying it,' he said.

'Are you a member of the library?'

'Erm, yes. But I'm afraid my card is a bit worn.'

He dug his hand into a trouser pocket and brought out a dozen battered cards, a penknife and a wizened conker. She tried not to giggle.

'Here,' he said, passing the battered library card to her.

'Ah, yes. That is a bit tatty, isn't it? I'll get you a new one. It won't take a minute.' She opened a desk drawer and brought out a choice of three bright cards to choose from. 'We have red, purple or green.'

'Ooooh,' he said. 'Decisions.'

'I know. We like to make life as interesting as possible.'

'I think I'll go for the green,' he said.

'Good choice,' Megan said. 'Just sign the card to make it yours and I'll link it to you on the system.' She tapped a few keys, using the information from his old card. 'Rick Wildman, right?'

'That's right.'

'Are you still at the same address?'

'Kind of.'

She frowned.

'I'm in the process of moving out of one place and moving into another,' he explained. 'Only, well, the new one doesn't have a roof yet. Or walls.'

Megan smiled. 'Sounds like a project.'

'Oh, it is. Hence the books I'm ordering. I need all the info and tips I can get.'

'Well, good luck with it,' she said. 'You're good to go with your new card.'

'Thanks! I'll – erm – take a look around.'

'Let me know if you need anything else,' she told him and he gave her a big warm smile the like of which she'd never experienced before because it was the first smile she'd felt deep down in her belly.

Tea. That's what was needed. Maybe it was indigestion she was feeling in her belly. A cup of peppermint would put paid to that. She nipped into the little room at the back of the library where there was a sink and kettle. There was also a huge box of teabags donated by a local café and which any member of the library could help themselves to. This was also the room where board games were kept together with jigsaws, a box of Lego and a basket of wool for the Knit and Natter group. It always warmed Megan's heart that so much of what made people smile was very simple indeed: a cup of warm tea, a board game, a ball of wool or a book, and a few minutes of chat with a neighbour. These simple things could make all the difference especially if you were a member of the community living on your own or struggling through difficult times. The library was a wonderful hub, providing so much more than the next good read.

When Megan emerged with her steaming cup of tea a moment later, she saw that Mr Rick Wildman was still there in the library. He looked up from the non-fiction section and smiled that big warm smile again. Megan took a big slurp of her peppermint tea to combat the indigestion.

~

Rick Wildman left the library and simply couldn't stop smiling. Well, that had been a surprise, he thought. He wasn't sure what he'd imagined the little library at Castle Clare would be like. It had been years since he'd last visited. He certainly hadn't expected a beautiful young woman to be hiding away in such a place.

As he got in the Land Rover, he couldn't help recalling her pale skin. She definitely didn't see enough of the great outdoors, he couldn't help thinking. He thought of her long, dark, glossy ponytail and wondered what she'd look like with her hair loose. He shook his head, silently admonishing himself for the stereotypical image he was creating of the bookish woman who was all neat blouses and pinned back hair that needed untying.

Instead, he thought about the books. He'd been genuinely surprised by the selection there'd been considering how small the library was. There were several titles he'd wanted, but something had made him pause before he filled his arms with books. If he took just a couple, that would give him a very good excuse to come back again soon, wouldn't it? Of course, he also had those other books on order so he'd definitely be returning.

And there was something else he had to return to the library for – to find out the name of the beautiful librarian.

CHAPTER FOUR

When the delivery van pulled up outside Sam Nightingale's shop, he knew what the three boxes would contain – books! What else? Except, these were no ordinary books.

It had been a slow morning in which Sam and Grandpa Joe had dusted some shelves, completed three crossword puzzles and eaten far too many custard creams, so the delivery was very timely.

'Well, this is all very exciting,' Grandpa Joe said as he examined the boxes.

'It is, isn't it?' Sam said, getting to work with the scissors.

'It never gets old, does it? Taking a delivery of new – *old* books. Seeing them, handling them for the first time, getting to know them, dreaming about the new homes they'll go to.'

Sam smiled. It was one of the greatest joys of his job, and it was just as well that he loved it so much because his income was erratic at best. But these boxes of books should help there, he thought. He'd come across the books at an online auction and had spotted some nice titles in amongst the job lot. The only downside was not being able to handle them. He had definitely been taking a punt as they hadn't been cheap, but he hoped to turn a decent profit selling them on.

As Sam cut and ripped the tape off the first box, excitement filled him like a little boy at Christmas. But it was short-lived.

'What's the matter?' Grandpa Joe asked.

'Take a look. Or rather, take a *smell*.'

Grandpa Joe came forward and his nose wrinkled in alarm. 'They smell damp.'

'They smell more than damp,' Sam said. 'It's like they've lived in a cave since the time they were published.'

'Open the next box.'

Sam nodded and got to work. A moment later, the same damp smell rose up and Sam glanced at his grandpa.

'Third time lucky?' Grandpa Joe said.

Sam slit the third box open with the scissors and his heart sank. All three boxes were full of damp books.

'Well, I hope you can get your money back,' Grandpa Joe said.

'I'm not sure I can,' Sam said. 'The lot was "sold as seen".'

'But you didn't see them!'

'I know.'

'Did it say they were damp?'

'Not exactly.'

Grandpa Joe scratched his chin. 'So you can't send them back?'

'I don't think so, but I'll check.'

Sam walked over to his laptop on the shop counter and called up the website where he'd bought the books.

'What's it say?' Grandpa Joe asked.

'Just give me a sec.'

A moment later, Sam's heart plummeted. 'The seller's account has been closed.'

'What does that mean?'

'I think it means they knew exactly what they were doing and took the money and ran. These books are well and truly mine.'

Grandpa Joe mumbled something colourfully rude that lightened the mood a little, but the truth was that Sam had spent more than he'd really wanted to on these rare books in the hope of making a profit. But the only profit had been made by the corrupt seller.

'Well, we'd better make the best of them,' his grandpa said gamely, digging into the first box and picking out an old hardback with a faded blue cover and fine gold lettering along the spine. 'We'll dust them all and give them a jolly good airing.'

Sam nodded. He loved his grandpa's optimism, but he wasn't feeling it himself yet because he'd really needed to make some money this month – not for fripperies like new clothes or entertainment – Sam wasn't the sort to spend on such luxuries. Besides his utility bills and weekly groceries, there was little other than books that Sam actually bought. However, there was one thing he'd desperately hoped to buy this summer. He'd set his heart on it. But the likelihood of being able to afford it now was fast slipping away.

Bryony Nightingale loved the long summer evenings when there were still hours of daylight left to enjoy after she'd closed the children's bookshop for the day and headed home from Castle Clare. She sometimes took a walk, following the footpaths across the pretty countryside, but she didn't have time for one tonight because Ben would be arriving home as soon as he'd finished teaching at the college. He'd texted to say that the Ipswich traffic was a nightmare and he'd be later than he'd hoped, so that gave Bryony the opportunity to pay a quick visit to a friend.

Cuckoo Cottage was within walking distance of Bryony and Ben's place at Springfield Terrace. It was a pink delight that sat on the main road into Great Tallington and looked – at least to Bryony – like a French Fancy with its rounded thatched roof and confection pink plasterwork. It was the home of Flo Lohman and her great-nephew, Sonny. Bryony always loved her visits there, helping out in the garden and with the animals whenever she could. Ben would often join her. Just last month, he'd helped to fix the roof of the donkeys' stable. Belle and Beau had been so appreciative that they'd eaten a hole right through his shirt sleeve when he'd stripped off because of the heat.

Bryony knew that she would be wasting her time knocking or ringing the bell so went straight round to the garden via a little path to the side of the house which was overgrown with weeds. She made a mental note to do something about that as soon as she had time.

'Flo?' she called. 'Sonny?'

'Bryony?' Flo came out of her potting shed, her white hair circling her face in a sort of Brigitte Bardot meets the Medusa kind of style.

'Hi Flo! I've come to buy some eggs.'

Flo waved a hand at her. 'You don't need to buy them. I've got plenty in the house. Come and get a box.'

'How are you? I've been meaning to come over. It feels ages since I've seen you.'

'We're fine, my dear! How are things with you and Ben? Is he driving you up the wall yet?'

'It's only been a couple of days, Flo!'

'That can be enough with some men!' Flo said with a grin.

They left the bright garden, entering the cool of the cottage kitchen.

'Cup of tea?'

'Oh, no thank you,' Bryony said quickly. She'd learned that hygiene was not Flo's strong point and the first cup of tea she'd accepted – the one with the potato peeling stuck to the bottom of the cup – had also been her last.

They walked through to the living room and it was then that Bryony saw there was yet another addition to the Lohman household.

'You've got a dog!'

Flo nodded. 'It does seem that way, doesn't it?'

'Is it a dachshund?'

'Mostly. He's a cross, though, and I'm not sure what the other half is.'

'He's *adorable*!' Bryony said, bending to give the animal a fuss.

His coat was a silky chestnut and his eyes were calm – friendly but assessing.

'He's a dear thing,' Flo said. 'A good friend of mine – Edie – just got him, but then she had a bad fall. Well, I should say, she had *another* bad fall. Anyway, her family persuaded her to go into a home and she asked if I'd take her little dog.' Flo sighed.

'You never could turn down an animal in need, could you, Flo?'

'I do find it rather hard,' Flo admitted. 'But I'm not sure I can look after him properly. He's a lively little thing and of course, Sonny adores him! But he chases after the hens and I can't have that. It's cruel to keep him locked inside and I do like my girls to free range.'

'Didn't Edie's family want him?'

'Edie said no. They all work full-time and didn't want the responsibility anyway.'

Bryony nodded and, before she could think about the consequences, burst out, 'I'll take him!'

'What?'

'It'll be the perfect solution – he'll be just across the road and you and Sonny can visit him whenever you like. I know it's a sudden decision, but my family's always had dogs and I'd love to have one. It's the perfect time with Ben living with me now. We'll be a real family with a dog!'

'But your work, my dear?'

'That's no problem. I can have him with me in the shop. It'll be wonderful. The customers will love him,' Bryony said, thinking of all the children who came into the shop each day after school. 'What's his name?'

Flo pursed her lips. 'He doesn't actually have one. Edie couldn't make up her mind, and me and Sonny have been arguing about it. I want Fudge, but Sonny wants to name him after some singer I've never heard of.'

'We'll think of something,' Bryony assured her. 'Do you want me to take him now?'

Flo gasped. 'Really?'

'Does that work for you?'

Flo looked thoughtful. 'I think it might be less confusing for the dog. Don't want him getting his paws *too* firmly under the table, do we?'

'Good idea.'

'We have all his things. There's a lovely new soft bed he adores. Some toys. His food and water bowls are in the kitchen and we've got two leads, a bag of food and several packets of treats. He even has a little jacket for the colder weather. There's all his brushes too. His long coat needs a bit of attention.'

'Like my hair!' Bryony laughed and then suddenly felt excited. 'I can't wait to see the look on Ben's face when he gets home.'

'I hope I'm not going to get you into trouble!'

'No, of course you're not. Ben loves dogs. We've actually talked about getting one.'

It was just then that Sonny came running into the room.

'Hi Sonny!' Bryony chimed. 'How are you?'

His face was full of summer freckles and his eyes sparkled with joy. 'I've got an egg!' he said, holding up the long pale egg in his hands.

'So you have!' Bryony said with a laugh as she saw a white hen feather stuck to the top of it.

'It looks like Marie Antoinette!' Flo said.

Sonny looked confused.

'Pop it on the rack in the kitchen, Sonny,' Flo told him and the boy left the room. Flo turned back to Bryony and said in a whisper, 'Don't say anything yet about the dog.'

'Will he be upset?' Bryony asked.

'You'd be surprised. He's a very resilient lad. I'm sure he'll understand when I explain that I can't have a dog chasing my hens. He's just as attached to my girls as I am. I was watching him the other day. He was sitting by the coop cuddling one of the ex-bats we rehomed last month.' A smile spread across Flo's face as she recalled the scene. 'Chattering away to her, he was. You know, I think those hens know more about my great-nephew than I do!'

'He looks so happy these days,' Bryony told her.

'He really has blossomed, hasn't he? Remember the pale, sullen lad he was when his no-good thieving father just dumped him here one day?'

'Oh, yes!' Bryony said, recalling the first time the little boy had come into her bookshop and how shy he'd been.

'I didn't know it at the time, but that day was the best thing to happen to the both of us. I don't know what I'd do without my Sonny now.'

'He's so lucky to have you, Flo.'

Flo smiled. 'And this little dog will be lucky to have you. Come on – let's get his things put together so you can make him comfortable at yours.'

Later that evening, after taking her new companion for a walk and letting him sniff around the tiny patch of garden at the back of the house, Bryony sat nervously on the sofa in the front room. It felt funny having a dog in the house, but it was a pretty good feeling. Bryony had grown up with dogs. There'd always been at least two at any time at Campion House and, at one stage, there were even seven after Shelley the Labrador had had puppies many moons ago. But Bryony had never had a dachshund before. She grinned. Who'd have thought that a sausage dog would enter her life? It always amazed her how exciting and unpredictable life could be.

When she heard Ben's car pull in the driveway, she leapt up from the sofa. The little dog was on instant alert and she bent to fuss him. Fingers crossed, he seemed to have settled very quickly, but what would he make of Ben? And what would Ben make of him?

Bryony made her way to the front door.

'Hello!' Ben said as he got out of the car. 'Have I told you how much I love coming home to you?'

'Have I told you how much I love you coming home to me?'

He approached her and they kissed.

'What have you been up to?' Ben asked as he came into the hallway.

'What do you mean?'

He grinned. 'You've got that impish look you have when you've done something naughty.'

Bryony's mouth dropped open in shock. '*Impish!*'

Ben nodded. 'Come on – out with it!'

There was no hiding from the man who knew everything about her so she led him into the living room, watching his face closely as he clocked the dog standing in the centre of the room.

'Is that a dachshund?'

'Yes. A dachshund cross.'

'What's he crossed with? A drainpipe?'

'Don't be mean!'

'I'm not! It's just that he's...' Ben looked at the little creature, 'well, he's very long, isn't he?'

'Yes, quite the long fellow.' Bryony laughed and then her face turned serious. '*Longfellow!*' she cried.

'What?'

'That's what we'll call him. Longfellow – after the American poet. You know – the one who wrote *The Song of Hiawatha*. It's perfect! In the great tradition of dogs being named after writers in our family.'

'Oh, right!' Ben said. 'Like Brontë, Hardy and – what's Polly's spaniel called?'

'Dickens!'

Ben frowned as realisation dawned. 'Wait a minute – is he *yours*?'

Bryony shook her head. 'No – he's *ours*!'

'But where did he come from?'

'Flo's. She took him in for a friend, but he's chasing her chickens and she doesn't feel she can cope.'

'He's just a youngster, isn't he?'

'Yes.'

'It's quite a commitment, Bry.'

'I know.'

Ben bent down to give the dog a fuss. 'Wow! He's so soft. Have you felt his coat?'

'I gave him a brush after we had a walk. He loved it. He's a very good little boy.' She bent down next to Ben and placed a hand on his shoulder. 'You don't mind, do you? I didn't think you would.'

'Mind? No! He's gorgeous!'

'Not as gorgeous as you, though.'

Ben turned to face her. 'You don't need to butter me up. I think he's brilliant.'

Bryony kissed Ben and then turned back to the dog. 'Longfellow,' she said with love in her voice. 'It took a few goes, but you've definitely found your forever home.'

CHAPTER FIVE

Rick Wildman was getting to know Oak Farm Cottage intimately. Since the property had become his on a sleety sullen day back in early spring, he'd got to work clearing the inside of the muck and debris that had accumulated over the years it had stood abandoned. How could anyone let a property get into such a state, he wondered? Mind you, if it had been in immaculate condition with shiny floorboards, a nice fitted kitchen and thick curtains at the windows, there would have been no way Rick would have been able to afford it, and he wouldn't have wanted it anyway. He'd wanted a project and he didn't mind putting in the time and effort because that's what he had to give. Everything he had, all of his resources – physical, mental and material – would be lovingly given to this place.

But those first months of spring had been hard. The weather had been wet and cold, making conditions uncomfortable and even dangerous. He'd had to bide his time, taking a few paid jobs for other people in the meantime, and had only been able to make a start outside on the roof once summer had truly arrived.

The roof was made of thatch. At least, it had been. It couldn't really be called thatch these days because there was so much moss and mould. It was a rotten messy mass that had to be completely removed. Rick had chosen to replace it with tiles instead – a less expensive material in terms of original outlay as well as insurance in the years to come. He didn't want the worry of maintaining a thatched property. Besides, he liked a bonfire and a garden barbecue and wouldn't want to be constantly worrying about sparks flying up on the merest breeze.

It had been a filthy job to remove the old thatch. He'd roped in a good friend, promising a slap-up meal at The Happy Hare in Castle Clare and as much beer as his friend could drink as payment. Once the thatch had been removed, there'd been a mad rush to secure a tarpaulin over the exposed rafters as the sky had darkened at an alarming rate.

'I'm sure that wasn't forecast!' Rick had complained, looking up into the inky depths from his position on the top of his new home.

It had been a great relief when they'd both come back down to earth safely at the end of a long day's work, the house sealed from the elements and a large pile of thatch ready to be burned.

Now, at the height of the summer, Rick was beginning to find out what the garden and grounds had in store for him. Since the recent rains, great ropes of brambles had twisted their way across the lawn and pernicious nettles had sprouted up around the moat. Rick had spent a small fortune on garden equipment and it was hard, hot work, but very satisfying when you stood back to see a piece of ground you'd cleared, taming it and making it habitable.

But he couldn't do everything himself. Luckily, working in the building trade, he knew who he could call to help him with the project. He might have wanted to do as much of the work as he could alone, but he knew that his skills would only go so far and that he needed to make good progress during the summer months. He was spending pretty much all his time at Oak Farm Cottage – getting there early each morning, walking Truffle and Blewit over the common, taking deliveries of materials and working until sunset. Sometimes, if the weather was good, he'd camp out in the garden and the dogs would sleep in the Land Rover. Rick had a small tent but, more often than not, he'd sleep on a ground sheet under the stars. And what stars there were above his home. Melton Green was far enough away from the light pollution of cities and towns to be able to fully embrace the night skies. What a joy it was to awake early on his makeshift bed on the lawn beside the moat. He'd often just lie still, listening to the birdsong and watching the movement of the wind through the trees that surrounded his property. It was certainly a more pleasant experience than waking up at the property he was still renting. There, he'd frequently be woken by the morning coughing of his chain-smoking neighbour who would proceed to put the radio on full blast. Rick couldn't wait to be shot of the place and move to Oak Farm Cottage full-time but, for the moment, he needed the amenities at his rental.

It was on one of his trips back to the old place to check his emails that he saw a message that made him smile. It was from Suffolk Libraries. He had two books ready to pick up from the library in Castle Clare.

Polly Nightingale had just taken Archie to school and given Dickens his morning walk in the woods behind the little terraced house on Lilac Row that they shared with Jago Solomon. She was feeling a little sluggish and wanted to check something. Dickens ran ahead to the kitchen and Polly went to the bathroom. A few minutes later, she emerged, tears misting her eyes. She'd been so sure this time. She would have made a bet on it. But it wasn't to be – she'd got her period.

She and Jago had discussed their future together and they'd agreed they'd love to have a child together, and Polly knew it was the right time because she had all the same feelings she'd had in the run-up to getting pregnant with Archie. Of course, this pregnancy would be different because the father would be different. She'd been granted a divorce from her husband Sean after he'd gone missing again, and after the bruises he'd inflicted on her at their last fateful meeting. If it hadn't been for her beloved spaniel coming to her rescue that night, Polly dreaded to think how it might have ended.

Now, as she entered the kitchen, Dickens looked up from his basket and got up to walk towards her, as if instinctively knowing that his mistress needed the comfort of a wet nose and a waggy tail.

'I thought I was pregnant,' she whispered to him. His calm, freckled face looked up into hers although it was a little blurry because she was still crying. She sniffed and wiped her eyes on the back of her sleeve. She had to pull herself together. There was plenty of time. She wasn't exactly over the hill. But there was a desperation in her – a hunger to have a child with Jago and give Archie a little brother or sister. She felt as if it would make their family complete and create a bond that would thoroughly unite them all.

Since leaving her old home and moving in to the house on the outskirts of Castle Clare, Polly had felt more contented than at any time of her life. She was lucky to have left those dark days behind her. She'd even made the decision to change her name from her married one of Prior back to Nightingale. Archie had too although she'd told him it was his decision and he didn't have to change it if he didn't want to.

Like her, Archie had bloomed since Jago had come into their lives. She'd never forget the dramatic way it had happened – with Archie running out in front of Jago's motorbike because he'd seen a scrap of litter and was so focused on racing after it that he didn't see the bike at all. Luckily Jago had swerved in good time, running the bike across the village green and leaving a huge skid mark which the neighbours had complained about for weeks. But he'd quickly become a part of Polly and Archie's routine and she couldn't imagine life without him now.

Polly certainly hadn't been looking for love – especially not with someone so much younger than her. She'd known people would talk, but Jago just shrugged it off. Who cared if you were a mere thought in the mind of somebody else for a few miserable moments, he'd tell her? He always could make her smile, but she wasn't sure if he'd be able to pull her out of her current mood now that she'd found out she wasn't pregnant.

Stealing herself for the day ahead, Polly made a cup of tea and then returned to the bathroom to wash her face and apply a good coat of make-up. She might not be feeling colourful, but she could jolly well apply some brightness to her face to fool everybody else.

Alas, when she entered Bryony's bookshop half an hour later, her sister saw right through her.

'Oh, Pol! What's the matter?'

Polly sighed, her shoulders drooping in defeat and Bryony rushed out from behind the counter and wrapped her in a hug. No more words were needed.

'Listen,' Bryony said, 'I've got cheese straws from the bakery. Want to help me out with them?'

Polly nodded.

'And come and meet Longfellow.'

Polly looked around in confusion. 'Who? Where?'

'Behind the counter.'

Polly gasped as she looked at the little dog curled up in his basked. 'Oh, Bry! Is he yours?'

As Bryony went to get the cheese straws, she filled Polly in on Longfellow's story. 'I'm totally smitten with him and Ben even suggested we let him sleep in our room.'

'Oh, don't start something you might regret,' Polly warned.

'I put my foot down although I might have sneaked him in on his first night. Poor darling was crying and my heart just ached for him. We're his third home, you see, and it must be so confusing for him.'

'Well, he looks pretty settled now,' Polly said, taking the cheese straw Bryony held out towards her. 'How do you think he'll get on with all our dogs? They're a lot bigger than he is.'

'I know. But I think they'll be okay. Spaniels are gentle, aren't they? And Hardy's not got a bad bone in his body unless there's a rabbit in the garden. But I think I'll let him get properly acclimatised first before introducing him to everyone at Sunday lunch.'

'Good idea. It can be a lot for anyone to take in all at once. I still remember how you all pounced on Jago when I first brought him home.'

Bryony giggled. 'We do love a newcomer!'

The word *newcomer* hit Polly and she sighed again.

'Oh, Pol!' Bryony said, instantly understanding. 'It'll happen. You just have to give these things time.'

'I know. It's only...'

'You're impatient?'

Polly gave a little smile. 'Maybe. I guess I want this so much. You know when something feels right? Well, this feels right. *So* right!'

'Then it will happen,' Bryony told her. 'And, in the meantime, there are cheese straws.'

Polly laughed and took another. Bryony and baked goods were just what she needed this morning.

Sam pulled into the driveway of Campion House and sat for a moment. He felt completely flattened by the week he'd had so far despite Grandpa Joe's attempts to lighten things with his humour and determination. But he couldn't get over how he'd been hoodwinked by the online auction. After years in the book business, he really should have known better. Yet, you couldn't physically go out and vet every single copy of every single book you purchased. Sometimes, you had to take a chance. He still hadn't told Callie about it yet. She was up against a deadline for her latest children's novel and he didn't want to add to the stress she was under. Her publisher had brought the publication date forward. Apparently, that was to her advantage, they'd told her, but she was paying the price for it now with long days and late nights at the keyboard.

Getting out of the car and letting himself into his family home,

Sam was immediately greeted by Brontë the spaniel and Hardy the pointer.

'Hey, Mum!' he called down the hallway.

'Hi Sam. Come through to the kitchen. I've just put the kettle on.'

Sam walked through the house, the two dogs following. His mother turned around from the worktop and opened her arms to hug him. Sam entered her embrace. He'd long realised that there was no use protesting.

'You're never too old for a hug,' she'd tell him if he ever did dare to protest.

'Have you lost weight again?' she asked him now as she released him at last.

'I don't think so.'

'You're not eating properly. Is Callie not feeding you right?'

'Mum, it's not Callie's job to cook for me. She has work of her own to fill her time.'

'If you've a man in your life that you love, it's your job to feed him properly.'

'Blimey, don't let anyone outside these four walls hear you say that!'

She shook her head. 'I guess I seem horribly old-fashioned to you, but I couldn't see my man withering away in front of me.'

'I'm not withering away!'

'Then what is it?' Eleanor asked. 'Something's wrong, isn't it?'

There was no point in hiding it from her. If he didn't tell her, she'd find out somehow. It was just how it was in their family.

'I got hold of some bad books.'

'What do you mean by *bad* books?'

'They were damp. All three boxes of them.'

'*Three boxes*!' Eleanor looked horrified.

'I was hoping to make a little bit of money quickly.'

'Oh, dear! Are you in trouble? Is your plumbing up the spout again?' She gave a little laugh at the unintended pun.

'Very funny. And, no – it's not the plumbing. It's...'

'What?'

He sighed. 'I want to buy something. Something for Callie.'

'Not a first edition of anything ghastly?'

'No!' Sam said, grinning as he remembered the first edition M R James book Callie had bought him for Christmas and how much trouble it had stirred up in the family.

'Then what?' she asked and then the penny dropped. 'Sam!'

'*Shush*! I don't want everyone knowing about it. You know Bryony and Lara are terrible at keeping secrets like that.'

'Oh, Sam! I'm so excited for you.'

'She hasn't said yes yet, Mum!'

Eleanor suddenly looked anxious. 'You think she might say no?'

'Well, she's been married and divorced before, hasn't she?'

'But so have you and it obviously hasn't put you off.'

Sam smiled. No, it certainly hadn't. At least, it had for a while. He hadn't so much as even wanted to date again, but then Callie Logan had walked into his bookshop, picked up a book and sniffed it. Was that the moment he knew she was the right woman for him? It was a pretty good indicator – that much was certain.

'Look, come with me,' Eleanor said. 'I have an idea.'

Sam followed his mum out of the kitchen and up the stairs to the master bedroom. It was a beautiful room with two huge sash windows overlooking the front garden. Eleanor walked across to her dressing table on which sat a large oval swing mirror and a fabric-covered jewellery box which she opened. A moment later, she took out a blue ring box with gold lettering on it and handed it to Sam.

Sam opened it and looked down at the ring inside. It was a square sapphire surrounded by twelve diamonds, but it wasn't one of those sapphires which are almost black – it was a wonderfully milky blue, aged and achingly beautiful. And the diamonds looked more like pearls.

'It was my mother's engagement ring. Art Deco. You see the square shape and setting?'

'It's lovely. But I've never seen you wear it.'

'No. I've always been too nervous to. But that's silly, isn't it? It's wrong to keep something so beautiful trapped in a dark box. It needs to be worn.' She smiled and her message was clear.

'I can't take this!'

'You don't like it?'

'No, I *love* it, but – it's yours, Mum!'

'It's mine to give to you. And, if I know Callie, I think she'll adore something with a bit of history about it.'

Sam nodded. 'Yes. I'd already thought about an antique ring. I bought a new one for Emma, remember?'

'I remember.'

'It wasn't much and I don't think she ever forgave me for that particular slight. But I didn't have a lot of money back then.' He grinned. 'Or now!'

'The lot of a secondhand bookseller!'

'Yes. But I knew she wouldn't want a vintage ring.'

'If I may say, other than choosing you as a husband, Emma had very poor taste.'

Sam gave a wry smile. 'Mum?' he said a moment later. 'You've never spoken much about your mother.'

A sad expression danced across Eleanor's face. 'She died when you were very small.'

'Did I ever meet her? I can't remember.'

'Oh, yes! And she doted on you.'

'What was her name?'

'Mary Eliza Birch. But, when she married my father, she became Finch.'

'Finch?'

'Now, I *have* told you that before, I'm sure!' Eleanor said.

'Yes, but I'd forgotten,' Sam said. 'So you went from being a finch to becoming a nightingale?'

Eleanor laughed. 'Exactly so!' She turned her attention back to the ring. 'Now, I don't know what size it is – you might need to get it fitted especially for her.'

'She hasn't said yes yet, Mum!' Sam reminded her.

'But she probably will – at least, once she sees this ring.'

Sam gave her a reprimanding look and she laughed.

'You sure you shouldn't be giving this to Polly or Bryony or Lara?'

'Can you really see them wearing something like this? It's too old-fashioned for Bryony and Lara, and Polly rarely wears jewellery.'

'I don't know what to say.'

'Say yes!' Eleanor told him. 'Just like Callie will!'

Sam smiled and they hugged. 'Yes!' he said.

CHAPTER SIX

Leaving Truffle and Blewit at home because it was too warm to leave them in the Land Rover, Rick drove into Castle Clare, parking on Church Street and walking the short distance to the library, only he managed to miss the turn and ended up in somebody's front garden. Frowning, he tried again, finding the library at the next turn.

He paused before entering, catching sight of the dark-haired librarian inside. She was crouching beside a small boy and pointing to the shelves in front of him, nodding encouragingly. Rick watched as the young boy smiled and dared to reach out and pull a book from the shelf. Her hair was tied back in a neat bun and there was something about the thickness and glossiness of it that reminded him of Princess Leia – his first boyhood crush. He shook his head. That particular comparison wasn't helping matters. He felt tongue-tied enough around her already.

Entering the library, he smiled as she turned around from the children's section.

'Mr Wildman?'

'Please – call me Rick,' he said.

'Good to see you.'

'I've had a message saying there are a couple of books in for me.'

She nodded. 'They're on the shelf over there. You can scan them out on the machine and stamp them yourself if you like or I could do them at the desk here for you.'

'I'll let you do them. There's no telling what mischief I could do with one of those stamps,' he said, going to retrieve the books.

'A lot of people like to do it themselves,' she revealed as she took the books from him, 'although with varying degrees of success, it has to be said.' She stamped one of his books and then pointed out an upside-down stamp that straddled two columns above her own neat stamp. 'Shocking,' she said with a smile that made his heart skip at least two beats.

He cleared his throat. 'You know, I missed the turn to the library.'

'Ah! The sign's been covered by a hanging basket. Castle Clare in Bloom in all its confusing glory.'

She stamped his second book and pushed them both towards him. 'Anything else?' she asked. It was his cue to leave, only he wasn't ready to go. *Think*, he told himself. *Ask her something. Anything!*

'Can I get things photocopied here? I mean, from the books? If I need to?'

'Yes, of course. We have a photocopier here.' She pointed to the corner of the room. 'There's just a small charge per page.'

'Great.' He hadn't yet picked up his books, knowing that the minute he did so, he'd lose her and she'd probably go back to the young boy who was pulling out books willy-nilly, and he wasn't going to lose out to a toddler.

'Erm, I don't know your name. I mean, you know mine and, well, I have a feeling I'm going to be in and out of here borrowing books and it would be nice to know your name,' he said, feeling as if he was babbling. 'If that's okay?'

'It's okay. Most people know my name. It's Megan Nightingale.'

'Like the bookshop people in town?'

'That's right. I'm a cousin.'

Rick nodded. If he remembered rightly, his brother Leo had gone out with a young woman who was now seeing the Nightingale who ran the secondhand bookshop. Sam, wasn't it?

'She chose a bookworm over me!' Rick remembered his brother saying. He'd made light of the situation, but Rick could tell he'd liked her a lot. For a moment, he wondered if it was wise to have a crush on a Nightingale. Would it be disloyal of him?

Megan smiled as she pushed his books an inch closer towards him just in case he'd forgotten they were there, and any thought of loyalty to his brother went right out of the window.

'Megan!' he whispered.

She smiled again and he never wanted her to stop smiling at him. He wanted to stand there all day being smiled at.

'You know I'm doing up an old place?' he said, motioning to the books in between them. 'Hence these obscure titles.'

'Yes, you mentioned that before. I hope it's going well.'

'It's a bit of a wreck, but I think it could be beautiful. Well, I know it could. It's a bit of old England, you see. Sixteenth century, huge oak beams everywhere, a massive fireplace in the main room. And it's surrounded by fields and woods. It's even got a moat. Well, the remains of one.'

'It sounds wonderful. Exciting to have your own moat – even if it is just the remains of one.'

'It's a bit silted up. I want to get it dredged at some point so I can swim in it.'

Megan smiled. 'My brothers and I used to swim in an old moat during the summer holidays. Up on Melton Green.'

'That's where my place is! Oak Tree Cottage.'

'No! Really? That old place? We used to think it was haunted. It always looked so sad and unloved. I used to worry about it.'

'Well, you don't need to worry anymore. It's getting the attention it deserves.'

'I'm glad to hear that.'

Rick was delighted that they now had this connection. 'I can't believe you used to swim there.'

'We'd sneak through a hedge near the cottage. It was a great adventure.'

'And what was it like?'

'The water? Oh, it was always icy cold. It's fed by a spring. But it's wonderful in the summer when it's hot.'

'I've cleared a load of nettles so you can just about get in again.'

'But you've not swum in it yet?'

'No, not yet.'

'You should! A free swim is always worthwhile.'

The image of Megan swimming in his moat was just too adorable. 'Why don't you come over?' he blurted before having a chance to check himself.

Megan looked a little startled.

'Not to swim – I mean, unless you want to of course. Come and see the old place. See what I'm doing.'

She looked tempted, but bit her lip as if mulling over whether this was a good idea or not.

'I can show you what my plans are. I've got the roof off now. Walls too.'

'Sounds terrifying!'

'It's getting the proper attention it needs and, to do that, I have to take the building apart first. It's a bit scary,' he told her. 'I'd love to show it to you.'

It was then that Winston Kneller came into the library. Rick knew him from a small job he'd done on his terrace a couple of years ago.

'Good morning, Mr Kneller,' Megan said.

'Good morning, Megan. And,' he paused, tapping the air for a moment, 'Rick, isn't it?'

'That's right, sir.'

'How are you?'

'I'm good. How are you?'

'Can't complain. I mean I *could*, but we'd be here all day if we went down that rabbit hole!' He chuckled.

'No Delilah?' Rick asked and he observed a look pass between Winston and Megan that he didn't quite understand. A secret, shared history.

'Er – no. Best to leave the old girl at home on library outings,' Winston said, tapping his hat and going to sit down with the local newspaper.

Rick turned back to Megan. She was still chewing her bottom lip.

'Mr Kneller can vouch for me – if you need a reference,' Rick whispered, and was delighted when she smiled at that.

'Okay,' she said. 'I'd love to see it.'

'Yeah? Great. Shall we...' He got his phone out and they quickly exchanged numbers before agreeing on a date and time. Rick gave her directions because Megan wasn't convinced that she'd be able to find the old place again seeing as her childhood route to it had been across fields.

It was only then that Rick picked his books up. He still didn't want to leave the library, but at least he knew he was going to see Megan again. She was coming to Oak Farm Cottage!

He couldn't wait.

Lara Nightingale was home from university. She had one more year to go and she had an absolutely huge reading list for the holidays.

'It's not fair,' she complained to Josh as she sat in his shop. 'What's the point of a holiday if you have to keep working?'

'Ah, you love it!' he told her.

'Have you seen the size of some of the novels? *Vanity Fair* is the first on the list. It's over seven hundred pages, Josh!'

'I know. I read it in my final year too.'

'Maybe I'll get the audio book – get somebody else to read it for me.'

'Yes, but you can't highlight all the quotes you might need on an audio book. You really should read it properly.'

She sighed, obviously seeing that there was no easy way out of hard physical reading.

'Well, at least I've got the festival to distract me. Tristan's done most of the work, but I'll be able to take over the reins next year.'

'He said that? He's actually letting go of his grip?'

Lara laughed. 'I think he's a bit tired of it now.'

'And what are your plans?'

'Oh, you know – bigger, better!'

'Bigger? Castle Clare's only a small place.'

'I've got some ideas.'

Josh grinned. 'You always were the ambitious one in the family. But, in the meantime, you're meant to be helping me.'

She got up from the stool she'd been commandeering for most of the morning. 'Okay,' she said. 'I'm heading to the stock room. I may be gone some time!'

Josh watched her go. He loved having his little sister in the shop with him, but she could be a bit intense sometimes. Like Bryony, she had boundless energy and enthusiasm whereas he, Sam and Polly were much quieter personalities. Lara was also brutally honest and Josh had been nervous about introducing April Channing to her. But, luckily, Lara adored April. *Everyone* adored April, Josh thought with a smile. How could you not?

Josh thought back to the first glimpse he'd had of April when she'd been opening the shop across the road from his own. He'd always scorned the notion of love at first sight, but something had happened in that moment that had changed the direction of his life forever. Of course, there'd been a little confusion involving her twin sister May and a lot of anxious days when she'd disclosed her health condition to him, but they were now in a good place. Better than good, Josh told himself. Especially as it had all been so unexpected.

Josh had been married to his books. As he'd watched so many of his siblings falling in love, he'd secretly been relieved that that probably wasn't on the cards for him. And then April Channing had breezed oh so gently into his life and he'd been well and truly smitten.

Josh guessed it served him right. He'd been quite the pompous young man, stubbornly believing that he was above such things as falling in love. And now he and April were even talking about moving in together and maybe even starting a family. The trouble was, she was very close to her sister and the place they were renting together was too expensive for May to stay in on her own, while Josh's place was simply too small for the three of them and – well – even though April had given it a makeover, it was far too modern for April's taste. It looked like life was about to be shaken up for all of them if they were to move forward.

Josh glanced out of his window towards A Little Bit Bloomsbury – the shop April ran with her sister. April was on duty today, but he hadn't seen her other than to wave at from across the road. He could hold out no longer.

'Lara?'

'Yes?' her distant voice called from the stock room.

'Can you hold the fort while I head out?'

'No need to ask where you're going, is there?' Lara said as she appeared behind him.

He grinned. 'I won't be long.'

'Yeah, right!'

He didn't argue. He'd probably be ages.

Leaving his shop and crossing the road, he entered A Little Bit Bloomsbury a moment later. April was bent over a small coffee table, sanding it down, her sky-blue dress covered with a pink polka-dotted apron. She was wearing her pink glasses. She'd been having frequent headaches again and was going to make an appointment with her doctor. It was a subject neither of them liked to discuss, but it hung over them like a dark cloud on a sunny day.

'Josh!' she said as she saw him, standing up. Her long chestnut hair was held back by a colourful headscarf. She looked adorable and he instantly cupped her rosy face in his hands and kissed her.

'You okay?' he asked.

'I'm okay. You?'

'I've got Lara in today and she's doing nothing but complain about her reading list for the holidays.'

'Well, it is pretty miserable to have homework during the summer, isn't it?'

'I guess.'

'Do you want a cup of tea?'

'Not really. I just wanted to see you.'

They smiled at one another and April put her sand paper down and untied her apron. 'Do you fancy a walk?'

'Now?'

She nodded. 'I've got some sandwiches in the back. We could have an early lunch up at the castle. I'm sure Lara wouldn't mind.'

'Okay,' he said. He was very easily persuaded where April was concerned.

She grabbed her bag from the back room, turned the shop sign round to 'Back Before You Know It' and locked up. Josh waved across to Lara who'd spotted them. She was grinning widely and Josh could clearly see her *I told you so* expression.

Hand in hand, Josh and April walked through Castle Clare, crossing the main road and heading towards Castle Park and the ruins that towered over the little town. It was quite a climb to the top especially on a warm day, but the views across the rooftops and out to the Suffolk countryside beyond were worth it.

They had the spot to themselves and sat on a bench and ate the sandwiches April had made.

'How about we take the rest of the day off?' Josh suggested. 'This summer weather makes me lazy.'

'Really? I never thought I'd hear you say that.'

'Ah, life isn't all about work, you know? I've learned that since meeting you.' He leaned towards her and kissed her sun-warmed cheek.

'Josh?'

'Yes?'

'I'm pregnant.'

Josh, who'd been watching a distant buzzard, suddenly snapped his gaze back to April. 'What?'

'I'm pregnant.' April's face lit up with the most gorgeous smile he'd ever seen.

'Are you sure?'

'I did a test yesterday. Two tests. But I was pretty sure before.'

'But we...'

'I know we didn't really plan it,' she said. 'I know we said it would be better to wait. But, well – it's happening now!'

Josh's mouth had fallen open. 'I... don't know what to say. Are you feeling okay?'

'I feel fine! I mean, that could change, I guess. But I'm so excited, Josh. You know I hoped it would happen sooner rather than later?'

He reached out and stroked her hair. 'I know,' he said, realising how worried she was about her future and her failing eyesight. 'Does May know?'

She shook her head. 'I don't tell May *every*thing, you know!'

'I know.'

'I wanted you to be the first to hear.'

'So your parents don't know?'

'Not yet. But I can't wait to see their faces. Mum will be thrilled, of course. Daddy George will be ecstatic and Daddy Jeff will be getting spreadsheets out and making sure our finances are in proper shape to welcome a new life into the world.'

'Heavens! I guess we should be thinking about that!'

April laughed. 'I didn't say that to scare you.'

'Still, we should tighten our belts, I guess.'

'Yes, no more three course dinners at fine restaurants every weekend.'

'Or expensive holidays.'

'Or brand new cars.'

'I'll have to give up smoking, drinking and gambling,' Josh said.

'And I'll stop going to the nail bar every day and the hairdressers every week.'

They giggled for there were no such extravagant expenses in their simple lifestyle.

'Seriously,' Josh began.

'Since when were you anything *but* serious?' April teased.

'We should start saving.'

'I know. But there's a lot we can save money on,' April told him. 'I've just found a gorgeous little cradle online that I can do up.'

'You've been looking at cradles already?'

'I couldn't help it. As soon as I found out I was pregnant, I kind of went into nesting mode.'

Josh shook his head in wonder. 'I can't believe it.'

'You are happy about it, aren't you?'

'*Yes!* I'm just a bit stunned.'

'Me too.'

'Can I feel it?'

'I don't think there's anything to feel yet.'

Still, Josh put his hand out and April took it, guiding it to her belly.

'Definitely a boy!' he said a moment later.

'Oh, Josh!' She grinned.

'Do you want to know?' he asked. 'Should we find out?'

She frowned. 'I'm not sure. Do you want to know?'

'We could leave it as a surprise.'

'Yes, I like surprises.'

'You've certainly given me one today!' Josh said with a laugh.

'What do you think your family will say?'

'They'll be thrilled!' Josh said without needing to think about the answer. 'Especially Mum. I think she's been secretly hoping for another grandchild. Archie's getting so big these days.' He paused. 'But...'

'What?'

'Let's not tell anyone. Not just yet.'

'Why not?'

He put his arm around her. 'I want it to be our secret for a bit longer. It's such a good feeling, isn't it?'

She leaned in towards him, resting her head in the crook of his neck. 'Yes,' she said. 'It's a pretty good feeling.'

CHAPTER SEVEN

As Megan drove down the road that bisected Melton Green, she kept a close look out for the turn that would lead across the common towards Oak Farm Cottage. What had Rick said? She'd written it on a post-it stuck to her dashboard and she glanced at it now as she slowed down. She had to watch out for a farm on the right which was behind a large pond and an old oak tree. Then she was to take the next left down an unmade track and watch out for the potholes half-way down and park as soon as the house came into view.

It was quite exciting, but she couldn't help wondering if it was completely sane. And safe. She'd visited Bryony's shop during her lunch hour and told her about the invitation and her cousin had immediately rung Callie who was the fount of all knowledge when it came to the Wildman brothers seeing as she'd gone out with Leo when she'd first moved to Suffolk.

Megan had watched in alarm as Bryony told Callie that Megan was going to visit Rick at his secret country hideaway.

'What can you tell us about him?' Bryony had asked. Megan had waited, breathless, for the answer. 'Well, what can you tell us about Leo? They're brothers. There must be similarities.' There'd been another pause and then Bryony had nodded towards Megan for her attention. 'She said he's a good kisser!'

Megan tried not to think of the implications of that as she found the farm and took the next left across the common, slowing down so she could avoid the anticipated potholes. The common was baking under the summer sun, its bleached grasses blond and beautiful. She recognised the red seed of dock plants which she'd used to crumble in her hands as a child, and there were a few buttercups shining brightly.

It was a stunning place in the middle of the summer, but she couldn't help wondering what it would be like in the middle of winter with a north-easterly wind blowing all the way from Siberia. It would be pretty bleak then, she thought. Still, she noticed that there were mature trees and hedges all around the property as she approached it, providing shelter from the worst the weather could throw at it.

Parking her car a moment later, she looked at the trees that now surrounded her. And the cottage. She squinted. It really didn't look like a cottage at all – more like the skeleton of some great beast that had died in the woods many years ago. She wasn't sure what she'd been expecting, but it hadn't been something quite as extreme as this.

It was as she was getting out of the car that she heard Rick's voice and saw him coming out of a barn to her right, a huge saw in his hand. If it hadn't been for his promise that Winston Kneller could vouch for him, she might have fled right there and then.

'You made it!' he cried, the sun full on his face. It was no wonder he was so tanned, she thought. He was wearing khaki trousers with a dozen pockets up and down the legs, and a white T-shirt which made his arms look so brown.

'Your directions were great,' she told him.

'And you avoided the potholes?'

'I did!'

'Good!'

'I'd forgotten how much I loved it out here. It's like a whole other world.'

'Yeah, that's how I felt when I first saw this place. It really stole my heart. Come and see it all.' He put the saw down and led the way around the side of the cottage where a great brick chimney soared into the blue sky above. As they turned the corner, the property opened into a garden. There was an old greenhouse to the right and a couple of overgrown raised beds and, beyond, a meadow enclosed by thick hedgerows.

'Welcome to Oak Farm Cottage,' he said. 'What do you think?'

Megan looked around, taking in the tallness of the trees, the long golden grass in the meadow and the starry shapes of spent honeysuckle in the hedgerows.

'It's beautiful.' She felt Rick's eyes upon her.

'Yes,' he said.

She turned to face him, holding his gaze for a moment. 'You should be wearing a hat,' she suddenly said.

He frowned. 'Wait right there.' He ran into the house – if it could be called a house with no roof and no walls and only its basic wooden structure intact. In fact, now Megan could see that, on this side, there was probably more scaffolding than original structure.

She silently cursed herself. What had she been thinking, telling him he should be wearing a hat? Honestly! What would he think of her now? That she was a bossy, uptight librarian – that's what. And serve her right too.

A moment later, he was back out on the lawn holding two sky-blue caps in his hand. 'Promotional caps from a mate of mine. I knew they'd come in handy.' He popped one on his head. 'My mum's always on at me to wear one, but I seem to spend most of my time wearing a hard hat round here and, when I take it off, it's such a relief that I forget to put a cap on.'

'The sun's so strong today,' she said, a little more gently.

'And so you should be wearing one too,' he said, moving closer so that he could put the second cap on her.

Her breath caught at the sudden nearness of him and she felt his hands against her hair as he secured the cap.

'Shouldn't we both be wearing hard hats?' she asked, glancing at the cottage.

'Not unless you're going up the scaffolding.'

'I hadn't planned to,' she said, looking down at the dress she was wearing. Maybe she should have worn something a little more practical, she thought. But the sunny day had insisted upon a summer dress so she'd chosen her favourite one covered in tiny blue cornflowers.

'The house is pretty safe. The only danger is if a pigeon poops on you from a cross beam.'

Megan bit back a smile.

'It looks so... bare. So vulnerable like this. Was there nothing else salvageable?'

'Not really. The roof was completely rotten and the walls were just crumbling.'

'Poor house!'

'It does look odd with no roof. I had tarpaulin over it for ages once the thatch was removed, but there's a run of good weather so we can keep it off for a while. I actually love working up there. It's a whole different perspective on the property.'

Megan glanced up at the roof structure. 'Can you see the common from up there?'

'Oh, yes. You can see as far as Castle Clare. You should have a look some time – if you're up for that sort of thing.'

'I might be,' Megan said.

'You know, I'm seriously thinking of not having a roof. I love the way the birds fly in and out and through, and I've always felt easier sleeping outdoors.'

'You know we're in the UK, right?'

'Yeah, I know,' he said, almost in frustration. 'I'll just have to enjoy the roofless look for the summer.' He motioned for her to follow him inside although it was barely inside at all because you could see right through.

'The front door will be here – looking out across the back lawn towards the moat and my favourite view of the meadow.'

'I can see why it's your favourite,' Megan said, looking at the tall grasses dancing gently in the summer breeze.

'I'm going to build some shallow steps here so I can sit in the sun and just look.'

She liked that. People who took the time to just sit and look were few and far between. Unless they were sitting looking at screens, of course.

'The kitchen will be along this side. I'm going to have a big old Aga which will warm the place up in the winter. I've got one lined up from a job I was doing in a house near Sudbury. They're letting me have it for free, but I'm in charge of getting it over here which is a pretty big job.'

Megan tried to imagine the country kitchen of the future, but was finding it hard without any walls or windows.

'It has good bones,' she told him, looking around at the very impressive stud walls, beams and rafters. 'Is that the right expression for a house?'

'Why not? It has a face, don't you think? Or it will have once the door and windows go in. And the main fireplace is the heart and the kitchen is the soul. Or is it the other way around? Anyway, it's definitely a living, breathing thing.'

Megan nodded. 'You must be very patient to take on something like this,' she said.

'I've never really thought about it like that. I just – I don't know – have a vision, I guess. Does that sound big-headed?'

'No, not at all. I'd say you'd *have* to have a vision,' she said and they held each other's gaze a while. 'So, what is your vision?'

He took a deep breath, his hands on his hips as he looked around the space.

'I suppose it all centres around this fireplace – take a look.' He bent and stepped into the huge hearth and looked straight up.

Megan followed him and gasped. 'You could fit the whole Nightingale family in here. And there are a lot of us!'

He smiled and they stepped back out into the room. 'So I'm going to put a wood burner in – more efficient than an open fire. Have one or two big sofas here and – don't laugh – a rocking chair.'

'I'm not laughing,' Megan said, thinking it sounded absolutely perfect.

'I found one in an old barn on the land. It's a bit tatty, but I think I can sort it. Then…' he motioned for her to follow.

'I'm going to extend this end of the house behind the fireplace and I want my study and office area there – overlooking the moat where I can look up and watch the wildlife whenever my invoicing or tax return is getting me down.'

'Good idea.'

'And then, upstairs – once there's a floor and staircase in obviously, there'll be three good-sized bedrooms, a bathroom and – well, I'm still deciding. Three windows facing this way, though,' he said, pointing towards the moat again. 'Dormer windows.'

'Oh, I like dormer windows. They look so right in a cottage.'

'They do, don't they? And I want to make the most of this view and get plenty of light into the place.'

They stepped back outside and Megan turned to look at the house with renewed interest. It was going to be the perfect country retreat, she could see that now. And, yes, she could see roses around the door – even though there wasn't actually a door yet.

'How long do you think it'll take you?' she dared to ask.

He scratched his chin. 'I don't want to put any time pressure on myself with this project, but there's a deadline to get it watertight – probably towards the end of October when the weather changes with the clocks and we lose the daylight. It's no good leaving all my tools outside then. I'll have to be working indoors.'

'Do you think you'll make it?'

'I think I've got to.' He grinned. 'Yeah, I'll make it. Unless the weather turns now, of course. We can have some pretty erratic weather here, can't we?'

'I think you might get lucky,' Megan said as she walked towards the moat and peered down into the green depths.

'Is it as you remember it?'

'It looks smaller.'

'Just overgrown, I imagine. I'll get it opened up as soon as I can. Take some of the elder and brambles back.' He grinned. 'How would you like a tour of the rest of the land?'

Megan smiled. 'Yes please.'

'Great!' He clapped his hands together as if in excitement to show off what was now his. 'I'll just let the dogs out. You okay with dogs?'

'Yes. I love dogs.'

She watched as he walked over to the Land Rover parked in the shade of a great oak tree. Two furry faces were looking out of the back and a volley of happy barks sounded as he opened the tailgate and they jumped out.

'Meet Truffle and Blewit – mother and son. They belong to Leo, but I'm their dad while he's away. And he might have to fight me for custody if he ever comes back.'

'I can see why,' Megan said, bending to fuss them as they made a big fuss over her. 'I bet they love this place.'

'It's spaniel heaven – lots of rabbits and pheasants. Their noses are permanently fixed to the ground here.'

Megan followed as Rick strode out into the golden meadow beyond the garden, the two dogs running ahead of him. She did her best not to stare at his tanned arms, but it was hard not to. They looked so – well – healthy. She looked down at her own pale, library-worn limbs. She really didn't spend enough time outdoors, she knew that. Her whole life seemed to revolve around books. Books made her happy, but she could see how they could also lead to a very unhealthy sort of lifestyle. Being here, though, with Rick, in a secret little pocket of the Suffolk countryside felt good. She loved being surrounded by the trees and the hedgerows. It was all so green and lush. Even the air smelled green, she thought fancifully.

Rick was telling her something about coppicing, but she wasn't really listening. She watched his face as he talked. His hair didn't look quite so dark out in the fullness of the sun. She could see tawny streaks waving through the conker-brown curls and there were freckles on his face too – just a few. Enough to be cute, she thought.

'What do you think?' he asked.

'Pardon?' She swallowed hard. She felt as if he'd caught her counting his freckles.

'The shepherd's hut? It came with the land. I didn't spot it at first. Crazy, huh? There's so much land here – so much to take in – that I completely overlooked a shepherd's hut.'

'Oh! It's wonderful,' Megan said, noticing it now.

He walked up the steps and opened the door and Megan followed his lead.

'It's in a bit of a state, but I'll get round to it at some point. Make a fun place for a mate to stay. Or even to spend a night out in the meadow. At this time of year, it looks like a sea of grasses from this window, doesn't it?'

Megan took a step closer towards him to look out of the cobwebbed window. The view was, she had to admit, pretty special.

'It's lovely. The window frames–'

'Oh, that needs replacing. Rotten!'

'No – I was going to say that the window frames the view perfectly.'

He grinned. 'Right, I see!'

They laughed together and then he reached out and touched her shoulder lightly.

'Follow me.' He jumped down without touching the steps, but Megan was more careful.

'Are these rotten too?' she asked, wondering if that was the reason he'd jumped.

'I don't think so. But I can help you down if you're unsure.'

'It's okay,' she said, stepping down lightly, and then silently cursing herself for it would have been a chance to be touched by him again.

Heavens, what was happening to her? Maybe the heat of the day was affecting her. Maybe she should drive back to the safety of her library where it was cool and void of temptations.

Rick was striding ahead again.

'There are all sorts of things hiding on and *in* the land here,' he said. 'I was thrilled to find this old barn.' He pointed to his right. 'Although, like the shepherd's hut, it needs almost as much work as the house does. Good storage, though. It's pretty watertight, I think. You'd be amazed what I've found. The hedges are hiding all sorts of things. Old cars and bikes. There's what looks like a carriage too and part of a tractor.'

'You could open a museum.'

He laughed. 'The Museum of Broken Vehicles. But there's a lot of useful stuff too – bits of furniture, floorboards and windows stacked up in the barns. I'm sure I'll be able to use most of it at some point. I've also been pilfering bits from skips – with permission, of course. The other day, I found a pretty decent little chair. One of the legs had a crack in it, but that's easily fixed. And, if it isn't, it'll go on the fire to keep me warm in the winter.'

Megan smiled. 'It's good to recycle.'

'Absolutely. That's what this place is all about, I think – using the materials close to hand. I want to run it that way too, using wood from the land as fuel in the winter.'

They marched on through a second, larger meadow towards a small wood.

'This is the boundary.'

'You have your own wood?'

'Well, I actually own part of a wood already – with Leo. But this feels different.'

'Has Leo seen this place yet?'

'Only photos. I can't wait to show him around, but I don't know when he's coming back.'

'Do you miss him?'

'Yeah, I do. He's my best friend. But he needed to get away.'

'He went out with Callie Logan, didn't he?'

'You know about that?' Rick said. 'Of course you do. It was your cousin she ended up with, right?'

'That's right. Is that one of the things he needed to get away from?'

'I think so. He went out with someone after her and that didn't work out either.'

'Poor Leo. He seems unlucky in love.'

'Maybe he'll meet someone while he's away. I hope he does.'

'Ouch!' Megan cried suddenly as her cap was pulled off her head by a long bramble. 'I think I'm caught!'

'Don't move!' Rick was by her side in an instant, peering closely. 'It's got its hooks in your collar, I'm afraid.'

'Oh, no! I love this dress.'

'Just hold still,' he told her. 'I must hack these things back, but I was waiting for some free fruit before I did that. Sorry!'

'Don't apologise.'

'I'll make you a blackberry crumble when the fruit's ripe.'

'I'll hold you to it,' she said, trying desperately not to move as he carefully unhooked each thorn from her collar, his fingers touching her bare skin as he did so.

'There – you're free,' he said, bending to pick up her cap and placing it gently on her head. They gazed at each other and Megan felt the heat of the whole summer in that one moment.

And that's when it happened.

She wasn't sure who made the first move because they both sort of crashed into each other in a kiss. Her cap fell to the ground again and she felt Rick's hands around her waist, hot through the thin fabric of her dress. She pressed her hands against his chest. He felt so warm and wonderful. She couldn't remember the last time she'd been so thoroughly kissed. All she could think about – and it wasn't really a moment for thinking, not even for a librarian – was that she didn't want this kiss to end. Not ever.

But it did.

'Wow,' Rick said as they broke apart. He removed his own cap and ran a hand through his hair. 'I – I wasn't expecting that today.'

'You weren't?'

He frowned. 'Were you?'

'I... I don't know what I expected.'

He leaned his forehead against hers and she could feel his breath on her face. 'Can I tell you something?'

'Yes?'

'I wanted to kiss you that first time I saw you in the library,' he confessed.

'You did?'

'Yep.'

'Can I tell you something?' she said. 'I wanted to kiss you as soon as you pulled that funny old conker out of your pocket!'

Rick laughed and they kissed again. It was gentler this time. Sweeter. Tender. Megan's heart was still racing and she allowed her fingers to tiptoe up his bare arms as he held her face in his hands.

'You're so pale,' he whispered.

She nodded. 'I don't get out enough.'

'I can see that.'

She touched his tanned face, her fingertips seeking out his freckles. 'You're so...'

'What?'

'Outdoorsy!'

He smiled and, because her fingers were still dancing over his face, she felt his smile.

'How about you spend more time outdoors – with me?'

'Here?'

'Well, for starters, I've got some lunch waiting for us.' He bent to kiss her again. It was quick this time. Too quick, Megan couldn't help thinking. And then he took her hand in his and they walked back from the meadow towards the house.

'Who's this?' Megan said as she saw a ginger cat walking across the lawn towards them.

'Just a cat,' Rick said, bending to tickle it behind its ears. 'Must belong to a nearby farm.'

'Don't the dogs chase him?' She turned around to see that both Truffle and Blewit had flopped down in the shade.

'Nah! Old Ginger's in charge here.'

'Every country cottage needs a cat on a windowsill, I think.'

'It would be nice to have one.'

'I suppose you'll need to make a few windowsills first.'

'Well, there is that!'

'Do you think you'll keep animals here – in time, I mean?' she asked.

'I'm not sure. I hadn't given it much thought. It might be fun to have a few hens scratching away in the garden. It would certainly make a home of this place.' He clapped his hands together. 'Right, I promised you lunch!'

She watched as Rick walked towards the barn near the house. A moment later, he brought out a cool box and a picnic rug which he spread across the lawn in the shade of one of the oak trees. They sat down together and he opened the box to reveal a heap of sandwiches.

'These are amazing!' Megan told him, impressed. 'You made all these this morning?'

'Not exactly. When I make sandwiches, they tend *not* to look like these! I got them from Castle Clare.'

'So what do yours look like?'

'They're big and ugly with knuckle marks left in the bread where I've tried to make the slices stick together.'

Megan laughed.

'Would you like a drink?' He brought out two glasses wrapped in napkins together with a bottle of pink lemonade. 'I wasn't sure what you'd like so I got this.'

'It looks wonderful!'

'I hope it isn't too – you know – pink!'

'I love pink!'

'Oh, good.'

'And bubbles!'

'I thought about wine, but I wasn't sure it was a good idea in the middle of a hot day.'

'Especially if you're climbing ladders and things.'

Rick poured the lemonade into the glasses and handed one to Megan.

'To – er – to new...' he hesitated and she wondered if the word *friendship* had been on its way and if he'd had second thoughts after the kiss in the meadow.

'To whatever summer brings,' Megan finished for him, clinking her glass against his. He smiled and she could still feel that smile under her fingertips.

There were many other treats in the cool box – crudités, samosas, jam tarts and doughnuts.

As they ate, they chatted easily.

'So is Rick short for Richard?'

'Nope. It's just Rick. Does everyone call you Megan or do you get Meg or Meggie?'

'No, it's definitely Megan. Meg is a bit witchy, don't you think? And Meggie is too like a cat. But my family calls me *Min* after my initials.'

'So what does the 'I' stand for?'

'Iris.'

'That's one of my favourite flowers. We have them at the edge of the moat here.' He grinned. 'We have minnows too – another kind of *Min*. Maybe I could call you Minnow.'

Megan could feel herself blushing. It felt far too early to be giving each other nicknames even after that kiss in the meadow.

'What's your favourite thing about doing up an old place?' she asked, trying to distract herself from the kiss.

Rick gazed across the lawn towards the bare bones of the house. 'I love the intimacy through physical contact. My hands – they've touched every inch of this place.'

Megan swallowed hard and wondered if he knew the effect his words were having on her.

'What are you reading at the moment? Do librarians always have a book on the go?'

'Well, I can only speak for myself but, yes, I'm pretty much always reading two or three books at once.'

'And right now?'

'A book of poetry by Mary Oliver and *84 Charing Cross Road* for the second time.'

'You've read it before?'

'I think the best books deserve more than one outing.' She told him a bit about the book and why she loved it so much. 'People just don't write letters to each other anymore, do they?'

'I guess not.'

'Or even notes! Or – if they do – they're practical things like, *Get bread on the way home*. It's so sad!' She puffed out her cheeks in consternation at a lost world.

'I'll write to you, Megan.'

She gave him a teasing smile.

'No, I *will!*' he insisted. 'I'm not promising anything literary. It won't be written in fountain pen or on fine coloured paper or anything like that.'

She laughed. 'You don't have to write me a letter!'

'But I want to. Or at the very least a note.'

They smiled at one another and his expression was one of excitement and sincerity. She wasn't sure she believed him but, as he leaned in to give her another kiss full of memories from the meadow, she really wasn't thinking about promises.

It was when her phone beeped a moment later that the spell broke. She brought it out of her bag, her face falling as she read the message.

'What is it?' Rick asked.

'Nothing,' she said, quickly putting her phone away.

CHAPTER EIGHT

When Megan Nightingale received the first message on her Facebook page, she'd simply deleted it. The next one too. Then, when similar messages started to appear on her other social media platforms, she'd done her best to block them. She'd even reported a few of them. But up they would pop again from different accounts.

It was when they started to arrive on her work account that she began to get seriously worried. That was much more serious and she couldn't simply write it off as some random attack on the internet. This was personal now. They were targeting her as an individual. And they were getting progressively more threatening.

In the beginning, the messages had been annoying but vague.

You're so pretty.

I love your smile.

Want to chat?

Megan had had similar ones in the past – usually purporting to be from military men or surgeons, their avatars clearly stolen from somebody else's profile. Didn't every woman get those? But, within a couple of weeks, they'd grown more sinister as well as more frequent.

I'm watching you.

Don't think you can stop me.

I know exactly where you are.

She'd had several sleepless nights and spent her working hours watching the customers who came into the library with a little more attention than normal. But surely it couldn't be anyone she knew? Even the man she called The Loner wouldn't do something like that, would he?

But, no matter how many hours she spent fretting and trying to work it out, Megan simply couldn't understand who'd be sending her such messages. And *why*? It wasn't as if she was a public figure or anything unusual like a singer or an actress, and she'd always thought of herself as fairly ordinary to look at especially when compared to her beautiful cousins Bryony and Polly or the vivacious Lara. There was nothing vivacious about her, she thought. She'd always lived such a quiet life even by the standards of her own quiet family, and had never – to her knowledge at least – ruffled any feathers. She'd certainly never flirted with anyone who might have misconstrued her actions. She never got into arguments either in real life or online. So why would someone be targeting her so cruelly in this way?

The worst thing about it all was that she hadn't told anyone what was going on. The truth was, she felt too ashamed to show the messages to her family – even though the crude content had nothing to do with her. She'd nearly mentioned them to Bryony once, but had lost her nerve. And she certainly wasn't about to mention them to Rick in case she scared him off.

She simply tried to forget about them, hoping that they'd stop as quickly as they'd started. But, as her phone pinged again with another message to darken her day, she feared that the end would never come.

~

Polly had just patched a hole in Archie's school trousers and had given Dickens's ears some much-needed attention with a brush when Jago came in.

'How did it go?' she asked with a smile.

He put his guitar case down and ran a hand through his unruly hair. 'Okay, I guess. It was a good crowd, but the landlord went back on his promise about payment.'

'He didn't pay you?'

'No, he paid us, but half what he said he would.'

'Oh, Jago! What did you say?'

'We let him know how we felt, but he's got his own issues going on. I kind of felt sorry for him. Prices are going up on everything.'

'I know! That's why we need to be paid for *our* time.'

'Yes! But what can you do?'

'Well, don't book another evening there.'

Jago pulled out a chair from the kitchen table and sank down into it. He looked exhausted.

'Want a tea?' she asked him.

'No, thanks, sweetheart.'

She pulled out the chair next to him and sat down, taking his large hands in her much smaller ones.

'I'll have to get some more pupils, Polly. Especially if – you know.'

Polly swallowed hard. 'It's not happening. Not this month.'

'Oh, Polly! You were so sure.'

She nodded, feeling tears welling up in her eyes. 'Maybe it's for the best. If things are tricky right now.'

'Don't say that! We'll get by. We always do. We'll find a way.' The passion in his voice gave her renewed hope and she sniffed her tears away.

'I always feel so strong with you, but I have these moments of doubt when I'm alone.'

He brought her hands up to his lips and kissed them. 'You've been through a lot. You're still healing. But look at how far we've come.'

'You mean to the other side of Castle Clare?' She gave him a wry smile.

'It might only be a few miles from where we were, but doesn't it feel a world away? It does to me.'

Polly knew what he meant. They couldn't have gone on living the way they had been: Jago in his mother's poky terrace and Polly and Archie in the one they'd shared with Sean. There were too many bad memories there. They'd needed a fresh start.

'So things are a little bit tricky at the moment. They are for a lot of people. But look at what we've got here.' He gave a laugh. 'And, if things get really bad, we'll always get at least one square meal a week at your parents' each Sunday!'

'Very funny!'

'Seriously, Pol. I've never felt richer in my entire life even if there's virtually nothing in my bank account!'

Polly could feel tears threatening again at his sweet words. She felt so comforted by them.

'Come on,' he said a moment later. 'It's late. Let's go to bed.'

They got up from the kitchen table, said goodnight to Dickens and went upstairs.

Owl Cottage was a tiny white-washed thatched home facing the green at Newton St Clare. Sam always loved his visits there particularly in the winter when they'd draw the thick curtains and light the wood burner and chat together about the latest books they were reading – or, indeed, writing. For Callie was always writing and, since getting her new contract, she'd been working harder than ever. Sam was worried about her. He knew she adored her work and was never happier than when immersed in the world of her stories, but Sam felt she had crossed a line recently and that wasn't good for her.

When she answered the door to him, his concern deepened further. Callie's fair hair looked dishevelled and her blue eyes looked sore.

'Hey – you all right?' he asked, entering the cottage and kissing her.

'Just tired.' She pushed her hair out of her face. She looked pale as well as tired, he noticed.

'Isn't the writing going well?'

'It's going *brilliantly!*' she said. 'I was up half last night writing.'

'Callie – that's not good for you.'

'It felt good getting all those words out of me.'

Sam just shook his head. 'I don't know how you do it.'

She shrugged. 'I don't know how *not* to do it!'

'You should take more breaks – get out! See the world. Well, at least the Suffolk coast.'

Callie looked down at her baggy T-shirt and leggings and sighed. 'You're right. But you know what it's like when I'm up against a deadline.'

'But you're *always* up against a deadline, Callie! You finish one book and then launch straight into another. There's barely a weekend between them. It never ends.'

'I'm sorry.'

'No need to apologise.' He wrapped her up in a warm hug. 'Listen, we should have a day out.'

'Where?'

'Well, I was thinking of the seaside, but it doesn't matter. We haven't taken a day off together in months, have we? You've been so busy with your book and I... I don't have any excuse. I just got into a routine, I guess.'

Callie smiled and nodded in agreement as they went through to the tiny kitchen at the back of the cottage where she put the kettle on. Sam glanced around, noting the plates in the sink and a couple of crumpled biscuit wrappers on the worktop. A midnight feast perhaps while she'd been working. He had to get her out of here, he told himself.

'Polly could use the extra day's work anyway,' Sam added.

'Is everything okay?'

'I think she and Jago are just a bit stretched at the mo.'

'Yes, I think a lot of people are feeling the pinch. Food prices have soared, haven't they?'

'Like everything else. My electricity bill's horrendous.'

'Oh, Sam!'

'But we all plough on, don't we?'

Callie made them both a cup of tea and they went through to the living room where they sat side by side on the sofa.

'I love how quiet it is here,' Sam said.

'Me too. Although Castle Clare isn't exactly a metropolis, is it?'

'No, but there's usually some kind of traffic or pedestrian noise,' Sam said. 'Last night, there was a cat fight in the yard behind the bookshop.'

'You mean a real cat fight or a couple of girlfriends having an argument after too many drinks at The Happy Hare?'

'A *real* cat fight!' Sam said with a laugh.

'I heard a fox last night. It sounded pretty close.'

'I bet it was coming to tell you it was time to switch your computer off and go to bed.'

'Probably!'

Sam gently touched her pale cheek. 'I wish you wouldn't work into the night like that.'

'It's okay. It's not all the time.'

'But these things catch up with you.'

'Oh, Sam! You make me sound ancient!'

'Well, you'll *look* ancient before you know it if you don't get proper sleep.'

Callie's hands flew to her face. 'Are you saying I look old?'

'No. I didn't say that. But you do look tired. Pale too. You definitely need some sea air.'

'Doctor's orders?'

'No. Sam Nightingale's orders. *Strict* orders. No wriggling out of them.'

Callie stared at him intently. 'Are you planning something?'

Sam frowned. 'What makes you say that?'

'I don't know – you've just got a look about you.'

He shook his head. 'Just a regular day out.'

She continued to stare at him some more and he began to feel nervous – as if she could see the cogs of his mind turning and planning.

'Okay,' she said at last. 'Let me finish this book–'

'Callie!'

'No – really – I'm *so* close, Sam! Then I can give you my full attention and enjoy a proper day out.'

'And you promise not to leap right into another one the minute you send this one to your editor? You'll at least have a day out first?'

Callie chewed her lip and nodded.

'Promise me!' Sam insisted.

'I promise!'

They kissed and Sam felt a bubble of excitement begin to build for the day he had planned and the question he wanted to ask Callie.

CHAPTER NINE

It was lovely to be back with Bryony, Megan thought as she sat on the familiar sofa where they'd shared so many confidences in the past. Ben was out for the evening at a concert in Ipswich so it was just the two of them together with Longfellow who had taken to jumping up on the sofa when Bryony was in the house on her own. Not that she'd encouraged it, she'd sworn to Ben. The little guy had somehow found his way up there and she hadn't had the heart to evict him after all he'd been through.

So here he was now, sitting to Bryony's left as she turned to face Megan.

'Tell me everything!' Bryony insisted, desperate to be filled in on what was happening with Rick Wildman since she'd last seen her.

'Well, he's very handsome,' Megan began slowly.

'More details please!'

Megan thought carefully. How could she describe Rick?

'He's tall. Strong. I think he spends his entire life outside up a ladder. He's *so* tanned and he has these cute little freckles over the bridge of his nose.'

Bryony sighed wistfully.

'His eyes are warm. Chestnut and amber. And his hair's dark with these warm streaks through it. And it's wonderfully messy and wavy.'

'The sort you want to run your fingers through?'

Megan couldn't help smiling and then she thought of the perfect way to describe Rick Wildman.

'He looks like the kind of man who'd drag you into a hedge, kiss you thoroughly and then write a sonnet about it.'

Bryony roared with laughter. 'And was Callie right?'

'About what?'

'That the Wildman brothers are good kissers?'

Megan didn't have to think about her answer. She simply nodded.

'Details! I want all the details!'

'Oh, Bry! I'm not going to kiss and tell. But...'

'What?'

'They were the best kisses of my life.'

Bryony swooned back on the sofa. 'There was more than one?'

'And I'm hoping there'll be more!'

'You're seeing him again?'

Megan nodded.

'When?'

'I don't know. He said he'll write to me.'

'*Write* to you? You mean text?'

'No. He said he wanted to write me a letter. I told him about *84 Charing Cross Road*.'

'Oh, the book club pick for September?'

'But I don't expect he really will. Nobody writes letters these days, do they?'

'Ben used to write me postcards.'

'Yes, they were wonderfully romantic.'

Bryony nodded. 'Even though I hated him at the time for leaving me.'

'He's back now, though. And you have Longfellow to take care of together.' Megan smiled. 'You're a little family.'

'I know! I love that. I was chatting to an old school friend and she couldn't believe I was still living in Suffolk near my parents.'

'Why couldn't she believe it?'

'She couldn't wait to leave. She used to talk about it all the time. "When I grow up. When I leave home…"'

'So where is she now?'

'Norfolk!'

Megan laughed. 'She only made it across the border?'

'Yes! Yet she still manages to make me feel like a hopeless case for still loving Castle Clare.'

Megan shook her head. 'But you've found your place here,' she told Bryony. 'Maybe your friend's one of those restless people who never truly finds out where they belong.'

'Maybe.'

'But you know where you belong.'

'I do.' Bryony gave Longfellow a little cuddle. 'More wine?'

Megan glanced at her watch. 'No, I'd better not, thanks.'

'How about a hot chocolate then?'

'Now, that's a good idea!'

As Bryony disappeared into the kitchen, Megan was left alone on the sofa with Longfellow. He was a dear little thing and he looked so completely at home already. Megan reached out to stroke his silky ears.

'You are *so* handsome!' she whispered. 'And you are so loved!'

He looked up at her, his dark eyes sleepy but alert.

And then Megan's phone beeped. She reached forward to where she'd left it in her handbag. She'd thought she'd switched it off for the evening. She was doing that more now and earlier and earlier each day.

As she looked at the latest message, she felt the colour drain from her face.

'Are you okay?' Bryony asked as she came back into the room

with the mugs of hot chocolate which she placed on the table in front of them.

Megan looked up from her phone.

'What's wrong?' Bryony was by her side in an instant and Megan handed her her phone. Bryony read the message.

'Who's this from?'

'I don't know.'

'Delete it. It's horrible.'

Megan swallowed hard. 'There've been others.'

Bryony frowned. 'You mean like this?'

'Yes.'

'For how long?'

'Two months.'

'*Two months*! Why didn't you tell me?'

Megan sighed. 'I didn't think they were that bad to begin with. I just thought it was a joke so I deleted them. I've been getting them via all my social media too, and, recently, via the library email address.'

'You think it's the same person?'

'It's the same sort of message.'

'Does Rick know?'

'No, I've not told him.'

'Have you any idea who it could be?'

Megan shook her head. 'Maybe they'll stop soon. It must be pretty boring for whoever it is, surely? I mean, I haven't responded in any way except...'

'What?'

'I did reply to one in the early days.'

'What did you say?'

'I just wrote, *Please stop*.'

'Oh, Megan! I don't think that was a very good idea.'

Megan could feel tears in her eyes now. 'I know!'

'It just shows that the messages are being read and – more than that – having the desired effect.'

'I don't understand. Why are they doing this?'

Bryony shook her head. 'They're just twisted. I've read a bit about this sort of thing. They're the kind of people who like causing chaos especially when it's online so it's hard for them to be traced.'

'But why me?' Megan asked in frustration.

'I don't know. Maybe they don't either. But one thing's certain – you've *got* to report this.'

'I know. I was kind of hoping it would all stop so I wouldn't have to.'

'What have you done with all the messages? Have you got a record of them?'

'I've deleted most of them.'

'I can understand why, but perhaps you should keep them. Print them out.'

'But they're so horrible!'

'I think that's all the more reason to have a record of them. You've got to go to the police and show them this stuff.'

Megan sighed, feeling so depleted by it all. She'd hoped that nobody would find out and that it would all go away. She certainly hadn't planned on telling Bryony any of this tonight. But, seeing the fear and anger in her cousin's face, Megan knew she couldn't hide away from it any longer.

On the same evening Megan was confiding in Bryony, Josh and April had decided that they should tell May their news. Josh had longed to keep the secret between just the two of them for a little longer, but April had been anxious that May would find out and then feel slighted for not being told.

Josh had to admit that it was pretty hard keeping the smile from his lips in the shop during the day. He wasn't known for his excessive smiling and it had been remarked upon by both his customers and his sister Lara who was helping him out during the summer holidays.

'You're *definitely* hiding something,' Lara told him as she unpacked the latest delivery of paperbacks. 'You're just not naturally happy like this.'

'Thanks a lot!'

'You know what I mean. You're Mr Serious. Mr Nothing's as Important as Books.' She mulled it over for a moment. 'Something's going on. Have you proposed to April? Are you planning to elope or something? You can tell me. I won't breathe a word to anyone!'

Josh didn't believe her for a moment. 'It's nothing like that,' he assured her.

'You've definitely changed since you met April.'

'Have I?' he asked. He didn't need to be told that, of course. He knew he'd changed. He could feel it on almost a cellular level. But it still surprised him to hear it from others.

'Yes, you're... softer!'

He frowned. 'Softer?'

'Gentler. Nicer.'

He rolled his eyes. Lara had the knack for making compliments seem like insults.

'Oh, you know what I mean!'

Josh sighed in exasperation. 'For a student of English Literature, you should be able to say exactly what you mean *succinctly* and without personal injury to others.'

Lara laughed. 'Now there's the Josh I'm used to! You're so funny!'

Josh hadn't meant to be funny. Only his family could wind him up like this. Perhaps that was one of the reasons that he was so happy to have found April. There was none of that Nightingale nonsense about her.

Now, sitting at the dining table at the place April shared with May, Josh wished with all his heart that he and April could run away together and not have to share their news with anyone. It was supremely selfish, he knew that. But it was just the way he felt.

April gave him a little nudge as May got up to clear the plates away. Josh nodded reluctantly.

'May?' April began. 'We have something to tell you.'

Josh could hear the hesitancy in April's voice and knew she felt the same way as he did. He'd been surprised when she'd agreed that they should keep it a secret – even from May – but she'd soon back-pedalled, insisting that her twin would be sure to find out. April had been careful to hide the pregnancy testing kits from May, but she knew she was bound to slip up with something sooner or later and she couldn't bear the thought that May would feel wounded if she wasn't told openly and honestly.

Having popped the plates into the sink, May came back to the table. 'What is it?'

'Sit down and we'll tell you.'

'Oh, heavens – it's sitting down news, is it?' May sat down, looking serious.

April looked at Josh and he squeezed her hand tightly.

'We're going to have a baby!'

Josh watched May's eyes widened. Was it joy, shock or horror? He couldn't tell.

'April!' she cried and she stood up and hugged her sister.

'Steady on!'

'I can't believe it! You're having a *baby*?'

'Well, Josh had something to do with it. I didn't do it all on my own!'

May released April from her hug and turned to Josh. He gave her a smile, she approached him cautiously and the two of them hugged. It had always been a little awkward between them not least because Josh had mistakenly taken May to Campion House instead of April one time. And he couldn't help feeling like he'd inserted himself between them in a way that the two sisters hadn't experienced before. But he trusted that he and May would become closer in time. He knew how protective May was of April and he couldn't say that he blamed her.

'Congratulations,' May told him.

'Thank you!'

'How long have you known?' May asked. April had told Josh that would be her first question.

'Just three weeks.'

'Blimey! You guys didn't hang around!'

Josh snorted. He couldn't help it. May's bluntness never failed to amuse him.

'You know we hoped for this,' April said, 'but it has surprised us a little.'

'Does anyone else know?' May asked. Again, April had told Josh to expect this question.

'Just you.'

May smiled, satisfied.

'When are you going to tell everyone?'

'I don't know. Soon, though.'

It was then that the joy drained from May's face. 'But everything will change now, won't it?'

'I guess it will.'

'Will you be moving out?' May gasped as the thought hit her properly. 'You'll be leaving me!'

'We haven't really discussed our plans yet,' April said quickly.

'But of course you will. You'll want your own place together, won't you?'

'Very likely,' Josh chimed in.

'Unless we could live like *our* family,' May said, suddenly looking excited. 'Only with two mothers instead of two fathers!'

Josh felt horrified by the idea. 'I don't think that will work,' he said quickly. 'Not for me personally.'

'Nothing's been decided yet,' April said. 'It's very early days. But we wanted to share the news with you.'

May nodded, a little placated. 'And you're feeling well? I've not noticed any changes in you.'

'I'm feeling fine.'

'That's good.' May breathed a sigh of relief. 'Well, I wasn't expecting this tonight.'

'I hope we haven't shocked you!' April said.

'Oh, no! It's the best news ever,' May declared. 'I'm going to be an aunt!' She laughed. 'Now, who wants dessert? There's a big bowl of trifle in the fridge and I'm betting a certain somebody will be able to manage a couple of portions *at least* now she's eating for two!'

CHAPTER TEN

Antonia Jessop could be a tricky customer at the best of times, Megan couldn't help thinking. But that morning, when she opened the library, Miss Jessop was ready to pounce. She was wielding a copy of the latest crime novel in a bestselling series, her manicured nail tapping near a jam stain on page two hundred and sixty-three. Megan fixed what she hoped was a concerned look on her face, but she really wasn't in the mood. She'd had seven messages that morning from the mystery stalker – a new record – and she really didn't need to listen to Miss Jessop's tirade.

'Disgusting!' she was saying. 'Right on a key scene too. I couldn't read it, of course. Ruined my whole experience of the book.'

'I'm sorry to hear that,' Megan told her.

'You'll have to order another copy so I can finish the story before I forget it all. I do find these crime plots hard to hold in my head.'

Megan wasn't about to order a new copy of the novel that – other than the jam stain – was still perfectly readable. She'd take it into the back room later, give it a quick wipe and hope that Antonia Jessop would forget about the whole thing.

It was then that the library door opened and Rick Wildman

walked in. Megan felt her heart skip a beat as he caught her eye and winked at her before disappearing behind the fiction shelves.

'You really should keep a better check on your books! If this was *my* library, I'd take care of things like this immediately – or at least before customers borrowed the books.'

'Well, it's rather hard to check every page of every book each day,' Megan tried to explain as Rick's head popped out from behind the cookery books. He rolled his eyes theatrically and Megan bit her lip to stop herself from laughing.

'It looks like a crime scene itself, this jam stain. At least, I *hope* it's jam!' Antonia Jessop shuddered theatrically. 'I dread to think what the alternative might be.'

Megan glanced over Miss Jessop's left shoulder to see that Rick had pulled out a copy of *Flavour* by Ottolenghi with one hand while holding a folded piece of paper in his other hand.

'I shall just have to check each page myself in future, shan't I?' Miss Jessop was saying.

Megan nodded, but she wasn't really listening now. She was watching as Rick placed the piece of paper he was holding into the book, leaving just a hint of it showing. He then turned the book to face her so she got a good look at the cover and then he replaced it on the shelf.

'Miss Nightingale? I don't think I've got your full attention!'

'I'll replace the book right away,' Megan told her, feeling just a little guilty about lying.

'Well, I should think so.'

Rick was leaving the library now but, just as he reached the door, he turned and gave her another wink that made Megan feel quite light-headed. She was disappointed he hadn't talked to her, but maybe he had an appointment in town to get to. And what was all that about the cook book?

As Antonia Jessop left her alone at long last, Megan approached the shelves where Rick had stood just moments before. She looked at the colourful spines of the cook books and pulled out the Ottolenghi that Rick had held in his hands. She could see the piece of paper sticking out of the top and she bit her lip as she pulled it from the book and unfolded it.

It was a letter!

Dear Minnow, it read, and her breath caught at the nickname he'd given her.

> *I can't stop thinking about you and our day together. I've never felt so much for someone so quickly. When we kissed in the meadow, I felt as if I was burning. I didn't want you to leave. It was like you belonged there with me. I've never felt like that before. Maybe I'm being a romantic fool. I don't want to scare you away if you don't feel the same. But maybe you do feel the same. If you do, come back to OFC after you close the library tonight. The days are long and I want to show you somewhere very special to me. And I want to kiss you again.*
>
> *Yours (because that's what I long to be!)*
>
> *Rick x*

She stood fixed to the spot as she reread his words feeling, once again, the heat of that summer day flowing through her.

As the doors of the library opened again and a delivery of books arrived in a large blue crate, Megan quickly folded her letter into quarters and tucked it safely in the pocket of her skirt, her heart racing. Rick had said he wasn't literary, but his words were lovelier than any poetry she'd ever read because they had come from the very depths of his being. She could sense that. He had not only kept his promise to her, but he'd laid himself bare by telling her how he felt. It was a huge responsibility to hold a man's heart in her hands, she thought. But it was also such a thrill.

The rest of the day in the library stretched interminably with Megan counting down the hours until she could close up and drive out to Melton Green. At last, when the moment came, she dashed home first to shower and change her clothes. Once she'd changed, she stared at herself in the mirror. What was happening to her? She'd never felt like this before. Was this just a summer romance? Did it matter? All she knew in that moment was that she was caught up in something so powerful that it could take her in any direction it wanted to and she would willingly go.

As she drove out to Oak Farm Cottage that evening, it was still warm and the sky was still blue – a little hazier than earlier in the day, perhaps, but just as beautiful. The trees had a languid look about them and the blonde grasses on Melton Common were still and silent as if they didn't have the energy to dance.

After bumping down the unmade track to the cottage, Megan parked her car and got out, walking round the side of the building. Truffle and Blewit were sitting together in the shady doorway of one of the sheds and each wagged a tail in greeting, and then she spotted Rick. He was up a ladder propped against the main chimney breast. He was wearing a hard hat and no shirt. Megan gasped at his bronzed body which looked naturally toned with all the hard labour he obviously undertook.

'Megan!' he cried as he saw her, quickly coming down the ladder and removing his hat before crossing the space between them and kissing her. Megan practically melted into him, her hands daring to touch his body.

'Gosh, sorry!' he said. 'I'm a bit hot and – well...'

'It's okay,' she said as he turned to put on a checked shirt slung over the stump of a tree. She tried not to stare at the raw broadness of his back, but it just wasn't something you saw in the library at Castle Clare.

He turned back to face her as he buttoned up his shirt. 'You get my letter then?' he asked, his eyes bright with mischief.

Megan saw an opportunity for some fun. 'What letter?'

Rick's face fell. '*Please* tell me you found it and that I haven't given some old dear a heart attack when she was trying to cook a curry!'

Megan laughed. 'Of *course* I found your letter!'

Rick shook his head. 'You are a cruel woman, Megan Nightingale!'

She laughed. 'I'm sorry! I couldn't resist!'

He took a step closer to her again. 'And I can't resist you.'

They kissed again.

'Was it okay?' he whispered.

'I love your kisses.'

He grinned. 'I'm glad to hear it. But I meant the letter. Was *that* okay?'

'It was... it was beautiful.'

'Really? You're not just saying that?'

'I never lie when it comes to words.'

He smiled. 'I believe you.'

'I've never had someone write to me like that. Actually, I can't think of the last time anyone wrote me a proper letter.'

'Well, I'm not sure mine was proper! More *improper*!'

She laughed. 'If that's what improper is, I'll take it!'

They kissed again.

'What did you do today? Tell me *everything*. Did you sort out that busybody this morning?'

'Oh, let's not talk about her. I don't want to think about anything outside of this place,' she said, glancing back at the naked oak frame of the house and up into the leafy canopy of the trees. 'It's all so perfect.'

The truth was, she didn't want to think about the day she'd had which had started with horrible messages and threats sent via her social media. She didn't want to think about the uppity Miss Jessop and she certainly didn't want to think about the stack of washing and ironing she had at home.

Rick put his arms around her waist. 'Okay,' he told her. 'Nothing else exists.'

'No.'

'Just us and this place.'

'I like that.'

She leaned her head against his shoulder and felt his fingers combing through her ponytail. It was a moment of tenderness, of peace, of love.

Megan closed her eyes. This was all moving so fast, she thought. It was almost frightening and yet she felt utterly content and – more than that – she felt safe. Even though she barely knew this man and had spent so little time with him, that didn't seem to matter. Some might call her crazy or foolish or even naïve that she was being led purely by instinct. But, in that moment standing on the sun-bleached lawn between the naked house and the overgrown moat, with his arms around her, instinct felt pretty darned good to her.

'There's something I want to show you,' Rick said at last. How long had they been standing there in each other's arms, Megan wondered? 'Are you up for a walk?'

She looked into his sunny face and nodded.

'It isn't far.'

He whistled for the spaniels and the four of them walked down the track together, turning left as it crossed the common and then left again into a shady bridleway.

'This is an old drovers' lane – or "long green"', Rick told her. 'It's about six miles long and links some of the market towns around here.'

Megan took it all in, luxuriating in the greenness of it all. 'It's beautiful. It has a real ancient feel about it, doesn't it? I can imagine the farmers and their cattle on their way to market.'

Rick nodded. 'Places like this are so important to preserve – not just because they're part of our history but because they act as wildlife corridors. It's great for flowers and fruit too. There were violets and primroses in the spring and there'll be bullaces and blackberries come late summer. There are orchids in the meadows here too.'

'It's another little paradise – just like yours!'

He stopped walking and turned to her. 'You're forgetting – this is all *ours*. Our little world.' He stroked her hair. 'Nothing else exists.'

She stared into the chestnut brightness of his eyes and wondered if he was going to kiss her or, indeed, if she should kiss him, but he started walking again.

'There was a section of trees lost in the eighties just before the Tree Preservation Order came into force.'

Megan frowned. 'Why would they cut down the trees?'

Rick sighed. 'Farming machines were getting bigger and trees and hedges were being destroyed to make the fields easier to work.'

'All in the name of progress,' Megan said sarcastically. 'Everyone thinks bigger is better and that it's all about making money, but it isn't! Take my library.' She smiled. 'I mean, take the library at Castle Clare – it's tiny and it's perfect. It just suits the needs of the community, but we've been threatened with closure so many times. You know it's a charity these days? And many others in the country are run by volunteers? So many have been shut down and sold off and for what? Because somebody somewhere wants to make money. Or even *more money*, I should say! It's just greed. Most of the bad decisions in this world come down to a handful of greedy people who just want more!' She took a deep breath. 'Sorry!'

'No, no! I admire your passion. And I feel the same way. That's why I took this place on. I want to try and make a difference – even if it's just on a tiny patch of land. I want to protect it. I feel lucky that I was able to buy the place at all. Apparently, the owner wanted to knock it down and just widen the fields. That would have meant pulling up all the hedgerows and cutting down the trees too.'

'What stopped him?'

'The money, I think. Selling the property to an idiot like me meant a big lump sum straightaway rather than him having to invest more and take the risk of making money on the land in the future. Farming can be a hazardous way to earn a living.'

They'd reached a stile now and Rick stopped and grinned. 'What happened to us shutting out the world and just being us?'

Megan returned his smile. 'The world has a way of creeping back in, doesn't it?' She closed the space between them, snuggling in to him and feeling the warmth of his breath on her face.

'Let's not let it,' he whispered. 'Let's just be us. Right here. In this moment.' He lifted her face in his hands. Hands which smelled of oak beams and sunshine. And they kissed and the magic of that moment was wholly complete. Nothing else was needed – no words or opinions, no memories or projections.

Rick and Megan. Megan and Rick. They were enough.

CHAPTER ELEVEN

Mid-July on the Suffolk coast was always going to be busy. Sam was wondering if he'd made the right decision in taking Callie to Walberswick, but the centre of the village was so pretty, the ice creams they'd bought after their pub lunch were delicious, and the walk along the shore was bracing but beautiful. Callie was wearing yellow striped shorts, a navy cotton jumper and had a floppy straw hat on that kept threatening to fly right off her head and take a dip in the sea.

They'd stopped at Blythburgh church on the way and Sam had shown Callie the scorch marks on the great wooden door which were said to be the scratches of Black Shuck during a wild attack on a stormy night hundreds of years ago.

Callie had been fascinated by the story, remembering the legendary dog had been mentioned when the Nightingales read and recounted ghost stories on Christmas Eve.

Sam had wondered if he should propose to her in the church under the great wooden angels which decorated the ceiling. It would have been lovely to have their blessing, he thought, and he had the ring in his pocket, safe in its box. But Callie hadn't stopped talking.

She was so caught up in the beauty of the building and the terrifying legend attached to it that the opportunity for a romantic moment simply hadn't happened.

So, here they were on the beach at Walberswick only it wasn't quite the scene Sam had imagined. There were just so many people – all enjoying the sun and sea. Great camps of tents, stripy windbreaks and colourful umbrellas, along with rugs, towels and hampers littered the stony beach. He certainly didn't want this to be the setting for his proposal.

'Shall we head into the dunes? There's a footpath further along. If we cross the road from there, we can walk out over the heath,' he suggested, remembering the walk he'd done a couple of times before.

'Sounds lovely!' Callie said, the wind almost taking her hat again.

'It'll be less windy away from the beach,' Sam promised her and it was. After they'd crossed the road in the village, a path took them past some pretty cottages before opening out into heathland. Sam was relieved to find that it was a lot quieter than the beach. There were a few walkers around, but they'd left the hordes of holidaymakers behind, and Callie's hat now transformed into a very well-behaved sort of a hat, freeing up her hand so Sam could hold it again.

'It's good to get away from screens, isn't it?' she said as they followed the footpath through the thick gorse.

'And the shop,' Sam added.

'We should do this more often.'

He smiled. 'We should, shouldn't we? Make an appointment with ourselves.'

'Yes. If it isn't in the diary, it just doesn't get done. I'm learning that. In fact, I'm going to buy some bright felt tip pens and write, *Day out with Sam* in pink or orange in my diary *every* week from now on!'

He laughed. 'Why not twice a week?'

'Or three times a week?'

They stopped walking for a moment and he kissed her. 'I'm afraid we're both too addicted to our work, aren't we?'

'I think you might be right. But let's make more time for days like this.'

Sam cleared his throat. He wasn't sure if he could promise more days *quite* like this in the future.

'Callie?'

'Yes?'

'There's something I want to ask you.'

She frowned. 'I've switched my phone off. I haven't even looked at it today – I promise! And I've not even *thought* about starting a new novel!'

'I know!' he said. 'It's not that.'

'What then?'

Sam glanced at the ground wondering about the practicalities of going down on one knee but thought better of it when he saw just how stony it was. So he took Callie's hands in his.

'Excuse me?'

A woman's voice came from behind Sam's left shoulder.

'Oh, sorry!' Callie said brightly, springing away from Sam to let the woman by.

Sam looked behind him to see there were five more walkers following the woman so they stood aside until they passed. They took their time, one of them was examining a map and Sam couldn't help admiring that it was a good old-fashioned fold out map rather than one on a screen.

'What did you want to ask me?' Callie said. Sam glanced at her. The walkers were still within earshot.

'I... erm... I've forgotten.'

Callie laughed. 'It'll come back to you.'

'I think it probably will,' Sam whispered to himself as they continued their walk.

It was a beautiful footpath which brought them out by the boats along the River Blyth which flowed into the harbour between Walberswick and Southwold. The path was busier here and Sam cursed his missed opportunity to propose back on the heath but, after the walkers, he'd been on edge in case they were interrupted again.

'You look thoughtful,' Callie said to him as they stopped to take in the scene.

'No, I'm just…'

'Are you okay? You look – I don't know – concerned.'

The sweet look in her eyes touched him deeply. Here was somebody who cared about him – *truly* cared. How had he got so lucky as to have her walk into his bookshop that day? And then, even though there were walkers approaching on the footpath and people on boats on the river, Sam couldn't wait any longer.

'Callie – marry me!' he blurted.

'What?' She laughed.

'Will you marry me?' He ran a hand through his hair. It was tousled from the sea breeze. Actually his whole body felt tousled. 'I've been trying to ask you all day, but it's not been going very well.'

'You have?'

He dug his hand in his pocket and pulled out the ring box, opening it to reveal the sapphire and diamond ring.

Callie's hands flew to her face. 'Sam, it's beautiful!'

'It was my grandmother's.'

'Grandma Nell?'

'No, my mother's mother, Mary.'

'I love it!'

'I hoped you would,' Sam said. 'So, is that a yes or is it just the ring you're interested in?' he asked with a laugh.

'It's most definitely a yes!'

They kissed as a family of four passed them on the path, and then Sam took the ring out of the box and put it on Callie's ring finger.

'Does it fit?'

She nodded. 'It feels wonderful. Just look at it!'

Sam smiled. 'It's you I'm looking at.'

Callie gasped. 'If I'd known about this today, I'd have made more of an effort. Just look at me in this old hat and these funny shorts!'

'You look perfect!'

'Oh, Sam!'

They kissed again, locked in a little world of their own as another group of holidaymakers walked right by them. One of them even took a photo.

~

Rick was making good progress at Oak Farm Cottage. He got up early each morning, working hard before the heat of the day forced him to take a break. He hadn't yet braved a dip in the moat; he hadn't had a chance to get in there and sort it out. But he could see how tempting it would be if he cleared it all.

One particularly hot lunchtime, he downed tools and jumped in the Land Rover with Truffle and Blewit and drove to Cavendish on the other side of Castle Clare. It pained him not to call in at the library en route, but he was due somewhere.

Parking outside a modest-looking terrace, he and the dogs got out. His mother was at the door to greet him.

'Look at the state of you!' she chided with a smile and a shake of her head.

'What?' Rick said, running a hand over his face. 'Ah!'

'Just like your father when he was caught up in a project! Forgot to shave, forgot to get his hair cut. He'd have forgotten to eat if I hadn't been there to remind him!'

Rick leaned in to kiss her cheek and then he and the dogs followed her into the cool interior of the house. It hadn't changed much over the years. The wallpaper in the hallway was peeling and faded, the carpet was worn and the kitchen could easily be used in a period drama now. But it was home. Rick and Leo had grown up here. There hadn't been much room for the family of four and the garden was woefully small too, but they'd always found an escape in the Suffolk countryside – exploring the woods, fields and footpaths together.

Rick had so many fond memories of growing up in Suffolk. His father might have had a dull office job, but his passion for life outside the office walls had been infectious and he'd instilled a love of the natural world in his sons which had never left them.

When Daniel Wildman had been taken from them woefully early, Rick and Leo had been understandably concerned about their mother. Elaine Wildman still worked part-time in the local garden centre, bringing home endless plants that had been deemed dead but which she'd resurrect. It was one of the reasons there'd never been room for Rick and Leo to kick a ball around in the garden.

'Have you heard from Leo?' Rick asked as they got on with making a spot of lunch in the kitchen.

She nodded. 'We had a chat online the other night. He looked well. Very tanned.'

'Good. Where is he?'

She frowned as she tried to remember. 'Somewhere like Romania. Or was it Montenegro? Somewhere with mountains. He's got a thing about mountains again.'

'What – climbing them?'

'Probably!'

Rick smiled. That sounded like Leo. He always was the slightly more adventurous of the two of them.

'And has he met anyone?'

'He said he was hanging out with a couple of Canadians. But I don't think he's met anyone in particular, if that's what you mean.'

As Rick prepped two plates of salad, he decided to tell her his own news.

'Mum?'

'Yes?' She turned around from having just put a homemade pizza in the oven and Rick felt his stomach growl at the prospect of lunch coming soon.

'I've met somebody.'

Her rosy face lit up with a smile. 'A woman?'

'Yep!'

'What's her name?'

'Megan. Megan Nightingale.'

'The librarian at Castle Clare?'

'You know her?'

'Well, only as the librarian. She's been in that place forever, hasn't she?'

'She's one of the Nightingale family and they're all crazy about books, aren't they?

'That's right. Who's that one in the secondhand bookshop? He's a bit shy, but he's always nice and polite.'

'Sam.'

'Yes, that's it! Didn't Leo have some sort of to-do with him?'

'Well, they didn't exactly come to blows or anything, Mum!'

'No doubt about a girl. I forget the details now.'

Rick saw no point in reminding her.

'You'll have to bring Megan here,' she said. 'And, if you don't, I'm sure I'll find a good excuse to start borrowing books every week.'

'Oh, Mum! You mustn't embarrass me!'

She laughed. 'You are just too easy to tease! But you really should introduce us, don't you think? If you think that's appropriate. If things are... serious.'

Rick bit back a smile. Were things serious if you couldn't stop thinking about someone? If their face was before you when you woke in the mornings and if the memory of their kisses haunted you all day long? Was it serious if you counted the hours and the minutes until you saw them again? And if you cursed every second of the day that wasn't spent in their company?

'Yes, Mum. I think it's serious.'

'Oh, Rick!' She beamed him a smile of pure delight.

'Now, don't get too excited. We haven't talked about the future or anything like that.'

His mother nodded as she grabbed knives and forks from a drawer and Rick was grateful when she didn't push for more details.

She'd always been good that way – never putting any pressure on her sons with talks of weddings or grandchildren.

'If you don't mind me saying, I always knew that Colleen girl wasn't the one for you.'

'Mum, that was *years* ago!' Rick said, thinking of the odd relationship he'd had with a woman who'd worked in a nail bar of all places. She'd forever been trying to give him a manicure, despairing at his builder's hands.

'And that's why I'm so happy for you now,' his mum went on. 'You and your brother – you seem to have rotten luck in love. I don't know what it is!'

'Probably just bad timing,' Rick said as he took the plates of salad to the table.

'But you think you've got the timing right now?'

He reached across the kitchen counter for a baguette which his mum had cut into slices.

'Well, I don't want to jinx anything,' he said as he thought about how Megan Nightingale felt in his arms, the scent of her skin, the silkiness of her hair and the way she made him feel when they kissed. 'But, yeah – things feel right this time.'

CHAPTER TWELVE

Sunday lunch at Campion House was always special no matter what the season. But the summer months were particularly glorious because the kitchen and table would be filled with produce from the garden from early tomatoes, crisp salad leaves to pungent rocket and sweet courgettes – sweet, that is, as long as you picked them before they turned into bulky hulking marrows. Frank always took pride in picking produce for Sunday lunch.

To go with offerings from the garden, Eleanor had made two huge quiches and Grandpa Joe had made a luscious-looking three-tiered cake decorated with strawberries and blueberries. Cake making had once been the domain of Grandma Nell, but she struggled to concentrate these days. Still, Eleanor was thrilled to see that Nell's secrets had been passed on to her husband and the resulting cake really was something to behold. Lara had popped out to buy a big tub of vanilla ice cream and some meringues just in case there wasn't enough to go around. One never quite knew how many people would turn up for lunch on any given Sunday. Everybody – bar Lara – had partners now and the table was always full. Mind you, Eleanor was always happy to squeeze in an extra chair or even set a new table alongside theirs.

The dining room doors had been opened into the garden and a gentle breeze stirred the curtains. Eleanor took her time laying the table with her favourite crockery. Frank had picked some pink and white cosmos and it was now dancing above the white linen tablecloth. There was something about a summer meal, she thought. Winter was a celebration too with heaps of roast vegetables and jugs of delicious gravy, but Eleanor also took joy in the intense freshness of summer food – the colours and the crispness of it all. It was definitely something to celebrate.

She glanced at the carriage clock on the mantelpiece, gauging when the first of her children would be arriving. There was still plenty of time. In fact, there was more than enough time to pour her and Frank a glass of something cool and delicious and enjoy a few quiet moments in the garden together before the chaotic delight of lunch began.

~

'I think you should tell them,' Sam said as he struggled with a button on his shirt sleeve.

'Me? But they're your family!' Callie said, looking a tad shocked as she stepped forward to help him.

'Don't you think it would be better coming from you? After all, you'll be wearing the ring.'

'I intend on hiding it until you break the news! Look!' Callie was, indeed, wearing the ring, but had twisted it round so that the stone was hidden, nestling above her palm as if cradled.

Sam didn't look happy. 'I hate making a fuss.'

'But you won't be making a fuss. You'll be telling them something they all want to hear.' Callie frowned for a moment. 'They *will* want to hear it, won't they? Oh, my goodness. I hadn't really thought about the alternative!'

'Of course they'll want to hear it. They love you almost as much as I do!' He kissed the tip of her nose tenderly.

'I hope they'll be happy.'

'You do know you're already a member of the Nightingale family whether we marry or not! A piece of paper isn't going to make any difference.'

'Then why do you want to get married?'

Sam looked thoughtful. 'I don't know. I guess I'm just a traditional kind of guy.'

'I have to say, I'm kind of surprised.'

'You are?'

'Well, I know you had a pretty awful experience with Emma.'

'But you did too – with Piers.'

'Yes! We haven't learned a thing, have we?' Callie said laughing.

'I think we've learned *every*thing!' Sam told her. 'Everything about who is wrong for us... and who is *right*.'

They kissed.

'I'll tell them,' Sam said.

'You will? Oh, good!'

He ran a hand through his hair, looking like an anxious schoolboy who knew he was going to have to give a presentation before the class.

'At lunch, do you think? Or as soon as I get the courage. Get it over and done with as quickly as possible.'

'Oh, Sam! You are funny!'

'Otherwise I'm sure to get indigestion from the nerves!'

Callie cupped his face in her hands, kissing him tenderly. 'I do love you, Sam Nightingale!'

'And I love you Callie Logan!'

'Ready to face the family?'

'As ready as I'll ever be!'

The two of them smiled conspiratorially and, holding hands, left Owl Cottage together.

~

April stood staring at her reflection in the full-length mirror in her bedroom.

'I'm not showing, am I?' she asked May who was standing next to her.

'I don't think so. Isn't it about the size of a poppy seed at the moment?'

'A poppy seed?'

'I saw this chart comparing a baby's size as it grows to different things like seeds and vegetables.'

April stifled a giggle and turned to get her reflection in profile just to make sure.

'I don't think a poppy seed is going to give the game away,' May told her.

'Good!' April gave her tummy a gentle pat. 'Because I'm not ready to share the news with the whole Nightingale clan just yet.'

May cocked her head to one side. 'What does it feel like having a baby inside you?'

'Well, it's quite hard to imagine at the moment. I feel mostly normal.'

'You do?'

April nodded. 'Except...'

'What?'

'I'm getting this uncontrollable urge.'

May frowned. 'What for?'

'Hot chocolate fudge sundae!'

'Oh!' May seemed relieved by this revelation. 'That's nothing to do with being pregnant. That's just being a woman!' May hugged her. 'I'll make sure we have plenty of ice cream in the freezer for the months ahead.'

~

As Eleanor had expected, it was a full table that Sunday at Campion House. As well as herself and Frank and Grandpa Joe and Grandma Nell, there was Sam and Callie; Polly, Jago and Archie; Bryony and Ben; Josh and April; and Lara. A full fourteen. Eleanor couldn't have been happier.

Three glass jugs of elderflower cordial filled with ice were being passed around the table and Frank's salad and Eleanor's quiches were going down a treat. It was a delightfully summery spread.

'Did you know Megan's seeing somebody?' Bryony announced.

'I had heard *some*thing,' Josh said. 'Who?'

'Rick Wildman.'

There was a brief moment of silence as this information was taken in.

'Leo's brother,' Bryony continued although everybody seemed to have guessed the connection.

Eleanor noticed that Callie suddenly looked fidgety.

'Are they serious?' Lara asked.

'I think so,' Bryony said. 'She sounds really smitten.' She grinned.

'What?' Lara asked. 'You know something, don't you?'

'Only things we talked about in confidence!'

'Oh, you spoilsport!'

'Well, I'm happy that she's happy,' Josh said. 'She's always been a bit of a loner.'

'Like you before true love struck!' Lara teased.

Josh blushed to the very roots of his hair and everyone laughed.

It was then that Sam cleared his throat. 'We have some news.'

The Nightingale family clattered their cutlery onto their plates and put down their glasses to give Sam their full attention because they knew that he never announced anything unless it was of the utmost importance.

'What is it, Sam?' Frank asked, leaning forward slightly.

Eleanor saw Sam glance at Callie who, she couldn't help noticing, was looking decidedly nervous and a little flutter of excitement filled her body.

'Earlier this week, I asked Callie if she'd do me the very great honour of being my wife and she said yes!'

A great communal roar of joy erupted around the table and Callie proudly held her hand out to show the ring to everyone.

Bryony smiled. 'It's Grandma Mary's!'

'You don't mind, do you?' Callie asked quickly.

'Oh, no,' Bryony said. 'It's perfect on you!'

'But that means you knew, Mum!' Lara said. 'Unless Sam stole it from your jewellery box!'

'I didn't steal it!' Sam cried.

'Well, I did know what Sam was up to,' Eleanor admitted, 'but I didn't know when. Oh, congratulations, darling! And Callie – I'm so thrilled. Really, I couldn't be happier! Haven't we got a few bottles of that lovely wine in the basement?' Eleanor said.

'I think so,' Frank said, getting up.

'I'll give you hand, Dad,' Lara said.

'Shall we clear the plates for dessert?' Polly asked.

'Yes, I think we're all ready?' she glanced at Archie who'd just popped another slice of quiche onto his plate.

'Mum says I'm a growing lad,' he announced and Eleanor smiled at his earnestness.

A few minutes later, Grandpa Joe's fabulous cake was being distributed along with ice cream and meringues while Frank and Lara poured wine for everyone. However, April put her hand over her glass.

'You're not pregnant, are you?' Lara asked with a laugh. Eleanor's head shot up at the question. She could see that Lara had meant it as a joke, but the look of horror on Josh's face caught everyone's attention.

Eleanor gasped and then frowned. 'Josh?'

Josh simply shook his head.

'You are, aren't you?' Lara said, clapping a hand on April's shoulder.

April glanced at Josh and he shrugged.

'I am!' she said and everyone cried congratulations again.

'What's going on?' Grandma Nell asked. 'It's so noisy today!'

'Josh and April are having a baby,' Frank told his mother.

'Already?' Grandma Nell declared.

'Well, not this very minute, Grandma!' Josh said, wondering if she even remembered who April was.

'But you've only just met the girl!' she retorted. Grandma Nell might be in the early stages of dementia, but she could still surprise everybody.

Eleanor felt herself welling up. 'An engagement and a baby in one afternoon!' she exclaimed. 'We are so blessed!'

In the great tradition of Sundays at Campion House, the Nightingales took off for a walk after lunch had settled, falling into happy conversations with one another as they crossed the golden fields, climbed over stiles and picked a few of the early blackberries they discovered. Eleanor had stayed at home to keep an eye on Nell as she'd dozed off in her favourite chair and Callie took the opportunity to approach Grandpa Joe.

'How is Nell?' Callie asked as she watched the three Nightingale dogs trotting down the path ahead of everyone.

'Oh, she has her moments,' he told her. 'Bright ones. Brutal ones.'

Callie nodded. She hadn't been witness to any of the brutal ones, but Sam had told her about a recent visit when his dear gentle grandmother had become quite violent. It had been scary to see her like that, he'd said.

'When you've been married as long as we have, you have to expect anything and everything,' Grandpa Joe went on. 'It's not easy, of course. Especially the forgetting. She sometimes looks at me as if I'm a stranger. It doesn't always last for long, but it cuts so deeply.'

Callie placed a hand on his arm. 'I'm so sorry.'

'But you, my dear! You're just starting your life.'

'Well, I had a bit of a *false* start, I'm afraid.'

Grandpa Joe shook his head. 'Let's call that a starter marriage. Both you and Sam have found your way through those to each other, and I couldn't be more delighted to have you in the family.'

Callie beamed him a smile. 'I still can't believe it!'

'What does your own family make of the news?'

Callie frowned. 'I haven't told them yet.'

'No?' Grandpa Joe looked surprised.

'I think I might have mentioned before that we're not...' She paused, not quite knowing what to say. It was always hard to explain her parents to other people especially to people like the Nightingales who all adored one another and made sure they spent quality time together. Callie had always felt such an oddity. Her parents simply didn't care. They were just two people who'd had a child and had sent her out into the world without really getting to know her at all.

'You're not what, dear?' Grandpa Joe prompted when she hadn't answered.

Callie hesitated before answering, knowing that she couldn't retract the words once they were out.

'We're not close,' she confessed at last.

'Ah, yes. I remember you telling me that.' He nodded as if trying to understand. 'Well, you have us now and you may soon regret just how close we all are!'

Callie smiled. 'No!' she told him. 'I absolutely *love* that about you all!'

~

'Well, I *had* hoped we'd keep our little bit of happiness to ourselves for a bit longer!' Josh said as he pulled up outside April's house.

'It was your face that gave the game away!' April smiled at him.

'I'm sorry.'

'It's okay. I'm just happy that everyone's so delighted. Not everyone would be, you know. It is a bit sudden, isn't it?'

'I suppose so.'

'We should tell my parents next. It's only fair, I guess.'

'Yes. We shouldn't leave them out.'

'Do you want to come in?' April asked, stifling a yawn.

'No, I'll head on home if that's okay. And you should have a rest!'

'I'm fine. Just a bit tired after all that food.'

'You know, perhaps we should think about getting engaged and married too,' Josh said, thinking of his brother's announcement.

'It wouldn't be a bad idea, I suppose.'

Josh grinned. 'Listen to how romantic we sound!'

April giggled. 'Yes, that wasn't exactly the proposal of the century, Josh Nightingale.'

'Or the acceptance of the century!' Josh said. 'So are we engaged?' He was genuinely confused now.

'Shall we say we are? Only, we don't have to tell anyone *that* piece of news yet, do we?'

Josh leaned forward to kiss her. 'No. We can definitely keep that little nugget to ourselves!'

It was a relief to get back to Lilac Row and close the door behind them. The afternoon had been a strain on Polly. Jago had seen Eleanor's tears of joy at the news of April's pregnancy, but he'd also been aware of the tears shining in Polly's eyes. Everyone would have mistaken them as mirrors of her mother's happiness, but he could feel the sad sting behind them and he hugged her close to him as they entered the house together. Archie had run up to his room and Dickens had curled up in his basket in the kitchen after a walk through the fields surrounding Campion House.

'You look exhausted,' Jago told her as they sat down in the living room together. 'Are you okay?'

Polly nodded, her forehead creased into a frown.

'It's not that I'm not happy for them.'

Jago sighed inwardly. He knew what was coming.

'I know April's worried about her condition and wants to experience everything she can,' Polly went on. 'But they've virtually just met! When was it?'

'A couple of months ago, I think.'

'Even Grandma said how quick it was!'

Jago nodded, remembering the old lady's declaration.

Polly pouted. 'It's just come so easily for them.'

Jago stroked her hair. 'And it'll happen for us too. It's still early days, Pol!'

She rested her head against his shoulder. 'It feels like it's never going to happen.'

'That's because you're impatient. You need to relax. Here – let me give you a massage. You're all tensed up!'

Jago positioned himself so that he could work on Polly's shoulders, but she kept fidgeting.

'You're tickling me!' She laughed.

'I'm tickling you, am I?'

'Yes!'

'What – here?'

'Yes! Stop it!'

'Or here?'

'Yes – there too!'

For a few moments, they laughed, tickled and shrieked on the sofa and then they fell into a tight cuddle and Jago could sense that Polly's eyes were filling with tears again. He sighed, holding her close to him and kissing the top of head as he whispered to her.

'It'll happen, Pol. I promise!'

CHAPTER THIRTEEN

Megan was crouched in the children's corner, reading to her young charges as part of Toddler Time. It was a weekly event that she adored. To witness the burgeoning book lovers of the future was a true honour and she loved seeing the expressions on their faces when she read aloud to them. There were just four youngsters today together with their parents: Henry who always had a stern expression and was the last to laugh at anything, Joseph who had pudding-plump cheeks and was utterly adorable, Maya who was a true beauty with her bright blue eyes and a sweet nature, and Ruby who had decided from the first that she only liked stories featuring unicorns or bunnies. Luckily, there were always plenty of those in the library.

Megan had just finished a book about a particularly truculent bunny when someone entered the library.

It was Rick.

He glanced in her direction, winked and then moved towards the shelves in the children's section. Luckily, the four mothers were too busy with their children to notice what Rick was up to and Megan watched, spellbound, as he pulled out a copy of Michael Rosen's ever popular *We're Going on a Bear Hunt* and took a folded piece of paper out of his pocket before placing it inside, making sure Megan got a good look at the book before he replaced it on the shelves. He then gave her a smile which she felt in the very centre of her belly. It was agony not to be able to go over to him and kiss him right there and then, but she was working and Ruby was begging her for another bunny story.

Once she'd read that story, Toddler Time was over, Megan got up from her home on the carpet, brushed her skirt down and returned her selection of books to the shelves.

'That was wonderful!' Joseph's mum told her. 'We'll see you next week.'

'Thanks for coming,' Megan said.

Ruby and her mum made a beeline for the toilet and Maya was raiding the picture books. There was always a certain amount of tidying up to do after the toddlers had departed, but Megan never minded. She loved their enthusiasm even if it was accompanied by runny noses and sticky fingers.

As Megan made her way back to the front desk, she saw that Henry had only just got up from his place on the floor.

'Shall we get some books first?' Henry's mum asked him. He gave a sullen look as she pulled a few titles from the shelf including the latest in a bestselling series about naughty baby elephants.

'Have we had this one, darling?'

He shook his head.

'Oh, look! Here's your favourite. Shall we get this out again? You always love it at bedtime!'

Megan gasped as she saw the title Mrs Burns had pulled out for young Henry. It was the Michael Rosen book Rick had placed his note inside. *Don't open it*, she begged silently. *Please don't open it!*

She swallowed hard as Mrs Burns and Henry approached the desk with the books they'd chosen.

'Nice choice,' Megan said, her eyes fixed on the Michael Rosen title.

Mrs Burns reached in her bag for the library card and Henry grabbed the book from her.

'Want it now,' he said, his expression defying his mum to take it away from him.

'We have to get it stamped first, Henry.'

He hugged the book to his chest and shook his head.

'It'll only take a moment,' she told him.

Megan watched anxiously as a tussle followed with both Mrs Burns and her son vying for the book.

And then it happened – Rick's letter fell right out and fluttered down onto the floor.

'Goodness – what's that?' Mrs Burns asked as she bent to pick it up.

Quick as lightning, Megan leapt around the desk and grabbed it first.

'Some nonsense, I imagine,' she said quickly, stashing the note behind the desk.

Mrs Burns blinked in surprise and Megan realised how odd she must have looked.

She cleared her throat. 'I try to keep a watch for this kind of thing – secret notes. You know? There's been a spate of them recently. Not always – erm – suitable reading for the youngsters.'

'Ah, right,' Mrs Burns said. 'I remember passing those sorts of notes under the desk at school when the teacher wasn't looking. Always felt so naughty!' She gave a giggle which made her look, once again, very like a schoolgirl.

Megan smiled, relief filling her as she stamped the books and watched Henry and his mum leave the library. Finally, she had a moment to herself and retrieved Rick's note which young Henry had almost got his grubby fingers on. Carefully, she unfolded it, taking in the neat slope of his writing in blue ink as she sat down to read his words.

Dear Minnow

I miss you. Even though I've just seen you, I miss you. Thank you for visiting me again and for letting me show you the drovers' road. I loved sharing that with you and I loved talking to you. And – more than anything else – I loved kissing you and being kissed by you!

I slept out under the stars last night. I say sleep, but I kept thinking about you and I'm not sure I actually got much sleep. It's a magical thing to do – to be outside as the sun is going down and the moon is coming up. There were all sorts of strange noises, but I felt so safe and comfortable. Warm too. Maybe it was thinking of you that kept me warm!

And I want to ask you something. Come and spend the night under the stars with me, Minnow! I want to share it all with you!

Yours, always, Rick x

Megan gasped as she finished reading. It was one thing to visit Oak Farm Cottage in the daytime and to take a walk; it was quite another to arrive for sunset and to stay the night.

She read the letter again and hugged it to her chest just as little Henry had hugged his favourite book minutes before. And she knew what she was going to do.

~

A few days after the great pregnancy revelation at Campion House, Josh and April took the day off, handing over their keys to Polly and

May respectively and heading up to see April's mother and the two daddies.

Josh still hadn't quite got used to the unconventional way that Arbella Channing lived with Daddy Jeff and Daddy George, but he was always made very welcome whenever he visited the artistic apartment in the commune deep in the Norfolk countryside. There was usually something interesting going on there whether Arbella was working on a sculpture or Daddy George had a new painting on the go. The eyes and the mind never got a chance to be bored.

Josh loved the drive through Suffolk up into Norfolk. It seemed to be a forgotten place, sparsely populated compared to the bustling coast and the busy broads. It was a landscape dotted with farms, church towers and traditional thatched cottages huddled around duck ponds.

As ever when he was with April, Josh had that holiday feeling – as if he had skipped school. He still wasn't quite used to taking time away from his bookshop to simply live. But it was a fine feeling and, glancing at April now as he approached a crossroads, his heart swelled with love and gratitude for the place he now found himself in.

As the country lanes narrowed further, Josh began to recognise where they were and, after they passed a windmill, he knew the next turning would be the tree-lined driveway that led to Fairley Hall – the big country house where April's family lived. The house itself had been split into numerous apartments and the grounds had been turned into a community farm. There were goats, sheep, chickens and pigs, and a huge area where fresh produce was grown with the biggest compost heaps Josh had ever seen. He couldn't help thinking that his father would be very envious indeed.

'They've just branched out into beekeeping,' April said as they parked. 'So there'll be honey in due course. And a retired carpenter's just moved in and he's fixing all the old stables.'

'Doesn't sound like much of a retirement.'

April laughed. 'That's the problem when you love your work. I guess you never really retire from it.'

They parked, entered the old building via a green-painted door and made their way upstairs which was where Arbella and George could usually be found.

'We're here!' April called as Josh hit his head on a particularly large windchime.

'Come in! Come in!' Arbella called.

Josh smiled as he entered. He couldn't not smile. It was all so colourful and wild. There were books and plants and art absolutely everywhere. Heaps and stacks of it all, jostling and jiving for attention.

Arbella appeared from behind an easel, a large paintbrush in her silver hair which was piled on her head in a mad sort of bun. She crossed the space between them and hugged them both at once.

'My gorgeous gorgeous people!'

'You're squashing us, Mum!'

'Squashing you with all the love in my heart!'

Josh's nose was lost somewhere in Arbella's hair which smelled wonderfully fruity like apricots or apples.

Finally, she let go of them, but it was then that Daddy George appeared and the whole hugging business started again.

Josh was slowly getting used to just how demonstrative the Channing family were. His own family weren't averse to hugging, but it was much more gentle an art.

When the hugging was out of everyone's system, Arbella showed them both what she and George had been working on. George, whom Josh always thought looked like a lion with his tawny hair and golden stubble, talked them through the massive canvas that was on the easel.

'We're not sure if the perspective is right,' Arbella said.

'But it's an abstract,' April said. 'Can perspective be wrong in an abstract?'

Arbella looked confused by this and tipped her head first one way and then the other.

George stepped forward. 'I like it the way it is.'

'Me too,' Josh said.

'You do?' April said. 'I thought you said you didn't like abstracts.'

Arbella and George turned to stare at Josh and he felt his face heating up at the attention.

'I – I'm coming round to them,' he said quickly.

Arbella showed them a few other pieces they'd been working on.

'We have a collector who wants three more of these,' she told them, pointing to a series of paintings that looked kind of like the sky. Or the sea. Josh wasn't sure no matter which way he turned his head. But he knew better than to say anything. He simply smiled in appreciation at the beauty of it all. And it really was all beautiful even if he didn't understand it.

As well as making art, Arbella had made a cake for their visit – a rare treat as she detested the kitchen – and they had some of it with a cup of tea before taking a walk around the grounds as they waited for Daddy Jeff to get home from work before breaking their news. Josh and April had said there was something they wanted to share with them all and Daddy Jeff had promised to get away from work early, but it seemed that he was held up. When he did finally get home, he insisted on changing out of his stuffy office shirt and tie and took a shower before joining them wearing a forest green shirt and beige slacks. Josh noticed how immaculate he looked. He had once told Josh that, while he appreciated art and loved how Arbella and George dressed, he could never quite break out of his own conventional style.

When they were all gathered together in the living room, April broke the news about her pregnancy and Josh watched as all her parents cheered and whooped for joy.

Arbella clapped her hands together. 'This is just perfect! You girls grew up with two daddies and now *your* child can grow up with two *mummies!*'

Josh shook his head. 'We'll be getting a place of our own,' he said, quickly making sure that everyone knew exactly how they were going to do things. And how they *wouldn't* be doing things.

'How does May feel about that?' Arbella asked, her face full of concern.

'She knows it's coming,' April said gently.

'Oh, dear.'

'She'll be fine. She knows that we couldn't go on living together forever.'

Arbella looked confused by this. 'But you would have – if Josh hadn't come along. Wouldn't you?'

'Well, I don't know. Maybe I would have.'

Josh glanced at her. April was looking upset and he was feeling uneasy about the direction of the conversation. He knew, of course, that twins had a special bond and, with April's eye condition, he'd stepped into the middle of a very tricky situation.

'May will just have to adapt,' Daddy Jeff said. 'She's a grown woman. Sooner or later, one of them was bound to meet somebody.

'I hope we're on your books as babysitters,' Daddy George said.

'Of course!' April replied with a smile.

'He – or she – will have a paintbrush in their hand in no time!' Arbella said.

'But a book first,' Josh added, keen that he should have at least some input into how his child was raised.

'Of course!' Arbella conceded. 'Well, this is just the best news ever. Do your parents know, Josh?'

He swallowed hard. He'd hoped that particular question wouldn't arise.

'Yes.'

'It was kind of forced out of us,' April told them. 'We didn't want to say anything so early.'

'No. It was my big-mouthed sister Lara who guessed.'

Arbella seemed to take this on board. If she was upset at not being the first to be told, she was hiding it well.

'How about some more cake to celebrate?' Daddy George said, standing up. And everybody agreed that was a very good idea indeed.

CHAPTER FOURTEEN

Once she'd tidied up the children's corner after five-year old Tommy Johnson had had a full-on meltdown, Megan had closed the library and gone home. She was glad that the July evening was still warm. Clear skies were forecast which would be great for stargazing, but wouldn't that mean it could also get cold? The likelihood of needing to snuggle up together was very strong indeed, she couldn't help thinking.

She wasn't arriving at Oak Farm Cottage until eight in the evening so she had plenty of time to get herself ready. She made time to text Bryony so that at least one person knew where she was.

Don't do anything I wouldn't do! Bryony texted back

We will be stargazing! Megan replied.

Are you sure?

Megan shook her head. She wasn't going to overthink things and she certainly wasn't going let Bryony's naughtiness make her anxious. In fact, she was going to switch her phone off completely. She'd been trying to do that more and more because the messages she'd been receiving had increased dramatically.

She looked at a few of them now as she sat in her living room. It felt horrible to read such poisonous, nasty things in the privacy of her own space. It was as if this person – whoever it was – was right there with her calling her those vicious names to her face, infecting not only her mind but her home. She wished she could ignore them, but she felt herself drawn to reading them as if she was spellbound. She read the ones sent today. She'd lost count after the first twenty. They would start off in the morning fairly innocuously, almost jokey in tone. Then, as the day progressed, they'd get darker and were sent more frequently.

Suddenly, sitting there alone on her sofa, Megan realised she was crying and quickly switched the phone off. She would *not* read any more. She would not even think about them. She dried her eyes and blew her nose. She hated feeling like this – so helpless and alone.

She took a shower, hoping that the hot water would scorch some of the hateful messages out of her mind because she didn't want to carry the weight of them to Oak Farm Cottage.

Then she spent an inordinate amount of time trying to decide what to wear. An evening arrival when it might be turning chilly wasn't the time for a summer dress, she quickly decided. But she didn't want to look like an old bag lady in her comfortable leggings and oversized jumper. She settled on her favourite pair of jeans and a slim-fit jumper, and then she started to worry about what to wear for sleep and where she would change? When she'd texted Rick to accept his invitation, he'd told her he had two sizeable sleeping bags so maybe she could actually change *in* the sleeping bag. Oh, this whole sleeping under the stars was fraught with worry!

She was still worrying on the drive out there. Was there somewhere to wash? Other than the green overgrown moat? She might once have swum there as a child, but she couldn't say she fancied it these days. Besides, it would be icy cold. And what were they doing for supper and breakfast? And was there even a loo?

She shook her head as she reached Melton Green. It was still light, but the sun was low over the common and the grasses were more golden than green. Parking her car and getting out, she couldn't help wondering if she was doing the right thing, but there was no going back now – he'd spotted her.

'Megan!' he called through the skeleton of the building. She grabbed her overnight bag from the back seat and walked around the side of the house to join him. She could have actually walked *through* the house, but it somehow didn't feel right so they met round the back in between the house and the moat. Truffle and Blewit immediately ran towards her from where they'd been sitting on the lawn and she bent to greet them. When she stood back up, Rick was in front of her.

'Hi,' she said, suddenly feeling shy.

'Hello Minnow,' he whispered and she dropped her bag to the ground as they fell into a warm embrace.

'I received a letter,' she whispered to him a moment later. 'Asking me to spend a night under the stars. Am I in the right place for that?'

He smiled and whispered back, 'Yes. You are.'

'I thought I'd better just check.' She felt his arms tighten around her and knew that she was, indeed, in the right place.

When they finally moved apart and Megan glanced back at the house, she gasped.

'You have a wall!' she exclaimed.

'And some roof too – look!' He pointed.

Megan looked up and saw the difference he'd made. 'It looks wonderful!'

'I've got a pals helping me for a bit while he's between jobs so we're making good progress.'

'It's so exciting seeing it go up like this.'

'Yeah, it'll soon start looking like a real house!'

Megan saw his smile fading quickly. 'What's wrong?'

He let out a deep sigh. 'It's all going so quickly and I don't want it to.'

'But you need walls and a roof!'

'I know. But having the place like this – with the sun streaming right into it and the wind blowing through it – it feels special.'

'Oh, Rick! I thought we'd agreed that you can't live in a place that's just stud walls and beams!'

He nodded. 'I know. I'm just enjoying the weirdness of it while I can. It's a kind of freedom, I guess.' He took her hand and led her into the centre of the house. 'It's changing, isn't it?'

'But that's good. Don't you want to see it finished and furnished?' They walked towards the empty brick fireplace now. 'Just imagine it in winter with the fire going and something wonderful cooking on the Aga.'

Rick grinned. 'I can imagine that.'

'And a sofa here. A big squashy one with lots of cushions.'

'And a couple of spaniels.'

'Oh, of course!'

'And someone special,' he added and Megan felt that fluttery feeling she was becoming oh so familiar with whenever she was around him.

'It's going to be so beautiful,' she told him.

He glanced up into the rafters and the tiles that were up there now and to the evening sky beyond them where the stars were waiting for their moment to shine down upon them.

'Hey? Are you hungry?'

Megan nodded and the two of them left the house and walked towards the moat to where Rick had set up a stove and laid a campfire. It didn't take him long to get the fire going and Megan watched as he cooked a simple pasta dish over the flames.

'You've done this before, haven't you?'

'Once or twice,' he admitted with a grin. 'Dad taught Leo and me how to make a fire before we could tie our shoelaces. He said it was a life skill that should be taught in schools.'

'He's probably right,' Megan said. 'What does he think about this place?'

A look of sadness passed over Rick's face. 'I'm afraid he died some years ago.'

'Oh, I'm sorry.'

'But he would have loved it. I wish I could share it with him.'

'I'm sure he'd be proud of what you're doing.'

'He'd certainly approve of cooking over a real fire. He said that food always tasted better outdoors. And he's right, don't you think?'

'I think I'm about to find out.'

Rick looked up from stirring the pan. 'You've never cooked outdoors before?'

'Never!' She laughed at his shocked expression.

'Not even a barbecue? Everyone's had a barbecue surely?'

'Oh, well, yes then. But it's not quite the same as this, is it? I mean eating supermarket burgers on a patio can't compete with this.'

'Well, this is kind of from the supermarket, but I'm hoping to grow tomatoes one day in the greenhouse over there. Needs fixing up, like everything else here, but it'd be good to grow what I can.'

'I love your vision for this place,' she told him.

'Yeah, I'm pretty excited about it myself. I still can't believe I own it. Each time I drive out here and turn down the track over the common, it seems surreal that this is really mine.'

When the pasta was ready, Rick served it in bowls, its rich tomato sauce thick and glossy.

'Is that enough?' he asked.

'More than enough, thank you!'

'I wasn't sure how hungry you'd be. I've got all sorts in the cool bag over there you can help yourself to. There are two huge bottles of water in the Land Rover. There's a tap over by the house, but I'd use the bottled water for brushing your teeth and washing if I was you. And there's a compost loo over there.' He pointed to the area behind the Land Rover.

'Noted!'

They ate in companionable silence as the light slowly faded from the sky. Truffle and Blewit were sitting by the fire beside them.

'Have they eaten?' Megan asked.

'Hours ago. They're fed twice a day, but I caught Blewit snacking in between meals on the remains of something gross under the shepherd's hut. It's probably best not to talk about that while we're eating.'

Megan grimaced as she finished her pasta. Rick had finished his too and took their bowls.

'I bought a little something from the bakery in Castle Clare,' he said.

'Oh, now you're just spoiling me!'

Megan watched as Rick went to retrieve a box from the Land Rover.

'I had to hide it from the dogs,' he told her. 'Well, that's not totally true. They're pretty well behaved on that front. It was me I had to hide it from.' He sat back down on the grass next to her and opened the box.

'Treacle tart?'

'I got Colin to cut it into slices.'

'I *love* treacle tart!'

'That's what Colin said.'

'You *asked* him?'

'He's got an encyclopaedic knowledge of the likes and dislikes of the people of Castle Clare. I tested him!'

'Really?'

'And he told me that treacle tart was your particular favourite. He said you were also a fan of jam doughnuts, but I thought that might be a bit tricky – a bit *sticky!*'

Megan giggled. 'Well, now you know all my wicked secrets!'

He pushed the box towards her and Megan took a slice.

'Good?' Rick asked before he dived in himself.

'It's the best!'

Rick took a bite. 'Oh, my god! You're right.'

'I am, aren't I?'

'I think it's gone right to the top of my list too now.'

'What was top before?'

'Tarte au Citron.'

'Oh, well, that's a classic!'

They both agreed that it would be detrimental to Colin's reputation if they didn't have at least two slices of treacle tart each and, once they had finished eating, they snuggled up together, watching the flames of the fire dancing.

'It's cooled down a lot, hasn't it?' Megan said.

'I've got plenty of blankets. Shall I get you one?'

'No, I'm okay. Where do Truffle and Blewit sleep?'

'In the Land Rover. They've got baskets in there. I let them out first thing.'

'When you say *first thing*, are you talking about dawn?'

He screwed his face up. 'Kinda! It just seems so natural to work with the light. You'll see. You'll be awake with the sun.'

'I'm not so sure!'

'Well, just take your time.' He tightened his arms around her. 'Are you ready to get the sleeping bags out? I guess it's getting quite late now.'

Megan gazed up into the sky which had morphed from a gentle turquoise to a beautiful inky blue. 'Okay.'

Rick got up and, after putting the food things away, he rolled out a couple of mats and placed the two sleeping bags on top of them.

'I've got pillows in the Land Rover.'

Megan smiled. He'd really thought of everything.

'Where shall I get changed?' she asked, glancing around. If she walked away from the fire in any direction, she'd be able to change wherever she wanted in privacy because there was no light at all.

'By the barn?'

'Okay.' She took her bag and walked towards the barn. It was dark away from the light of the fire and Megan disrobed quickly. She'd brought a long-sleeved pink nightdress with her. It was one of her favourites, but she felt anxious about it now. Was it a bit too matronly, she wondered? A little old-fashioned? Well, it was too late to worry about that now. Anyway, there was no point trying to be anything other than who she was.

She found her toothbrush and retrieved the water bottle from the Land Rover. It was a new experience to be brushing her teeth outdoors in the dark of the Suffolk countryside. Although, as she looked around her, she realised that her eyes were adjusting to the darkness and she could see the darker shapes of the trees against the softer blue-blackness of the sky.

She took her hairbrush out of a bag and gave her hair a good going over, leaving it loose. She wasn't sure if Rick had seen her hair loose before and wondered what he'd make of it. Suddenly, she felt nervous. Nervous about what she was wearing. Nervous about what she was doing here. Nervous about what might happen. She took a deep breath. The scent of a nearby jasmine clambering up the side of the old barn was heavy on the night air. Megan inhaled its sweet aroma and instantly felt calmer.

When she returned to the fire, she saw Rick crouching beside it. He'd changed into a T-shirt and shorts. She couldn't tell what colour they were in the evening light but, when he glanced up, she saw his mouth drop open.

'What?' she asked.

'Your hair.'

She frowned, thinking perhaps there was a creature stuck in it or something. 'Is it okay?' She did her best to flatten it with her hand in case it had gone flyaway.

Rick closed the space between them and kissed her deeply. 'I've always wanted to see you with your hair loose. It's so beautiful,' he told her. They gazed at each other for a moment and then Megan shivered.

'You're cold.'

'A little.'

'Let's wrap up in these bags then.'

'Are the dogs in bed now?' Megan looked around for them.

'Yes – safely in for the night.'

The two of them focused on their own beds, unzipping the sleeping bags and crawling inside. Megan then reached for her overnight bag and got something out. She could sense that Rick was watching her as she sat reading.

'You've brought a book?' he said in surprise.

'Of course! And a torch. I don't go anywhere without a trusty paperback. You never know when you're going to be held up in a queue or traffic.'

'There are no queues or traffic out here,' Rick pointed out.

'No, but it's habit, you see. And I like to read a bit each night.'

Rick pushed his sleeping bag down his body and sat up. 'What are you reading?'

'Well, I've just finished *84 Charing Cross Road* again.'

'Ah, the book with all the letters!'

'That's right. And I've just started this travel memoir. It's very funny,' she told him, finding where she'd got up to with the help of her torch.

A moment later, she felt Rick inch closer to her as if about to lean in and kiss her. Instinctively, she held her book up a little higher to block him and heard him laugh.

'Sorry!' she said. 'This is a good bit.'

'I guess it must be!' he teased.

'Just one more page before I kiss you.'

'I know my place,' he said, sounding suitably chastised. She bit back a giggle, hearing the smile in his voice. But she knew she couldn't concentrate now. Still, she duly finished the page and placed the book and torch back in her bag, zipping it up for the night. Rick was staring up at the sky and Megan nestled into him and they watched as, slowly, more and more stars became visible.

'The moon will come up soon,' Rick told her.

'I feel so small looking at it all,' Megan confessed.

'The sky will do that to you. But I like that feeling.'

'Me too.'

'It kind of puts you in your place, doesn't it?'

Rick turned to face her and they kissed.

'My Minnow,' he whispered. 'My beautiful Minnow.'

That night, under the moon and the stars and the whispering trees, they kissed. They kissed a lot.

CHAPTER FIFTEEN

Rick had said that Megan would be awake at first light and she was. Almost. But she hadn't woken as early as Rick and she sat up in her sleeping bag looking around for him. She soon spotted him. He'd obviously got up and let the dogs out of the Land Rover and she watched as he walked the perimeter of the meadow with them, his long easy strides eating up the golden land. She liked watching him move. He truly looked a part of this place, she thought.

Quickly, she got up and visited the compost loo and brushed her teeth and hair before having a drink of water and returning to her sleeping bag. The fire had long died out and the stars were a distant memory but, somewhere, she could hear a blackbird heralding the morning and the first warm rays of the sun were stretching across the fields and making the dew sparkle on the lawn.

It felt strange and wonderful waking up outside and it felt especially wonderful after the night they'd spent together. Megan closed her eyes and took a deep breath, trying to commit it all to memory. When she opened them again, she could hear the frantic panting of Truffle from somewhere behind her and a wet spaniel nose was soon poking in her left ear.

'Awww, Truffle!' Megan laughed, unzipping her sleeping bag and crawling out, much to the spaniel's delight. Megan gave her a good fuss and Blewit soon joined in for his share of attention.

'Good morning!' Rick called as he came out of the meadow and walked towards them.

'Am I up horribly late?'

'Nah!' Rick said, flopping down on the ground beside them all. 'Did you sleep okay?'

'Yes! I didn't think I would, but it was so comfortable. I loved it!'

'I loved being so close to you,' Rick said, inching towards her now and kissing her. 'Sharing all this with you.'

'I loved it too,' she whispered back, thinking of the kisses they'd shared.

'Fancy some breakfast? I can get the fire going again in no time.'

'Lovely! I'll get dressed.'

She picked up her overnight bag, taking it to a spot by the side of the barn. For a moment, she wondered whether to tie her hair back, but there was something deliciously freeing about having it loose with the summer breeze flowing through it and so she left it down. There were no mirrors at Oak Farm Cottage but, again, she found that rather freeing.

She had brought a change of clothes with her and put on the summer dress now. Like her nightdress, it was pink and she wondered about getting back into her jeans as the morning was still a little chilly. Instead, she reached for her cotton jumper and popped it on over the dress. She was grateful that she didn't have to rush into Castle Clare as the library was closed today. Instead, she could enjoy her time with Rick.

She glanced back towards the lawn and saw Rick crouching over the new fire he'd got going, nursing the flames into life with passion and patience. It was such a mesmerising scene and she watched in silent admiration for a while, but she then decided she wanted to get a sneaky photo and so switched her phone on. It would be good to check the weather forecast too, she thought.

Instantly, she realised her mistake. Not only could you could see so much of the sky at Oak Farm Cottage that a weather forecast seemed redundant, but she had also inadvertently let the outside world in once more – a world that she'd blissfully forgotten about since last night.

And there they were. Dozens of messages.

They'd banked up overnight.

I know where you are.

I know who you're with.

I know what you're doing.

A sob suddenly left her as she glanced around. Was that possible? Was this person following her every move?

'Porridge is ready!' Rick called.

Megan quickly sniffed and wiped the tears from her face, but it was too late to hide her distress. Her hands were shaking as she tried to hide her phone quickly as Rick was walking towards her.

'Megan?'

'I'm okay!' she said a little too quickly and brightly to be convincing.

'No, you're not!'

Another sob left her and she felt his arms around her.

'I'm okay! I'm okay,' she insisted, but she was crying now – crying in fear and crying in frustration that this horrible thing that was happening to her had found its way to this special place. *Their* special place.

'What is it? Tell me!'

She shook her head, not knowing how to begin.

'Is somebody ill?'

She shook her head.

'Then what's upset you so much?' He leaned back, holding her face in his fire-warmed hands. She could smell the meadow on his skin and the smoke from the fire.

'I've... I've been getting messages,' she began, hating having to share this with him.

'What sort of messages?'

'On my phone, by email, on social media.'

'What are they about?'

Megan felt tears filling her eyes again. 'I didn't want this to spoil what we have here. It's so ugly and nasty so I tried to shut it out!'

'Oh, Megan!'

'They're horrible. And they're getting worse. I get dozens of them every day and I don't know what to do. My cousin Bryony said I should report it.'

'You mean you haven't?'

She shook her head. 'That would make it real, wouldn't it? And I was hoping it would all stop long before I even thought of reporting it.'

Rick brushed the tears from her face with his fingers, but his tenderness caused her to cry even more.

'I'm sorry! I didn't want you to know about this.'

'Why?' He sounded completely baffled by her declaration.

'Because it spoils everything.'

'But you can't hide something like this. If you're upset about something, I want to know. I *need* to know!'

'It's just that I wanted this – I wanted *here* – to be perfect,' she tried to explain.

'And it is! Nobody can take away what we have here. *Nobody*!'

He pulled her towards him and she felt warm and secure in his embrace.

'Come on – we'll report it today.'

'No! You're busy with the building work.'

'There's nothing more important than this.'

'But the cottage–'

'I've got my mate working with me this week. He can take care of himself.' He looked serious for a moment.

'What is it?' Megan asked.

'I've just remembered – there *is* something more important – the porridge!' He grinned and winked at her which made her laugh. 'We're not doing anything before the porridge, agreed?'

She nodded and they returned to the fire where she watched as Rick served up two warm bowls full of porridge, pouring a golden stream of maple syrup over each serving. For a few minutes, Megan tried to push all thoughts of the messages out of her mind, determined that they shouldn't spoil this time with Rick, but she was aware that he was watching her and she hated that she'd brought this problem into his life.

'I saw two herons this morning and a roe deer,' he said, distracting her wonderfully from any woeful thoughts.

'I wish I'd come with you.'

'I didn't want to wake you. You looked so peaceful.'

'Another time?'

'You want to sleep out here again?' he asked.

'Absolutely!'

He laughed.

'Only maybe not two consecutive nights. I do feel a bit stiff in the lower back.'

'There'll be plenty of time over the summer,' he insisted.

They finished their porridge and Rick then scrambled a couple of eggs over the fire, garnishing the dish with finely chopped chives.

'I found a patch behind the greenhouse,' he told her.

The eggs were followed by strawberries, ripe and rich from a neighbouring farm. Then Megan insisted on making coffee for them both.

'I feel so lazy letting you do everything,' she said.

'But I love it.' He smiled at her as she boiled the water. 'I love looking after you.'

The brightness of his eyes and the warmth of his smile made her feel as if she could fly. In fact, she was quite convinced if she stood up at that moment, she'd very likely take off and float high above the roof of the cottage, over the golden grasses of the common and on up into the blue depths of the sky.

Coffee made, they took their mugs out into the meadow where the fallen trunk of a tree provided a rough but comfortable seat from where they could gaze back at the cottage.

'I love this spot,' Rick said. 'It's become a favourite place to come when I need to plan all I've got to do. Although, if I'm honest, I'm not really into planning.'

'You're not?'

'Nah! I'm more of a dive in and figure it out as I go type of person.'

'Can you do that when building a house?'

'It's working out pretty well so far.'

She smiled. 'I'm a big planner. Notebooks, pens, lists – I love all that stuff!'

'And what sort of things do you plan?'

'Well, I've always got a "to do" list on the go. I've also got a "to read" list. A "to watch" list–'

'Really?'

'It's important to keep up to date with all the new films, isn't it? Especially book adaptations. You've no idea how many people come into the library asking for the book they've just seen on the TV or at the cinema and I'm expected to know what they're talking about.'

'Anything else?' he asked, sipping his coffee.

'I've got a...' she paused.

'What?'

'I don't know if I should tell you. It's kind of private.'

'You can't dangle a carrot like that, Minnow!'

She laughed. 'Okay! I'll tell you, but you mustn't laugh, all right?'

'I won't laugh,' he promised.

'It's a "life list".'

He frowned. 'What's that?'

'It's all the things I want to experience – not just the usual stuff like go up in a hot air balloon.'

'Is that usual stuff?' Rick asked. 'Seems pretty adventurous to me!'

'Yes, but that's the kind of thing on everyone's lists, isn't it? Mine's more... I'm not sure how to describe it. It's more to do with feelings, I guess.'

Rick had put his mug down now and was paying her his full attention.

'Tell me,' he said gently.

'I want to know what it feels like to walk through the desert and be surrounded by nothing but sand dunes.'

Rick looked surprised by her declaration.

'Don't laugh!' she told him.

'I'm not laughing. Go on.'

She took a deep breath. 'I want to swim in a sea so blue that it hurts just to look at it. I want to climb a tree and see the world as a nesting bird would. I want to find the source of a river and follow its path to the sea. And to stand on top of a mountain and feel the wind whipping around me. And I want to...' She paused again and bit her lip.

'What?'

She looked into his warm chestnut eyes and reached to touch the roughness of his unshaven skin.

'I want to fall so deeply in love that I completely lose myself – even if it's just for a minute.'

She gazed at Rick and the space between them seemed to vibrate with tension and tenderness, and then they kissed.

Megan closed her eyes. The sun was rising above the trees and she could feel the warm rays on her skin, but she didn't focus on it. She heard a skylark in the next field, but she was only half aware of its heavenly song as it rose higher and higher into the blue above.

Her mind had lost its grip on thought and she was living through pure emotion. Just for a minute. But that was enough.

~

One of the downsides to living in the middle of nowhere was that it was a long drive to the nearest police station and Megan hated that she was monopolising Rick's time in this way, especially when the sun was shining and they could have spent a wonderful morning together at Oak Farm Cottage. She cursed the sender of the messages, hating the way they'd stolen so much of her time, not just filling her head but actually taking great chunks of her life away dealing with it all.

And now Rick's too.

Truth be told, Megan was glad to have Rick's company as she sat in the police station, but she felt dreadful for taking his time when she knew he could be up on the roof under the sunshine. They'd waited for Rick's mate to turn up so he could keep an eye on Truffle and Blewit and then they'd left in Megan's car.

Rick had asked if he could see some of the messages and she'd reluctantly shown him. She really hadn't wanted to because, although none of this was her fault, there was still that underlying feeling of shame at being called such names by someone and being told such horrendous things.

She'd seen a look of horror cross Rick's face as he'd read them. He'd muttered something under his breath and then had passed the phone back to her. When she'd confessed how long it had been going on, he'd looked dumbfounded and had pulled her in to a hug so tight that she never wanted him to let go.

When they walked out of the police station an hour later into the blazing sunshine, Megan was both relieved and furious.

'Well, I'm not sure if that wasn't a *complete* waste of time,' she said as they walked back to her car together.

'It's important that they've got a record of this. He took down all the details, didn't he?'

'I suppose.'

'Now it's up to you to gather as much evidence as possible.'

'But the police aren't *doing* anything!'

'I don't suppose there's much they can do at the moment,' Rick said with a sigh.

'I just feel that they weren't taking me very seriously.'

'Yes, it was frustrating, wasn't it? But you heard what he said – screenshot everything in case things get deleted. Keep a record of *everything* you're sent. You need to have it all. And don't reply to anything because that could make things even worse.'

'I know. I haven't been – at least, not since the beginning.'

Rick put his arm around her. 'How about we find somewhere for lunch?'

'I don't know. I'm not very hungry.'

'Want to come back to the cottage with me?'

'I think I'll have to unless you want to walk,' she said.

'Ah, yes. There is that.'

They both laughed and it felt good that they were still able to find a moment of levity in the midst of the darkness.

When they got back to Oak Farm Cottage, Rick introduced Megan to Matt who'd been holding the fort in his absence and making good progress with the tiling. The sun was high in the sky now and Megan was glad that Rick had persuaded her to stop at a favourite chippie on the way home. Now, all three of them dived into their paper wrappings, the smell of hot vinegar wafting across the lawn.

Megan listened to Rick and Matt chatting about the work on the house. They were both so passionate about what they were doing. Matt had recently been working on a Tudor manor house in the Stour Valley, rumoured to have several ghosts. He said he'd always made sure to leave before dark during the winter months.

She listened to their shared stories about dark properties and damp properties, spacious ones and small ones, and she couldn't help thinking what wonderful people they were and how there wasn't a bad bone in their body. And yet there were bad people out there – the sort to harass and stalk a person and make them feel unsafe and fearful every time they checked their phone. Looking at Rick now, she felt an overwhelming sense of gratitude that he'd come into her life and that she had him by her side as she tried to navigate her way through everything.

CHAPTER SIXTEEN

Josh and Lara were trying to decide how to arrange the shop window for the upcoming Castle Clare Literary Festival. It was the same every August with the Nightingale family trying to make the festival the best one ever, but Josh just wasn't feeling the love this year.

'You've got that bunting the wrong way round!' Lara yelled at him.

'Really? How can you tell?'

'Because the print is stronger on this side – look!'

Josh sighed and handed the whole thing to Lara. He was done with bunting.

'Do we really have to have bunting again?'

'Of course! You can't have a festival without bunting. Come on, Josh! Get into the spirit of things.'

He shook his head. 'I'm sorry. I'm a bit distracted.'

Lara put the bunting down. 'Shall I put the kettle on?'

A few minutes later, the two of them perched on the stools behind the till, sipping their tea.

'You okay, big bro?'

'Yes, I'm okay. Just... there's a lot to think about right now.'

'I'll say! I still can't believe I'm going to be an aunt again so I can only imagine how you feel about being a father!'

He puffed out his cheeks. 'That's such an enormous thought, isn't it? A *father*!'

'It's about as big as they come,' Lara agreed and then her forehead furrowed. 'What does it *feel* like?'

Josh took a sip of his tea. He'd been having all sorts of feelings about the upcoming arrival and how his whole life was going to change, only he wasn't sure he knew how to put it all into words. But his little sister was watching him closely, her big eyes full of wonder and curiosity.

'It feels like everything all at once. Joy, wonder, excitement, fear, dread.'

'*Dread?*'

'At all the things that could go wrong.'

'Oh, you mustn't think about that sort of thing!' Lara told him quickly, shaking her head. 'Positive thoughts only. Law of Attraction and all that.'

Josh nodded. 'Do you want children?' he dared to ask.

Lara gave a half laugh, half snort. 'Well, not until I've graduated at least! Give me a chance!'

'You'll make a great mum.'

Lara's eyes widened at this unexpected statement. 'You think?'

'Yes, of course. You're just so enthusiastic about everything. And nothing seems to faze you.'

'Except reading *Vanity Fair*.'

'Well, that would faze anyone!'

'Are you *sure* I can't get away with the audio book?'

'Lara!'

'Okay, okay! I'll read it *properly*!'

'Audio is a completely different experience. I don't think you'll pick up on the nuances of the language so much if you listen to it.'

'Maybe I can get away with an audio version of the Dickens then? His writing's more theatrical, isn't it?'

Josh sighed and shook his head. 'Read the books, Lara!'

'Okay, okay!' She jumped off the stool and took their empty mugs into the back room. When she returned, Josh was standing at the window.

'Why don't you pop across and see her?' she asked.

'You don't mind holding the fort?'

'Course not! It'll probably be easier managing this bunting business with you out of the way!'

He smiled. 'You should give Tristan a ring too and tell him that idea you had for the festival.'

'I tried. He's not interested. He says it's too much upheaval having a new venue at this stage.'

'That's a shame. I thought it was a good idea.'

'It was and the annoying thing is, I told him about it months ago so there was ages to get things ready.'

'You'll have more say in things next year.'

'I hope so! But he's holding the reins pretty tightly at the moment,' Lara told him and then she smiled. 'You're not listening, are you?'

'No, I am!'

'Go on – get across the road!'

Josh nodded. His sister knew him so well.

As he left the shop, he couldn't help feeling slightly anxious. He'd not heard from April that day. Usually, they'd swapped a few messages by now and maybe even chatted over breakfast. Certainly, she would have waved a couple of times from her own shop window. But not today.

Josh crossed the road and opened the door into *A Little Bit Bloomsbury*. As ever, the smell of wet paint greeted him and he saw her bending over a bookcase, a can of yellow paint by her side.

'Are you okay, sweetheart?' he asked.

She stood up and turned to face him.

'Oh, May!' Josh said in alarm.

'Hello Josh.'

'I thought April was in today,' he said, thanking his lucky stars that he hadn't crept up on May and pulled her into an embrace. It wouldn't have been the first time, mind.

'No. She said she wasn't up to it.'

'Is she all right?' He took his phone out to check for messages, but there wasn't anything from her.

'I think it might be morning sickness. She was making some pretty gross noises in the bathroom first thing.'

'Oh, god! I should go and see her.'

Josh was already half-way to the door.

'Josh?'

'Yes?'

'Could you pop into the Co-op and get something first? It might help.'

~

When Josh arrived at the ground floor flat in the Victorian villa on the edge of Castle Clare which April and May shared together, there was no answer when he rang the bell. At least, not at first. When April finally made it to the door wearing a dressing gown Josh felt awful for having disturbed her if she'd been sleeping. Her face was pale and her long hair had been tied up roughly at the back of her head – probably in response to the morning sickness, he couldn't help thinking.

'Hey!' he said, entering the flat and wrapping her up in a gentle hug.

'Josh! What are you doing here?'

'May told me you weren't feeling well. Why didn't you tell me?'

'I didn't want to bother you. I know you're busy with festival stuff.'

'But nothing's more important than this,' he said. 'Come and sit down. You look so tired. Can I make you a cup of tea or something?'

She shook her head and they went into the living room and sat on the sofa together.

'I thought I'd got away with the whole morning sickness thing, but it looks like I'm just entering that phase now.'

'Is it awful?'

'It isn't pleasant!'

He picked up her hands which were pale and cold in her lap and gave them a tight squeeze. 'You'll get through it.'

She let out a huge sigh. 'What if I'm not cut out for this? What if I can't do it?'

'What do you mean?'

'My body – my vision. *Everything!* What if it's all too much for me? What if I lose my sight before the baby arrives and I never get to see its face? Or if it happens before it takes its first steps? Or on its first morning of school?'

Josh could see tears in her eyes and it distressed him that she was suffering so much.

'I'm right here with you, April. And you won't miss a single thing because I'll tell you every little detail, okay? I'm good at details – you've said that, haven't you? Well, I won't miss out a thing. I'll describe every single freckle on our child's face, and every expression – even the mean ones! I won't let you miss a single second, I promise!'

'Oh, Josh! I'm so scared!'

Josh felt terrified hearing the fear in her voice, but he couldn't show that.

'Hey!' he said gently. 'That doesn't sound like the courageous April I know!'

She sniffed loudly. 'I don't *feel* very courageous.'

'That's just your hormones talking. You're changing. *Everything's* changing. It's a lot to cope with. But you *will* cope! Think of all you've ever been through. All the battles you've had – the fear, the pain you've endured. You came through it all, April. Not *once* did you fail at anything! You have survived all of your worst days to be here now with me on this sofa, with our beautiful baby growing inside you.'

She gave another big sniff and wiped her eyes on a tissue. 'I feel so exhausted.'

'But that's normal, isn't it? I've been reading about all this.'

'You have?'

'Of course! I've even ordered some books. Or rather, I should say, *more* books. All the latest ones. You should always have up to date information on this sort of thing. I'll bring them all round once I've read them.'

'You are such a sweetheart.'

'It's about all I am able to do as a bookseller. I feel a bit useless in all this otherwise.'

'You're not useless! I couldn't get through any of this without you.'

'Actually, I did bring you something, but I left it in the car,' he said. 'Wait a minute.' He popped out to the car and came back a moment later.

'What is it?' April asked, standing up and looking at the carrier bag.

'I've brought you a big slab of dark chocolate. May said you were out of it for your chocolate fudge sundaes.'

April shook her head, suddenly looking paler than ever. 'That craving's long gone!'

'Oh, dear. Well, I'll leave it in the kitchen just in case it comes back.'

They sat back down on the sofa and April rested her head against Josh's shoulder.

'I don't want you to go,' she whispered.

'I'm not going anywhere.'

'But you will at some point.'

'I guess. May won't want me here when she gets home, will she?'

'No. Probably not. But...'

'What?'

'Maybe I can go with you.'

Josh turned to look at her and April sat up straight. A little colour had returned to her face and her eyes looked brighter.

'You want to come back to the shop with me?'

She laughed. 'No! I'm saying I think it's time.'

Josh frowned and then he smiled. 'You mean...'

'I mean, I don't want to put you through all this morning sickness business but, maybe when the worst is over, I could move in with you. Is that very forward of me?'

'April, we're having a baby together. I don't think you can get much more forward than that.'

She smiled and it was so lovely to see her looking happy again that Josh wanted to tell her to pack her bags right there and then.

'What about May? I think she's got it into her head that you're here until the baby arrives.'

'She has kind of hinted at that.'

'Hinted! She's turning the spare room into a nursery, isn't she?'

'How do you know about that?'

'I didn't!' Josh said. 'It was just a suspicion that you've now confirmed.'

'Josh Nightingale – that is the most underhand thing you've ever done!'

He laughed, but then his expression changed. 'You'll have to tell her if you're serious about moving out.'

April almost visibly squirmed. 'Couldn't I just leave a note?'

'You're not the sort to do that.'

She sighed. 'I know. It's just going to break her heart.'

'No it won't. She's a big girl.'

'But she's still my little sister.'

'Yes, but only by twenty-three minutes!' Josh said as if she needed reminding. 'Anyway, she knows this is going to happen at some point. Personally, I think the earlier the better.'

'Really?'

'Truly. Besides...' he paused. 'I want you with me. I want you *both* with me! And I mean you and the baby – not you and May. Just so we're clear!'

April giggled.

'May's had her turn and now it's mine.'

April sighed and she nodded. 'I'll tell her. As soon as... as soon as I get the nerve.'

'Well, just make sure it's before your waters break.'

'You've been reading about that too, have you?'

Josh could feel his face heating up. 'I intend to be fully up to speed on this baby business.'

April put her arms around him and gave him a big kiss. 'I do love you, Josh Nightingale!'

Ben Stratton had just finished teaching for the day. He'd taken on a new class recently, teaching English Language GCSE to adults. He had to admire his students – most of whom came to his class to study after putting in a full day's work. Now *that* was dedication. The only thing was, it took up one whole evening a week and he kind of begrudged that time away from Bryony. And Longfellow.

Ben smiled as he thought of them both. It was funny how quickly they'd become a happy family unit in the little terrace house. He loved their life there so much and he especially looked forward to the evenings when they'd pop over to Cuckoo Cottage to help Flo and Sonny out with the animals. Their latest project was fixing the hen run which was decidedly shabby and in danger of collapsing.

It still amazed Ben how quickly he'd settled into life back in Suffolk. After his travels around the world, he had been a little anxious that he'd get itchy feet again one day. But that hadn't happened and he was pretty sure it wouldn't now. For the first time in his life, he felt truly settled. Peaceful. At home.

Ben crossed the car park, waving goodnight to one of his adult students as he made his way to his own car. It was then that his phone beeped. As he was carrying a pile of books, he waited until he got in the car before pulling out his phone. The message was via one of his social media sites from an account he didn't recognise.

I hate to tell you bad news Ben.

And that was it. Ben frowned and tried not to panic because it sounded pretty spammy to him. For a moment, he thought about ringing the number and asking what was going on, but another message arrived before he could do that.

You know she's cheating on you, don't you?

At that, Ben felt his blood run cold. Who was this? And were they talking about Bryony? As he was deliberating what to do, a third message appeared.

You've always known this would happen, right?

I'm sorry I had to tell you this.

Ben watched in horror and confusion as message after message appeared.

She isn't worth it.

You should leave her now before things get worse.

Ben's fingers hovered over the keypad and then he typed.

Who is this?

There was a short pause before the reply came.

I can't tell you that. I'm just looking out for you.

Ben felt rigid with fear. The tone of the last message seemed sincere, didn't it? But who could it be? Was it someone he knew? It sounded as if they knew Bryony so it must be someone local. Ben wracked his brains. Was it someone they were both friends with? Someone in Castle Clare where Bryony had her shop? Had they been watching her?

But who was to say any of this was true? Firstly, it could be a scam. Secondly, it could just be a troublemaker. Thirdly...

Thirdly, what? Someone was telling the truth? Someone really was looking out for Ben? Then why had they contacted him anonymously?

He closed his eyes for a moment. Bryony. *His* Bryony. His one and only true love. The woman he'd carried in his heart right around the world and the one he'd come back to. He loved her with every fibre of his being and he'd never suspect her of deceiving him.

But what if she was? a little voice deep inside him asked. *What if she's back with him? You know who I'm talking about. He never went away, did he? He's in Castle Clare. He's right next door to her every day she's in the shop.*

Ben shook his head, intent on quashing the evil internal voice. But, as he left Ipswich and drove down the country lanes back home, he couldn't get the messages out of his mind.

You've always known this would happen.

You should leave her now before things get worse.

Pulling up outside his home half an hour later, he could feel the beginnings of a headache brewing. He cut the engine and pulled his phone out, looking at the messages one last time. And then he deleted them. He got out of the car, scooping up the books from the back seat and fishing his key out of his pocket.

It was still light but the sun was setting fast, leaving deep pink smudges across the sky. Ben let himself in.

'I'm home!' he called, walking into the living room and placing his books down on the coffee table before ruffling Longfellow's head. He liked being greeted by this sweet creature.

'Bry?' he called. She wasn't in the kitchen so he came back out into the hallway.

'I'm just washing my hair,' she called from upstairs. 'I'll be down in a mo!'

'Okay.'

'Oh, Ben?'

'Yes?'

'I got you a treat! I've left it in the kitchen in case Longfellow got any ideas it was for him.'

Ben smiled and returned to the kitchen where he spotted a bag he'd missed before.

It was from Well Bread. The shop run by Colin the baker. In an instant, the messages he'd just deleted came flooding back to him. Colin had been Bryony's sweetheart while Ben had been travelling, but Bryony had always said she'd never really been in love with him. But Ben had seen the way Colin used to look at her. Was he still smitten? Was he wooing Bryony again and was she cheating on him as the messages had said?

His hands were shaking as he picked the bag up and looked inside. It was a chocolate éclair. He normally loved those, but the thought of eating this one made him feel nauseous.

Just then, Bryony entered the kitchen, her long dark hair glossy after her shower. She approached him for a kiss and then looked down at the bag.

'I thought you'd have wolfed that down by now,' she said.

'No. I'm... I'm not feeling too good.'

Bryony looked concerned. 'Are you okay?'

'I might just have a lie down. Headache.' He walked out of the kitchen.

'You don't want the éclair?' Bryony called after him.

'No. You have it.'

'Really? Well, if you're sure. I've already had one, but I can't resist anything of Colin's.'

Ben stopped in his tracks and turned to face Bryony, but her back was to him now as she scooped the éclair out of the bag.

'Oh my goodness! These things are delicious, aren't they? Colin really can't be beaten, can he? I mean, how can a girl resist?'

CHAPTER SEVENTEEN

Sam smiled across at Callie as he started the car.

'I love having you with me,' he told her. 'I know it's not *exactly* a day out like I promised you, but I think you'll enjoy this.'

'I'm really looking forward to it,' Callie said. 'I'm not quite ready to start another book yet so my time is yours!'

Sam did a comedy double-take at this confession. 'Really?'

'I know that sounds completely unbelievable!' She laughed. 'But there it is. I'm taking a break between books.'

'It's good to take time off, Callie.'

'I know. Even Piers said I'd been working too hard over the last few years.'

Sam tried not to flinch at the mention of Callie's ex-husband. 'When did he say that?'

'During the last Zoom call. Don't worry – he's not editing me again! He just pops up every so often to keep an eye on things.'

'Okay,' Sam said reservedly.

'You're not worried about that, are you?'

'No, of course not. I trust you!'

'He knows I'm with you. Anyway, he's only interested in me as an author these days.'

'Good,' Sam said as he pulled out into the road.

'So, tell me about this place.'

'Well, I went there a few years ago as part of an open garden thing with Mum and Grandma. But I've never been in the house before. It's a moated Tudor manor house, but I don't know much more other than that. I just remember bits of it from the garden.'

'Can we look round the garden today?'

'We can ask. I'm sure they wouldn't mind.'

They left the village of Newton St Clare and headed into the Suffolk countryside. It felt good to get away from the shop if only for half a day, Sam mused. He'd been feeling a little anxious about everything recently and often wondered just how long his little shop could survive. But he didn't like to dwell on it. The truth was, he wasn't sure what he'd do if he wasn't able to sell books. What else was he good for? Recently, he'd met a young book enthusiast who had a YouTube channel. He'd done a little piece about Sam and his shop and, for a brief spell, Sam had seen an uptick in orders. There'd even been comments left under the video suggesting that Sam set up his own channel and he'd flirted with the idea. Would people be interested in that? The day-to-day running of a tiny secondhand bookshop? He couldn't imagine it really and yet something tugged at him to look into it.

Then he'd realised that, if he were to commit to a new project and do it properly, he'd not only need the right equipment but would have to invest a lot of time too. There was also the slight rub that Sam couldn't bear the thought of being in front of a camera. One of the joys of being a bookshop owner was that his job was rarely about him; it was about the books. Of course, he had his local faithful customers whose visits to the shop were just as much about seeing Sam as their latest acquisitions, but Sam wasn't one to court attention.

The truth was, Sam had no idea what the future might hold for him other than marriage to Callie. Then again, could anyone be truly sure what the future held? Recent years had shown that even those with jobs once perceived safe could no longer rely on them to provide lifelong security.

That's why days like today were so pleasurable. It was just as well that he had joyous moments like this to make up for his scant earnings. He was lucky in so many ways. He'd known when he took over the shop from his parents that he was never going to make his fortune, but he'd always somehow managed to make enough. And that was the essence of happiness surely – knowing when you had *enough*.

Sam glanced out at the view ahead as they passed through a village. The Suffolk landscape was always glorious even in the depths of winter, although a bare muddy field had less appeal than the verdant green and golden ones of high summer. Sam wound his window down and inhaled the sweet air. It felt good to be outside on such a day, leaving the dark interior of the shop for a couple of blissful hours. Polly had been glad to cover for him and, as an added bonus, she'd said she'd do her best to tidy up some of the damp books he'd purchased at auction. At least today, he'd actually be seeing and handling the books *before* purchasing them.

As the country lanes narrowed, Sam slowed down.

'I think we're nearly there,' he said, noticing the height of the summer hedgerows and the grass growing in the middle of the road.

'I hope they don't mind me showing up with you,' Callie said.

'No. I mentioned you were coming. You'll be useful for carrying boxes if I buy anything!'

Callie laughed and, a moment later, Sam turned into a driveway and the great Tudor manor house appeared.

'Oh, Sam! This is wonderful!'

'It is, isn't it! There are peacocks too – including a white one – so look out for those.'

Sam parked his car in the gravelled driveway and they both got out, gazing up at the barley twist chimneys, the latticed windows and the sheer size of the manor house.

They didn't need to ring the bell which was a shame because there was a wonderful old-fashioned pull to the right of the great oak front door that Callie was desperate to try. But an elderly gentleman had come round the corner of the house and waved a hand at them.

'I was listening out for you,' he called as he crunched over the gravel driveway. 'I've been in the herbaceous border.'

Sam tried not to laugh at that. It sounded like a line straight out of *Love on a Branchline* – a novel he adored.

'Mr Benson?'

'I do hope so,' Mr Benson said, coming forward to shake his hand.

'Sam Nightingale. And this is my friend – erm – my fiancée, Callie.'

'Friend... fiancé? Are you not quite sure?' the older man asked with a chuckle.

'Oh, I'm sure. Fiancée – it's just I'm not used to saying it.'

'Then congratulations must be in order,' Mr Benson said, reaching out to shake Callie's hand.

'Thank you!'

'Now, come on inside although I should warn you, it's a bit of a state. We're in the middle of sorting everything out, you see.'

'You're selling the place, aren't you?' Sam asked as they entered the house.

Mr Benson nodded. 'It's sad in a way, but life has different seasons, doesn't it? And our season here is done. Personally,' he said, whispering behind his hand, 'I'm rather looking forward to living somewhere warmer.'

'Oh, where are you going?' Callie asked.

'California.'

'That is a change from Suffolk,' Sam said.

'We're buying a little apartment overlooking the ocean. It's even got air conditioning – did you ever hear of such a thing? Air conditioning! After years of struggling to keep warm in this old place!' He gave a hearty laugh and then started coughing. 'Will be good for my lungs, that's for sure!'

'The house is certainly beautiful,' Callie said and Sam glanced at her, seeing her writer's eyes taking in the wide sweep of the staircase and the paintings hanging on the walls. Even with the hallway full of boxes and rolled up rugs, it still took the breath away.

'Just remind me again – you're the book man, aren't you?'

'Yes indeed,' Sam said.

'Forgive my memory. I've had the antiques woman, the painting chap and the piano guy all here this week. One gets a little confused.'

'That's understandable.'

'So, the library is through this way. Don't go getting excited by the term *library*, mind. It's only a couple of bookcases really and I'm not sure what's there to be honest. It was my father who was the collector and I think he sold a fair few in his own lifetime, but take a look and let me know what you think. I'll go and put the kettle on. Tea all right for you both?'

'That would be great,' Sam said, trying not to gasp as Mr Benson opened the door to the library and they walked inside.

'I'll leave you to get to know the books for a while and see you with some tea anon'

'Thank you,' Callie said and they both watched as he closed the door and left them to it.

'Wow!' Sam said as he took in the extent of the library for the first time. 'I've been in a fair few libraries in my time, but this is something else.'

'Do you think you'll find some treasures here?' Callie asked, daring to approach one of the bookcases.

'Oh, undoubtedly.'

'He said it was only a couple of bookcases as if he was talking about something from IKEA.'

'I know!'

'But these are enormous!' Callie said.

Sam ran his hands along the gleaming wood of one of the shelves. 'I'm not sure where to begin.' He let his eyes take in the glorious expanse of books. The cases were about eight feet tall and ran the length of one side of the room. And the room itself was pretty impressive with a huge mullioned window looking out across the garden and twin desks in front of it. There were lamps on little tables positioned around the room and a couple of squashy armchairs and a sofa all heaped with cushions. It was a book-lover's haven.

'Callie – look at this!' Sam cried as he reached for an old book.

'What is it?'

'It's part of a set of Sir Walter Scott's Waverley novels from the late 1870s. I'll count them all properly, but I think it's a complete set of all twenty-eight of the novels which will be forty-eight volumes if I remember rightly.'

'Are they valuable?'

'Well, they won't make me a millionaire, but they're worth a pretty penny and they're very beautiful – look.'

Together, they examined the green and gold covers and the fine creamy pages inside with delightful illustrations, and the beautiful marbling on the edges when the books were closed.

'They're lovely!' Callie said with an appreciative sigh. 'And – dare I ask?'

Sam grinned and brought the book up to his nose. 'Oh, yes!' He held it towards Callie who took an eager sniff.

'Oh, that's a good one!'

'Like a thousand glorious autumns!' he said and they exchanged a look of pure enchantment.

'Will you be able to sell them on successfully?'

'I've actually got a couple of customers who'd *love* these.'

Callie frowned. 'How will you choose between them?'

'Well, one is a real bookworm and I know she'd get a lot of pleasure from actually handling and reading these editions.'

'On a cold winter's evening beside a roaring fire!' Callie said.

'Exactly!'

'And the other?'

'They're more a collector of beautiful books. They appreciate the beauty of the spines on a bookcase.'

'And you're going to choose the bookworm, aren't you?'

'I do try not to sell my books by the yard, yes!'

'I love that about you,' Callie confessed. 'Among a great deal of other things, of course.'

They shared a secret kiss in front of the books. It was where all the best kisses happened.

Sam and Callie then continued to peruse the shelves, pulling out volume after volume to place on the tables behind them, cooing in enthusiasm at some of the discoveries.

'Oh, Sam! *The Wind in the Willows*!'

'Let me see!' Sam took it gently from her. 'It's a first edition. 1908. Not bad condition cover, but a lot of foxing.' He held it reverently, looking at the freckle-like blemishes.

'It's quite a spooky cover,' Callie observed. 'What is that?'

'It's Pan. Remember the chapter when he plays his pipes?'

'*The Piper at the Gates of Dawn*!'

'That's right.'

Sam placed the book carefully on the table.

'I might have to buy that one from you,' Callie said, stroking the cover with loving fingers. 'Even if it is a bit spooky. It's just so beautiful.'

The two of them spent several pleasurable hours looking through the books, liaising with Mr Benson over tea and then taking a look around the gardens, walking down to the lake and even spotting two of the peacocks one of whom gave them the privilege of seeing his magnificent tail. Sam then made an offer for the books he wanted which was gratefully accepted and the long job of packing began.

As they drove back through the Suffolk countryside, the car full of boxes stuffed with books, Sam felt relief flooding his system. He had, of course, had to invest in these books upfront, but he was confident that they would all find good homes at a decent profit to him. It was just the lift he needed after the disaster of the boxes of damp books he'd purchased recently.

'I've had a brilliant day, Sam!' Callie told him.

'Me too. How's about a celebratory bag of chips on the way home?'

'Sam Nightingale – you read my mind!'

They laughed. It was the perfect way to round off a perfect day.

~

Megan was attempting to fix the photocopier for the third time that morning when her older brother Tristan almost ran into the library.

'Megan! Are you okay?'

Megan looked at her brother's pale face. 'I'm fine. What's the matter?'

'I came as quickly as I could.'

She frowned. 'Why?'

'Why?' His face looked positively ashen now. 'I got your message. Or *messages*, I should say.'

'What messages?'

'Your messages,' he said, sounding quite angry now. 'Megan – I dropped everything and came straight here. You said you were in trouble!' He handed her his phone and Megan suddenly felt the cold grip of realisation as she looked at the screen. Her eyes filled with tears.

'These aren't from me.'

'What do you mean, they aren't from you?'

'I didn't send them. Any of them.'

Tristan ran a hand through his dark hair which was looking even more dishevelled than usual. Being self-employed and working from home meant that he always dressed on the casual side and he was wearing a shirt which clearly hadn't been ironed and a waistcoat that had once belonged to Grandpa Joe and which was frayed at the bottom and faded at the top.

'Look, come and sit behind the desk. I'll make you a cup of tea and try to explain what's been going on.'

'Okay, but I can't be long.'

'I know,' she said, aware that he was forever juggling deadlines in his job as a freelance editor. Plus there was the added stress of organising the Castle Clare Literary Festival. The chaos of trying to arrange all the publicity and venues as well as speakers from all over the country was enough to drive anyone potty.

Tea made, Megan took advantage of the quiet morning in the library to tell Tristan what had been going on.

'You've been to the police? Why didn't you tell me?'

'I didn't want anyone to know about it. It's so... horrible!'

Tristan shook his head. 'I'm your big brother, Megan.'

'I know. But I was trying to sort it out by myself.'

'How? How were you trying to sort it out by yourself?'

Megan sighed, knowing he wasn't going to like her answer. 'By ignoring it.'

'And since when did that ever work for anyone?'

'I know. Well, the police know now and I'm keeping a record of everything. Which means you should keep everything that you receive.'

'You think they're definitely connected?'

'It seems a bit of a coincidence otherwise, doesn't it?'

'Yes, I suppose so.' Tristan sipped his tea. 'Have you any idea who it is?'

'No. None at all.'

'Have you upset anyone recently?' Tristan glanced around the library as if looking for suspects but there was only old Winston Kneller sitting reading the newspaper and he probably didn't even have a smartphone.

'Of course not. Unless it's that seven year old boy I shouted at for throwing a book at his friend's face. Seven year olds are pretty tech savvy these days, aren't they?' Megan gave a tiny smile, amazed that she could crack a joke at such a time.

'All right. I was only asking,' Tristan said.

'I'm sorry. But I've gone over it so many times myself. Don't think I haven't!'

'Well, I'll block the account.'

'But do keep a record of them all.'

He nodded. 'Are you okay?'

Megan wrapped her hands around her mug. 'It's been pretty scary and upsetting.'

'I can imagine.'

'I've told Rick.'

'Ah! The mysterious Rick we have yet to meet. Lara mentioned you were seeing somebody.'

Megan could feel herself blushing at the mention of him. 'You'll meet him.'

Tristan smiled. He had a lovely smile when he wasn't being quite so serious.

'So, what's going on with you?'

Megan listened as he talked about the books he was currently editing. There was part two of a trilogy for a publisher. The first had been a *Sunday Times* bestseller and the pressure was on to repeat that success. He was also working with a couple of clients whose manuscripts were at different stages. One was a short autobiography and the other a novel.

'I don't normally take science fiction, but this author's an old friend and I told him to get in touch if he ever finished his novel,' Tristan told her. 'I didn't really imagine he'd see it through.'

'What's it like?'

'Well, it's unfair of me to judge a genre I don't really read myself. I'm not the right editor for it, but I can definitely nudge him in the right direction with his storyline and world building.' Tristan shook his head.

'What?'

'I don't know. It's all these weird names in science fiction, isn't it? People, planets, species. I mean, nobody's ever called Bob, are they?'

Megan laughed. 'There was Arthur Dent in *The Hitchhiker's Guide to the Galaxy*,' she pointed out.

'Yes, but he was kind of outside that world, wasn't he?' Tristan finished his tea and stood up. 'Look, before we start getting carried away with book talk, I'd better get going.'

'Thanks for rushing over here. It's good to know that I've got people looking out for me.'

Tristan gave her a big hug and she had to blink back her tears. She hated that he'd been caused distress because of her.

'Let me know if you need me. Only *ring*! Don't just message because I won't be sure if it's actually you or not.'

She nodded and watched him leave.

Winston glanced up from the local paper. 'Everything all right?' he asked.

Megan fixed a bright smile on her face, feeling so grateful that she was surrounded by people she loved and who cared about her.

'Yes, thank you, Winston. Everything's great.'

Only it wasn't, she couldn't help thinking. This person – whoever it was – was now targeting not just her but those connected to her and that was a very worrying development. Perhaps the police would take things more seriously now.

CHAPTER EIGHTEEN

The day might have started warm at Oak Farm Cottage, but the sun had disappeared behind a flotilla of clouds around midday never to be seen again. Rick and Matt were making good progress with the roof, but Rick was ever mindful of the weather, glancing up at the heavens from his precarious home high above the ground, praying they wouldn't get rained off. It was cooler today and Rick was wearing a beaten-up wax jacket that looked as if a terrier might have had puppies in it sometime in the spring. Its big pockets were handy for tools and snacks, though.

It was easy on days like today for hours to pass so quickly that he forgot to check his phone for messages. When he finally came back down to earth for a bite to eat that was slightly more sustaining than the crumbling remains of a packet of digestives, he saw that he had a text from Megan.

Call me when you can. X

Fear instantly flooded his system at the thought that something might have happened to her and he rang her without wasting a single moment.

'Megan?'

'Oh, Rick! Are you okay? You sound out of breath!'

'Are *you* okay?'

'Yes, I'm fine. It's just...' she paused.

'What? Do you want me to come over?'

'No. Don't do that when you're busy.'

'It's no bother. I've pretty much finished for the day.'

'Shall I come to you?'

Rick found himself smiling. 'Yes!'

'Do you need anything out there?'

'Some hot food would be great.'

Megan laughed and he felt himself exhale at the delightful sound. 'You got it!'

'And you're sure you're okay?'

'I'll fill you in when I see you. But – yes – I'm okay.'

Rick couldn't settle after that. He tidied his tools up and had a wash in cold water once his mate had left for the day. Then he whistled for Truffle and Blewit and the three of them set off across the common purely for the pleasure of walking back down the track to the property that was now his. He still couldn't believe that he got to call this place home. Well, it wasn't *quite* home yet although he had been sleeping and eating there and washing too. Wild washing, he thought. It was home in the sense of that feeling of belonging and that was the most important thing, wasn't it?

As soon as Megan's car pulled up, Rick made his way towards it and was there to kiss her as soon as she got out.

'Hi beautiful,' he whispered, her long dark hair whipping into his face in the wind. She smiled up at him and they kissed again. 'Are you cold?'

'Not when I'm right here,' she said, burrowing into him. He was wearing a large checked shirt that was at least a little softer than the old wax jacket. 'But I mustn't let your food get cold.' Reluctantly, she tore herself away from him.

'Oh, what did you bring?'

'Pizza!' she said, opening the back door of the car and retrieving the enormous box. 'Good – it's still warm. It's just a plain Margherita because I wasn't sure what toppings you like.'

'I like any toppings! Except pineapple which has no business whatsoever being on a pizza.'

Megan gasped.

'Oh, no!' he said quickly. 'You don't, do you?'

'I absolutely *love* pineapple on pizza!'

'No way!'

'It's just so juicy and it's the perfect blend with tomato.'

Rick shook his head. 'It's alien and just wrong, Megan!'

She gave him a look of mock dismay. 'Oh, dear! This could very well be the end of us. Well, it's been nice while it lasted!'

He laughed. 'I might be willing to rethink things, of course.'

Megan gave him a smile. 'No. I wouldn't want you to be anything other than who you truly are!'

They took the opportunity to kiss again.

'I've brought a couple of bottles too. White wine and pink lemonade. I wasn't sure if you'd finished up on the roof today so thought lemonade was a safer bet if you were still working.'

'Nah! I'm done.' Rick glanced up at the sky and then, grabbing the bottles from the back of the car, they took their picnic into the house where he'd set up a bench. It was a nicely sheltered spot now that a good chunk of the roof was on and it protected them a little from the wind. The spaniels were already in there, hunkered down against the unseasonal weather, and it was lovely to sit there himself after a hard day's work, with Megan by his side.

After they'd eaten, Rick listened as she told him about the latest slew of messages she'd received and also the ones Tristan had been sent.

'They're targeting your brother now?'

She nodded. 'It's scary, isn't it?'

'That's not good.'

'I know. I'm really worried. Where will this end? If they're reaching out to people close to me now?' She gave a weary sigh that

Rick could feel in his very heart. 'I'm actually thinking of shutting down my social media pages which is really frustrating. But it's my friends and family I'm most worried about because they're so reachable there and I guess it's easy to look up connections to people close to me.'

'I guess so.'

'Just after Tristan left the library, I got a call from Luke.'

'That's your other brother?'

'Yes. He said he'd had some weird messages on Facebook supposedly from me.'

'How were they weird?'

'He said he could tell they weren't from me. They were really scammy – saying I needed some money quickly.'

'Oh, god!'

'Now, that could be unrelated. I mean, people get scammy messages all the time, but it's a bit of a coincidence, don't you think?'

'Yeah, I do.'

'And I'm really worried how many other people might have had messages like this – purporting to be from *me*. And how many have responded to them?'

'I'm feeling pretty lucky now that I'm not on any of those sites.'

'I'm glad too. I'd hate them to be able to get to you.'

'But this is all definitely escalating,' Rick pointed out. 'I think we need to go back to the police, don't you?'

Megan nodded and he could see that her eyes were now bright with tears. 'I'm okay,' she told him, aware that his gaze was upon her.

'Come here,' he said and pulled her in to a warm embrace. 'It's going to be okay. We'll deal with it, all right?' He felt her nodding and they sat there together on the rough wooden bench, the wind dancing towards them through the exposed rafters of the house.

Polly had got into a horrible habit of checking the days off on the kitchen calendar. She knew she was fixating on trying to conceive and that she was probably causing herself a lot of unnecessary stress which wouldn't exactly improve her chances, but she just couldn't help it. She wanted this to happen so badly. She only hoped she wasn't scaring Jago with her earnestness.

She'd also been working hard. Not only had she been doing more shifts than normal in the family bookshops as well as her teaching, but she'd taken on a part-time job at Castle Clare's Antiques Centre. It wasn't much money, but every little bit helped and she enjoyed learning about the pieces she handled each day as well as chatting to the customers – some of whom knew her from the bookshops. The downside was that it was all so tiring. She was feeling exhausted and that was making her fractious.

After a day in which she'd covered for Josh who'd taken April to an appointment with her ophthalmologist as Lara also had a doctor's appointment, she'd got home with Archie, walked Dickens, and then had to clean the kitchen floor after an exploding yoghurt incident following Archie's attempt to juggle three pots at once.

She was just about to collapse on the sofa with a handful of custard creams and no guilt at all when her mother rang for a bit of sympathy after a rough day with Grandma Nell. It was a tough few minutes and Polly had to hide her tears from her mum because she was obviously turning to her for strength, but she couldn't help feeling relief when the call ended and she released her pent-up emotions. Of course, she'd managed to drop the custard creams onto the carpet so Dickens got that particular treat and Polly couldn't justify opening a new packet.

It was times like this that she wished Jago had a normal job with normal hours, but he had a couple of guitar lessons that evening on the other side of Bury St Edmunds so he was going to be late home. For a moment, she thought about texting him, but didn't want to disturb him when he was in teaching mode.

She was just checking to see if he might have texted her when a message popped up.

Hello Polly!

She didn't recognise the sender.

Pretty Polly.

She sighed. Wow! Weren't they original! She was just about to switch her phone off when another message arrived.

You know he's seeing her, don't you?

Polly frowned. Who were they talking about?

You've always known he would cheat on you.

She gasped. Who was sending her these messages? For a moment, her fingers itched to write something back, but she was too scared to. Instead, she watched in horror as message after message appeared.

He's not good for you, Polly.

I'd leave him if I was you.

You deserve better.

He doesn't love you.

Tears stung her eyes, her imagination spiralling out of control. Jago had once dated her sister Bryony, hadn't he? It had been brief and he'd always sworn nothing had happened. But what if something had happened? And what if things had started again? What if Polly's anxiety to have a child with him was driving him away? Driving him back into the arms of her sister?

No, that couldn't possibly be true. Bryony was madly in love with Ben – she knew her sister and had never seen her happier than in recent months.

Don't trust him, Polly.

She read the latest message before switching her phone off. It was lies. Lies told by some anonymous crank who had nothing better to do than meddle. Well, she wasn't going to pay any attention to it.

She got up from the sofa and went upstairs, brushing her hair and washing her face. She looked dreadful. She really couldn't blame Jago if he was looking at other women. Maybe he'd come to his senses at last and realised that he didn't want to be shackled to a mother and son. It was such a responsibility, wasn't it? And he was still so young. She'd seen the look in his eyes the other night when she'd asked him not to play his guitar because Archie was sleeping. And then there'd been that time when Polly and Archie had had flu and Jago missed a concert to stay home and look after them. Had he hated them for that, Polly asked her reflection now?

That evening, she went through the motions of making tea for Archie and tidying the kitchen. She couldn't face eating anything herself. By the time Jago got home, she had worked herself into such a state that he immediately saw that something was wrong.

'Hey, what's the matter?'

'Nothing,' she said all too quickly.

'Tell me, Poll,' he said when she turned her back to him, afraid that she might lash out at him.

'I'm okay. Just tired.'

'Are you sure?'

'I've said so, all right?'

'All right!' he said.

She heard him drop his keys on the kitchen table and turned to watch as he took his boots off by the back door and she felt a strange distance between them in that moment.

You've always known he would cheat on you.

The messages she'd been sent taunted her once again as she recalled them. Should she tell him about them? She opened her mouth but, when he glanced up, she shut it again. She couldn't. If the messenger was telling the truth, she didn't want the pain of knowing for sure. And, if they were lies, what would Jago think of her doubting him even for a second?

'I'm going to take a shower, okay?'

She nodded and, as he left the room, she felt an awful void open up inside her and all her insecurities and anxieties flood right into it.

~

Megan and Rick left the police station after reporting the latest incidents both feeling drained.

'I can't believe he wasn't able to do anything,' Megan said. 'It's ridiculous! What if it was happening to him? Or to his mother or daughter? I bet he'd be doing more then!'

She felt Rick's hand on her shoulder, giving her a comforting squeeze.

'Listen,' he said. 'How about we pop round to my mum's this evening?'

'Your mum's?'

'Yes. She's been wanting to meet you for ages.'

'Really?'

'Of course *really!*' he said with a laugh. 'Perhaps it's because I can't stop talking about you whenever I see her.'

'I'd love you to meet my parents at some point,' Megan suggested.

'It wouldn't be a terrible idea,' he said with a grin.

They both laughed and then he leaned in towards her, resting his forehead against hers.

'This is getting pretty serious, isn't it?' he whispered.

'Yes. Pretty serious.' She took a deep breath, her hands resting on his chest and she marvelled that she could feel so calm and content so quickly after quite an unsettling time in the police station just because she was in Rick's company.

'You are a miracle worker,' she told him.

'I am?'

'Yes. You make me feel...' she paused. She couldn't quite settle on the right word to describe how she was feeling.

'What? Tell me.'

She took a deep breath. 'Peaceful.' She put her arms around him and held him tight. 'I don't ever want to let you go.'

'Then don't,' he said.

CHAPTER NINETEEN

April was cooking spaghetti in the kitchen when May entered the flat.

'Hey! How was your trip?' April asked as May came towards her and they hugged.

'Good. Although the London Underground was chaos. I'd forgotten how much I hated it.'

'One tends to forget about crowds and noise living in a small Suffolk town.'

'Yes!'

'But was it worth it?'

'Oh, it was wonderful,' May enthused. 'I think it's the largest exhibition of Vanessa Bell's work ever and it's so amazing to see it all laid out like that – paintings, textiles, furniture, ceramics. You'd have loved it.'

'I'm sure.'

'You'll have to go,' May encouraged.

'Yes, maybe I could go with Josh,' April said, pouring in the tomato sauce she'd made and adding a twist of pepper.

'That smells so good.'

'I thought you'd be hungry. How about eating outside? It's still sunny in the back garden.'

'Okay. I'll just wash my hands and change my clothes. I feel horribly grubby after London!'

April laughed. They were both such country mice.

After taking the heated plates out of the oven and dishing up the spaghetti with a side serving of fresh vegetables, the sisters took their meal outside where a small table and chairs stood in a spot to catch the evening sun. April had set out a damask tablecloth and two plump cushions and there was a jug of iced elderflower cordial and two tumblers already there.

'What did I do to deserve this?' May asked.

April smiled, but she could feel a nervous twitch at the corner of her mouth as they sat down. Because, the truth was, April had planned this lovely meal to spoil her sister tonight because she needed to tell her something. But not just yet. She'd build up to it. Slowly.

First, they just enjoyed each other's company, eating and chatting together in the evening sunshine. It was something that April was going to miss – this easy companionship with the one person who'd been with her her entire life. The person who knew her better than anybody – who *was* her in so many ways. But life changed and people evolved and April had found somebody else who adored her and knew her – not in the same way as May, of course, but in a new and exciting way and she needed to be with him.

'May?' she began tentatively. 'There's something I need to tell you.'

'Oh, my god! Your eye appointment – I totally forgot! How did it go?'

'It was fine.'

'You're okay?'

'Everything's good. The recent headaches were just headaches, thank goodness.' April took a quick sip of her drink and started again. 'It's something else.'

'What? Is it the baby?' May looked concerned.

'No. Well, kind of.' April paused. 'I want to move in with Josh as soon as my morning sickness is over.'

May gasped. '*No!*' The single word came out like a wail. 'I thought you were staying *here*.'

'I thought so too, but it doesn't seem right now. It doesn't *feel* right.'

'But you need me to look after you. I thought that's what you wanted.'

April nodded. 'You've taken care of me your whole life, May. I think you should probably have a break!'

'I don't want a break. I want to take care of you – and the baby.'

'Well, the trouble is, Josh wants to do that too,' April said in a hushed tone. 'And I'd kind of like him to. Not that I need anyone to take care of me,' she quickly added. 'Because I can take care of myself – even if you don't think I can.'

'I never said you couldn't.'

'I know. But being here – with you – well, I feel like I'm not growing. Does that make sense? And I think it's probably time for a change. My body's kind of demanding it from me. I'm growing in so many different ways, I guess!'

May didn't say anything for a moment so April continued.

'You knew this was going to happen sooner or later.'

'So make it later!' May said. 'I want to be with you when you go into labour.'

'I know. And I promise I'll call you when it happens. Or maybe Josh will call if I can't quite make it to a phone.'

May sighed. 'This is making me very nervous.'

April smiled sympathetically and she reached towards May across the table and took her hand.

'You will always be my twin. My confidante. My very best friend. That won't ever change. You know that, don't you?'

May nodded. 'I know.'

'And this is good! *Change* is good.'

May looked genuinely perplexed by this. 'How?'

'Because you've got your own life to lead. We couldn't go on like this even if Josh hadn't come along.'

'Why not? It's a good life.'

'I know. I just think it's more natural to have our own identities.'

'But we're twins. Twins are meant to be together.'

'Not forever,' April said, watching as May picked up her glass and took a long, slow sip. 'Anyway, hasn't Colin the baker been paying you special attention recently?'

'Has he?'

'You *must* have noticed!'

May frowned. 'He's just trying it on. He's not serious.'

April laughed. 'Why don't you think he's serious?'

'Because...'

'What?'

'You're the pretty one, April.'

'May – we're identical!'

May shook her head. 'Men can always tell.'

'Josh couldn't. His family couldn't – remember?'

'They knew. They just couldn't work it out.'

'Well, you can be a little...' April paused, 'a little more abrupt than me, perhaps. You need to relax more. Enjoy life. Let Colin flatter you and feed you pastries! And go out the next time he asks you.'

'He wanted to take me to dinner last week.'

'And you turned him down?'

She shrugged.

'Oh, May!' April watched as May closed her eyes.

'Everything's changing, isn't it?'

'Yes.'

'I don't like change.'

'I'm afraid it's inevitable. And just think how exciting it will be to welcome this baby into the world. I can't help thinking that, if we hadn't taken a chance to open our shop together, I'd never have met

Josh and this little life inside me would never have happened, would it?'

'I guess not,' May had to admit.

'And remember how scared we were to pour all our resources into the shop with no guarantees that it would work out? Remember the sleepless nights we had trying to budget our savings and raise more money? We could have just stayed in our old jobs – safe, perhaps, but bored.' April shook her head, thinking about the administrative roles they'd both taken for a while. 'But we bet on change, didn't we?'

'That was the scariest thing I've ever done.'

'But do you regret it?'

'No, of course not!'

April smiled as she tried to tease a smile out of her sister.

'Okay – change can be good!' May said at last, the tiniest of smiles lifting the corners of her mouth. 'Just not when so many changes happen all at once. First it was our jobs, then the shop opening, then you meeting Josh. And now there's your baby and you moving out, *and* you want me to go out with Colin!'

'I know it's a lot to cope with, but isn't it all rather brilliant and exciting at the same time? And I just *know* we'll look back on this time as being really special. Something we'll tell the grandchildren about!'

The look that crossed May's face at the mention of grandchildren made April laugh out loud.

'But, before grandchildren, let's have dessert, okay?' April said. 'I seem to have got my craving back for hot chocolate fudge sundae.'

On the same August evening, Rick picked Megan up from her home and drove her the short distance to his mother's house in Cavendish. Megan had taken an absolute age choosing the right dress to wear, settling on a simple blue cotton one which skimmed her knees. It was silly to feel so nervous, she couldn't help thinking, because she'd met

Mrs Wildman several times in the past as a customer of the library. However, they'd never talked at any length. She simply came in, nodded, chose her books, said a polite few words about the weather and left. It just went to show you that you never quite knew what role a person might someday play in your life.

As Rick pulled up outside the house, he turned to look at Megan. 'You ready?'

Megan was clutching a bottle of rose pressé which Rick had said his mother had a special weakness for.

'I think so,' she said.

'You don't have to worry about a thing. Mum's as sweet as they come and I know she's going to adore you.'

Megan smiled but she couldn't help feeling nervous. It still felt as if everything was rushing forward at a pace she couldn't quite keep up with. Not that they were talking about wedding bells and settling down and starting a family or anything like that, but meeting parents was definitely a serious step forward, wasn't it?

They got out of the Land Rover and Rick knocked on the door of the terraced house. It was opened a moment later and the smiling face of Rick's mother greeted them.

She immediately ushered them inside, gave Rick a big hug in the hallway and then turned her attention to Megan.

'Welcome to my home, Megan.'

'Mrs Wildman – it's lovely to see you again.'

'So you two have definitely met before?' Rick asked.

'Of course we have,' his mother said. 'Although I don't make frequent trips to the library.' She came forward and the two women hugged. 'It's so good to meet you *properly!* And you must call me Elaine.'

'I've brought you a little something.' Megan handed her the bottle.

'My favourite! I'm guessing a little bird told you!'

'I might have had a bit of help, yes!'

They all walked through to the kitchen at the back of the house where the door stood open onto a tiny garden where a small table had been set.

'I thought we could eat outside. It's such a glorious evening, isn't it?'

'It was hard to tear myself down from the roof today,' Rick said.

Mrs Wildman shook her head. 'Don't you go overdoing it. And I hope you're wearing sunscreen and a proper hat!'

'Yes, of course I am, Mum!'

Megan watched their fond banter with delight as they all helped to bring the food out into the garden.

'Oh, dear,' Mrs Wildman said as they all sat down next to a sad-looking geranium. 'That's not looking very well, is it?'

Megan watched as her host went back into the kitchen and brought out a little watering can, giving the plant a good soaking.

'Not another of your patients, is it?' Rick asked.

'Nobody wanted this one,' she said.

Rick turned to Megan. 'Mum takes in all the strays of the plant world.'

'They just crave a little love and attention. Like that house you're restoring. You see – you make fun of what I do but you're doing it yourself on a much bigger scale!'

Rick laughed. 'I am! I guess there's something in our DNA that likes rescuing things.'

'Your father was the same only with old tools.' She nodded to the tiny shed at the end of the garden. 'He'd pick them up at car boot sales and secondhand shops. He used to love that they'd had a life before he found them.'

'Yes, I have quite a few of them now,' Rick said.

'It's good to keep things going,' Megan said. 'So many of us just throw things away these days and that puts so much pressure on our planet.'

Mrs Wildman nodded. 'And what do you restore, Megan?'

'Well, I do my best to restore books when they come in from enthusiastic readers.'

Rick and his mother laughed at that.

'A very noble cause,' Mrs Wildman told her. 'Now, let's eat.'

After enjoying a delicious courgette and leek lasagne served with locally grown salad, followed by a strawberry tart that was so good that Megan felt sure she was going to pass out from pleasure, they all gathered the dishes and took them back into the kitchen.

'Rick? Could you give the pots a good watering for me? There's water in the can outside.'

'Oh, sure,' he said, returning to the garden.

'No need to do that,' Mrs Wildman told Megan as she helped to load the dishwasher.

'I like making myself useful,' Megan told her as she continued to help.

'Has Rick roped you in to working on his house yet?'

'Not yet. I'm afraid I wouldn't know what to do. I'm more of an indoor person.'

'What do you think of his project?'

'I love it! I can't believe he's doing most of the work himself.'

'Yes, he isn't scared to pour everything he's got into a job.'

'Have you seen it?'

'I have. I saw it just after he'd bought it. I think he was too afraid to show it to me before he'd signed all the paperwork in case I tried to talk him out of it.'

'Would you have?'

Elaine Wildman shook her head. 'No point in that. Once Rick's made his mind up about something, he always sees it through.'

Megan felt a warm glow right in the centre of her being.

'He's like his father in that respect – very focused. Leo's the same.'

'He's travelling, isn't he?'

'I miss him.' Elaine looked thoughtful for a moment. 'I think he's working a few things out. He doesn't always open up about his feelings like Rick does, but he feels things just as deeply. You know about their father, don't you? He passed five years ago. Our boys might have been grown up, but they still needed their father.'

'Of course,' Megan said, trying to imagine what it must have been like for Rick and Leo.

'I still need him too.' Elaine's face softened and Megan reached a hand towards her and lightly touched her arm. 'What a sweetheart you are. I can see why Rick adores you so much.'

Megan felt herself blushing.

Just then, Rick came in the back door.

'All watered!' he said, glancing from one to the other. 'Oh, no! You've not been talking about me, have you?'

One of the joys of the long summer evenings was that it meant there was plenty of time for Bryony to visit Cuckoo Cottage and help out in the garden after she'd shut up shop for the day. It was just a short walk and Longfellow was always excited to make the little journey because he knew that Sonny had a tin of dog treats.

Bryony made her way straight to the back of the cottage as she guessed Flo would be in the garden, and she was mindful to close the gate behind her in case any chickens went walkabout.

'Flo? Sonny?' Bryony called as she and Longfellow entered the garden which was looking gloriously jungly at the height of summer with produce spilling out from the raised beds and towers of flowers humming with bees even as the sun dipped in the sky.

'Bryony!' Flo called back, her head popping out from the greenhouse. Her shock of white hair was spilling out from under a frayed sunhat that looked as if it might recently have been wrestled off a scarecrow. 'Come and have a cucamelon!'

After handing Longfellow's lead to a grinning Sonny and watching as they headed off down the garden together, Bryony entered the greenhouse.

'What on earth is a cucamelon?'

Flo proudly pointed out the row of plants, pinching off a small oval fruit. 'It's shaped like a tiny melon and has the texture and flavour of a cucumber. Cucamelon!'

Bryony took the fruit that was offered to her and, following Flo's lead, popped it into her mouth whole.

'Good?'

'Erm – it's quite sour, isn't it?'

'Me and Sonny can't get enough of them. Very good little hit of moisture when you're working in the garden and can't be bothered going back inside for a drink. Sonny spotted the seed packet and we thought we'd give them a go.'

'I remember you telling me that you like to grow something new each year.'

'That's right. Well, cucamelons are it this year.'

Bryony glanced around the greenhouse, inhaling the incomparable scent of warm tomato plants. She spotted the glossy leaves of peppers too with their small fruits promising treats for the kitchen come autumn.

'The aubergines are a disgrace even with all this glorious sunshine. I'm not sure they're going to ripen. If only aubergines grew as quickly as nettles!'

'How are you, Flo?'

'Good! And pleased to see you although...' she stopped. 'Come outside. I'm feeling a bit hot and bothered in here.'

They stepped out of the greenhouse and Flo looked at Bryony quizzically.

'What is it?' Bryony asked.

'You tell me!'

Bryony sighed. There was no point trying to hide anything from Flo. She could sniff out an anxiety at fifty paces.

'Ben's been acting a bit strangely.'

'Strangely? How?'

'I don't know. Distant. It's as if his mind's somewhere else.'

Flo nodded, her bright eyes crinkling in concentration at Bryony's words.

'I'm worried, Flo. What if he wants to leave again?'

'But he's just come back!'

'I *know*, but he might be one of those people who doesn't ever get the travel bug out of their system.'

Flo glanced around the garden. 'I wonder if there's a herbal cure for that. Maybe a few cups of nettle tea.' She'd meant to lighten the mood, but Bryony wasn't laughing. 'Have you talked to him?'

'I've tried but, when I ask him what's wrong, he denies that anything is. But I know him. I know when something's not right.'

'Maybe something's going on at work?'

'He always tells me when there is.'

'Do you think he's unwell?'

'Oh, god! I hadn't even thought of that.'

'Now, don't go panicking. He's probably fine, but it's best to be sure about these things, isn't it? Some men just aren't very good when it comes to talking about health stuff.'

Bryony nodded, suddenly wanting to get back home to talk to him.

'It'll work out,' Flo told her. 'Don't you go worrying!' She then motioned towards Sonny who was now sitting on the back doorstep with Longfellow beside him. The young boy was patiently brushing the dog's long silky ears.

'Is that your hairbrush, Flo?' Bryony asked.

She chuckled. 'Probably!'

Ben was home late that night – later than normal. When Bryony asked what the hold-up had been, he'd told her one of his adult student's had begged a word after class and then he'd got held up in traffic. She didn't know whether to believe him or not. It seemed to her that he was trying to avoid her. Even now, as he moved around the living room, he was doing his best to avoid eye contact.

'Ben?'

'What?'

'Are you okay?'

He crouched down to fuss Longfellow in his basket. 'Course.'

'Nothing's... worrying you?'

'What do you mean?'

'I mean, you've been acting strangely. Are you okay?'

He looked up then and gave her the smallest of smiles. It wasn't a Ben smile. It was the shadow of one of those.

'I'm just tired,' he said. 'I'm going up to bed.' He bent forward, kissing Longfellow on the head and then he got up and left the room.

He didn't kiss Bryony.

CHAPTER TWENTY

The Castle Clare Literary Festival was in full swing. All three of the Nightingale bookshops looked resplendent with posters and towers of books advertising the writers who were visiting and giving talks and signings during the week. There was everyone from the latest chart-topping thriller writer, to an adventurer who'd recently cycled the length of South America raising money for charity, a novelist whose latest book had been adapted into a miniseries on one of the streaming channels, and Castle Clare's very own children's writer supreme – Callie Logan.

The high street and market square fluttered with bright bunting and there were floral displays everywhere. Tristan Nightingale was flitting between venues making sure everyone had what they needed and that things were running smoothly. Lara was responding to all his barked orders and was doing her part handing out flyers all over town, and Josh was desperately trying to keep all his new customers happy as they queued to pay for their signed books.

Megan was extra busy in the library catering to the children's events that had been put on. Now that the summer holidays were underway, parents were more anxious than ever to find entertainment for their little ones, and the library during the literary festival provided the perfect drop-in centre. Luckily, Megan had a couple of volunteers to help with everything. She didn't know what she'd do without them. Even so, when she looked up to see Rick enter the library, there was little she could do from her home on the carpet in the children's corner supervising a session where everyone was making their own dragon out of the cardboard innards of toilet rolls. She so wanted to approach him if just for a few seconds' contact, but she was surrounded by children and couldn't move. Instead, she watched as he winked at her and took a small sheet of paper from his jacket pocket. He approached the shelves, pausing at History, and pulled out a Bettany Hughes title: *Venus and Aphrodite*. His choice seemed to make him smile and Megan could feel her cheeks heating up as she watched him place his letter inside, making sure she got a good look at the book before replacing it.

It was agony knowing that Rick's letter was there but being unable to retrieve it. She tried to keep half an eye on the bookshelf, hoping that nobody would pull the title out and find it. Luckily, the history shelves weren't favourites of the young patrons she had in today. They were far more interested in the box of buttons, ribbons and shells that Megan had brought out from her secret stash for the express purpose of decorating dragons.

Despite being anxious to read Rick's letter, Megan loved her time spent on the carpet with the little ones. Not only did it stimulate her own creativity but it helped her to be truly in the moment which meant that she wasn't thinking about the recent messages that had been sent to her phone. She'd had an upsetting morning recording them all and wished, once again, that the police hadn't asked her to do that because it meant reading them all which meant absorbing them all. That was one of the curses of being an avid reader – words sunk in and stayed with you. Luckily, her mind was occupied for the entire 'How to Decorate Your Own Dragon' session and, after an intense ninety minutes, twelve grateful parents and fifteen happy children left with their newly made treasures.

An exhausted Megan waved them all off, closed the library door and went to tidy up. It didn't take long. Everybody had done their bit to make sure the place wasn't left in a mess and Megan was grateful for that. She told her two trusty volunteers that she could cope and they should go home and enjoy the rest of the summer day.

Then and only then did she cross the room to the history shelves and pull out the Bettany Hughes book.

Venus and Aphrodite. She smiled. It was a good place to put a love letter.

Taking the single folded page out of the book, she read.

My gorgeous Minnow

I thought about telling you how much my mum adored you, but that's not really a romantic way to start a love letter, is it? So I'll tell you how much I adore you.

I adore your earnestness when you talk about books and your laughter when you play with Truffle and Blewit. I love the raven gloss of your hair and the paleness of your skin although I think the summer sun may steal that away from you. I love the brightness of your eyes and the way they close when I lean in to kiss you.

I love the time we spend together – the days and the nights and the long afternoons. I love talking with you and walking with you. I love cooking for you and cuddling by the fire. And sharing my dreams and listening to yours.

I have never written the word "love" so many times before but I want to write it one more time.

I love you!

Rick xxx

Megan gasped as she finished the letter. It was pure poetry and she couldn't believe she'd inspired such beauty. She clutched it to her chest wanting to absorb it fully.

~

Lara Nightingale was walking back to Josh's bookshop after an event in the village hall. It had been completely sold out and the writer had given a fabulous talk. Josh was still there so Lara let herself in to the shop and did a quick tidy around in preparation for another day of festival fun the following day.

Her cousin Tristan had just about been bearable, but he still treated her like a skivvy – giving her all the dull jobs when she knew she was ready to take on more responsibility.

'Next year,' she told herself through gritted teeth. He wouldn't have a choice then because she was stepping up!

A piece of bunting had come down in the window and she was just fixing it when her phone beeped. It had been beeping all day and she'd actually switched it off for a few hours which was very unlike her because she liked to keep in touch with all her university friends. It was probably one of them now having a crisis about something terribly important like what they should wear on a date.

Lara reached for her phone expecting to see a message from one of her friends, but there weren't any. Instead, there was message after message from – well, she didn't know.

I've been watching you.

You're so pretty.

I think we would be good together.

Lara winced and glanced out of the window as if she might be being watched at this very moment, and then she read on.

Are you ignoring me?

Please write back.

I don't know what I'll do if you don't.

Or are you still seeing Ben?

Lara gasped. Who was this? Angrily, she messaged back.

Keep away from me, you creep!

A reply came back almost instantly.

So you are there!

I thought you were ignoring me.

You've been seeing Ben haven't you?

Does Bryony know? I might have to tell her.

Lara was shaking as message after message popped up.

You shouldn't treat a sister like that.

What will she say when she finds out?

What will your friends think of you when I tell them?

Lara thought about messaging back, but instinct told her not to engage and she wished she hadn't already let this person know she was reading their messages.

She glanced out of the shop window into the street. There were a few people she recognised from the village hall event now making their way to The Happy Hare pub, Lara guessed. But there wasn't anyone out there who might be *watching* her.

She switched her phone off and went into the store room and boiled a kettle. She needed tea. Well, she really needed wine, but she didn't fancy going to the pub on her own so she reached for the tin and pulled out a jasmine teabag. The scent always calmed her down and she had regular mugs of it when studying at university.

She was just inhaling the sweet aroma when Josh entered the shop, the bell tinkling above him.

'Wow! That was some event!' he said as she walked back through to the front of the shop. His hair was dishevelled and his tie was crooked. 'Can you believe how many people turned up? We're going to need to think about bigger premises soon.'

'I know! I've been telling Tris that for ages!'

'Yes, well, when you're at the helm...' He stopped. 'Are you all right?'

'Yes, why?'

'You look pale.'

'I'm fine. I just – I think I'm done for the day.'

'Right. Well, you go home. I'll lock up here.'

'Are you sure?'

'There's not a lot to do. I think I can manage.'

She nodded, grateful to be able to go. She wanted to get back to Campion House and the sanctuary of her childhood bedroom. She wanted the knowledge that her parents and grandparents were there, and the dogs and the locks on the big front door. She wanted to get into bed, her pillows around her and a good book in her hands – even if it was *Vanity Fair* – anything to help her escape.

Quickly, she finished her tea and was just about to leave the shop when Josh called after her.

'Lara!'

'What?'

'Your phone.' He nodded to the counter and Lara's eyes fixed on it, but she didn't immediately go to pick it up so Josh did, handing it to her. 'You wouldn't want to forget this, would you?'

Megan had lost count of the number of times she'd reread Rick's latest love letter, but it was definitely more than twenty-three.

When she opened the door to him that evening and he stepped inside, she threw her arms around him and kissed him.

'You got my letter?'

She nodded. 'It was beautiful. I don't know what to say.'

'You don't have to say anything.'

'But I do.' She looked into his amber-flecked eyes and inhaled the sweet smell of summer grass that clung to his clothing. 'I love you,' she said.

He stroked her hair. 'I love you too. I think I gave that away in the letter, didn't I?'

She laughed.

'I love your laugh,' he whispered.

'You wrote that.'

They kissed again.

'You'd better come in,' Megan said, aware that she hadn't actually closed the door and that they were putting on quite a show for the neighbours. 'I'm afraid it's not as impressive as Oak Farm Cottage, but it's home.'

'I've been looking forward to seeing it,' Rick told her as he walked through to the living room.

'I can't believe you've not been inside here yet. Although I must say, I love visiting Oak Farm Cottage.'

'Wow! You have a lot of books!'

'This isn't even half of them,' she said, watching as Rick stepped forward to examine the titles on the shelves in the living room. She suddenly became very conscious of the information he was gathering about her by looking at something as intimate as her book collection. It was a strange kind of vulnerability.

'There are more upstairs and in boxes in the loft. I shouldn't keep them up there, only this place is so small and I don't want it to feel too crowded. But it would be lovely to display them all together one day.'

'You should. A librarian should definitely have their own library,' Rick said. 'Isn't that part of the job description?'

'It really should be,' she agreed. 'Perhaps when I can invest in some decent shelves. These ones were already here and it's a bit tricky making big changes when you're renting.'

'That's why I wanted to build my place myself. I can be totally in charge of everything from the bricks underneath my feet to the tiles above my head.'

'I definitely envy you that!' Megan said as she went into the kitchen and made them both a cup of tea. She knew exactly how he liked it now – black with one level teaspoon of sugar and, under no circumstance should she squeeze the teabag.

'Are you still getting the messages?' Rick asked a few minutes later as they sat down with their tea and a plate of shortbread.

She nodded. 'Yes, but let's not talk about them.'

He picked her hand up and squeezed it. 'You're keeping a record of them?'

'Every nasty one,' she said with a sigh. 'They said something really horrible last night.'

Rick frowned. 'What?' he asked gently.

'They said... they said that the police will never do anything and that they can do exactly what they want with me.'

Rick swore colourfully.

'They called me all sorts of names too which I don't want to repeat.'

'You do know that none of that is true?' Rick said and, when Megan frowned, he continued. 'They're not true because they don't know you.'

'How do you know they don't know me?'

'Because these messages are so vitriolic and anyone who truly knew you couldn't possibly have a reason for saying things like that, could they?'

'I don't know. What makes anyone do something like this? If they know me, it's really horrible because I genuinely believe I haven't done anything to upset anyone. But it's making me doubt myself now. If I don't know them, I can't work out why they'd pick me.'

'It might help if you look at it like they don't care who they're targeting. The problem is squarely with *them*. I don't really know much about all this, but I'm guessing it's some lonely person who hates the whole world and this is their way of getting back at it.'

Megan finished her tea and snuggled up closer to Rick, wrapping her arms around him and resting her head on his chest.

'Let's stop talking about it. Tell me something wonderful.'

'Something wonderful?'

'Yes – about your day. The dogs. The house. Your meadow. Anything!'

Rick took a deep breath which Megan felt as she cuddled him closer.

'You know I wasn't lying when I said my mum can't stop talking about you,' Rick began. 'I practically had to hang up on her this morning!'

'Oh, dear! I'm sorry about that.' She giggled. 'But I hope you didn't really hang up on her!'

'I had a roof to finish! I had no choice!' He laughed and Megan knew that Rick would never be anything but sweet and kind to his mother.

'And don't forget – you should meet my parents at some point,' Megan told him. 'Maybe go to theirs for dinner one evening. You should see the house – it's full of books. Floor to ceiling.'

'You don't say!'

Megan laughed. 'It is kind of a family thing. My aunt and uncle are the same and all my cousins too – there are always books everywhere. Sometimes at the expense of furniture.'

'Really?'

'My brother Luke actually had to make a bed from books because there was no way he was going to get a bed into the house.'

'No way! You're kidding, right?'

Megan sat up and gave him a smile. 'Yes, I might be. But it nearly is that bad.'

'Listen,' Rick said, 'about meeting your parents. How about they come out to Oak Farm Cottage and I show them around? We could have a barbecue.'

'You don't want to come to theirs first?'

Rick gave a little shrug. 'I'm not really an indoor sort of person. I always feel awkward in rooms especially with strangers. I don't want them to get a bad first impression of me.'

'But they wouldn't, Rick!'

'It might be easier at the cottage first.'

Megan nodded in understanding. 'Well, I'm sure they'd love to see it. Mum's passionate about old Suffolk buildings and I know Dad will love all the outbuildings and the land.'

'Great! Let's set something up, shall we?'

'But I'll make sure they don't stay too long.'

'Why?'

Megan snuggled into him once more. 'Because I want to spend another night under the stars with you.'

CHAPTER TWENTY-ONE

It was a bright Sunday morning when Megan arrived at her parents' house just a short drive through the country lanes from Castle Clare. They'd had several properties in Suffolk over the years, but were now happily settled in a seventeenth century cottage at the edge of a village. It had draughts and creaks and low ceilings and doors where you had to duck to avoid cracking your skull. It was listed so you weren't allowed to add or subtract anything to or from it without jumping through a number of conservation hoops, and the sloping ceilings upstairs meant less room for bookcases meaning Ralph and Bonnie had had to get creative with their collection over the years. But they adored the old house. There was something in the old walls and wonky floors that spoke to them, that held them and comforted them.

As Megan pulled up outside The Nook, she couldn't help wondering what it would look like if it was taken back to its bare bones as Rick's Oak Farm Cottage had been. It was timber-framed as Rick's was and was very much a traditional Suffolk home. Although Megan hadn't grown up here, she was very fond of the old place and always loved spending time there.

Her mother and father had retired from the bookshop in Castle Clare which they'd run with Frank and Eleanor. But, where Frank and Eleanor were happy to pursue other passions in retirement, Ralph and Bonnie just couldn't stop themselves from being involved in the world of books and had started an online publishing company after Ralph had had a short stint as a university lecturer. It wasn't very lucrative, but it was wholly absorbing and rewarding and kept them fully immersed in the written word.

Megan let herself in with her key. Her parents liked her to have one for "emergency purposes" even though they were only in their early sixties.

'I'm here!' she called politely as she entered. The radio was on in the kitchen and she made her way through, ducking at the door so as to avoid cracking her head.

'Megan, love!' Her mum turned around from a cupboard where she'd been putting crockery away.

'You look lovely, Mum!' Megan said, admiring her mother's linen dress in a cornflower blue. Bonnie's red hair, which came out of a bottle these days, was tied back and she was wearing an amethyst pendant which Megan had recently bought for her birthday.

The two women embraced.

'Is this all right?' her mother asked, her voice full of anxiety. 'I wasn't sure what to wear to a building site.'

'You'll be fine. We won't make you climb any ladders, I promise! And it's all perfectly safe and very neat. It doesn't feel like a building site at all.'

'It's very exciting, isn't it?' her mother said.

'It's the most beautiful place in the world – the house, the meadow, the woods! I can't wait for you to see it all.'

'And meet Rick, of course,' her mother added.

'Of *course*!' Megan laughed.

'Or is this an Elizabeth Bennet situation we have here?'

'Oh, Mum! No! I met Rick long before I saw his beautiful house,' Megan assured her, remembering how the heroine of *Pride and*

Prejudice started to soften towards Mr Darcy after seeing his fine home of Pemberley.

It was then that Megan's father entered the room. 'Ah, Megan!'

'Hi Dad.' They hugged. 'Are you okay?'

'I've just had a call from Ed. He's a new author we signed earlier this year. He's going to be late delivering his novel so we're going to have to push publication back.'

'Will that be a problem?' Bonnie asked.

'Only if we make it one, so let's not!'

Megan smiled at her father's level-headedness. He had always been wonderfully patient which, she believed, came from a lifelong love affair with the novel. For who could read so many works without learning to be empathetic towards one's fellow human beings?

'Right!' he said. 'Let's meet this chap of yours, shall we?'

With that, Megan and her parents drove out to Oak Farm Cottage.

It didn't take them long to reach Melton Green.

'It certainly is a rural part of Suffolk, isn't it?' her mother commented to Megan who was sitting in the back seat. 'I do love it out here. There's a part of me that still misses that old place we had out this way.'

'Yes, but remember the winters we used to get,' her father said. 'Bitterly cold winds right across those flat fields.'

'Yes, but remember the summers!' Megan countered.

'And Oak Farm Cottage is the place you and your brothers used to swim?' her mother asked.

'That's right.'

'I think we might have had something to say about that had we known at the time!' her father said.

'Oh, Dad! It's what kids in the country do. They climb trees and make dens.'

'And swim in ditches apparently!' her father added.

'It isn't a ditch – it's a proper moat. Although it does look more like a ditch at the moment, but Rick's going to clear it.'

'So he just walked into your library one day? Is that how you met him?'

'It's how I meet most people, Mum,' Megan said with a laugh, acknowledging the fact that she didn't get out much.

'And it's his brother who went out with Sam's fiancée?' her mother went on.

Megan rolled her eyes. Why did everybody fixate on that detail, she wondered? But that was small town life, wasn't it?

'Yes, Mum. Leo went out with Callie Logan – the writer.'

'She made quite an impression on the men of Suffolk in a short time, didn't she? Maybe it's all inspiration for her books!'

'She writes children's fiction, Mum!'

'Yes, but every story is a love story, isn't it?'

Megan considered this for a moment, trying to work out if her mother was being utterly profound or not, but didn't have time because they were almost at the turn for Oak Farm Cottage.

'It's the next left, Dad. Slow down or you'll miss the track.'

A moment later and their car was bumping over the unmade track, Ralph doing his best to avoid the potholes.

'What's this going to be like in the winter?' he asked.

'Muddy I expect,' Megan said. 'Rick has a Land Rover.'

'And wellies, I hope!' her mum said.

'Just park here,' Megan told her dad as they reached the house. Megan noticed that the back of the cottage which, rather perversely, was the one that faced the track, now had a complete wall so that it was no longer possible to see through to the meadow on the other side. Megan smiled at the progress, but it felt poignant that she would never again be able to see right through the house.

The three of them got out of the car and Megan could feel the butterflies in her stomach. They were dancing madly and she realised how important this visit was to her and how she longed for her parents to adore Rick and Oak Farm Cottage because this was the man and the place she loved more than anyone or anywhere in the world.

Truffle and Blewit were the first to greet them as Megan and her parents rounded the side of the house. The dogs ran across the lawn from the shade in front of a shed and danced around everyone's feet, demanding attention.

Rick, who must have heard the commotion, came out of the house and gave his hair a quick ruffle with his hand and Megan saw a shower of dust rain down from it. He quickly wiped his hands on his trousers and strode across the lawn to greet them.

Megan introduced everyone and hands were shaken.

'This is a pretty impressive set-up,' Megan's father said.

'Thank you. I'm rather attached to it.'

'Looks like a lot of work!' her mother said, glancing up at the roof which was very nearly complete now.

'It's one of the reasons I bought it.'

'Rick's not afraid of hard work,' Megan told them proudly.

Her mother nodded. 'I can see that.'

'It's what makes me happy – taking a building back to its bones and helping it breathe. Choosing the right materials for it and putting it all back together again.'

'So you've done this before?' Ralph asked.

'Well, little bits here and there on other people's properties, but nothing on this scale before. This is my first whole building.'

'And here's Megan's moat!' her mother said, walking across the lawn for a closer look.

'It's not *my* moat, Mum!'

'Actually, I think that's a very good name for it,' Rick said as they all peered into the murky green depths together.

'Did she tell you she used to swim here with her brothers?'

'She did. And she's promised she'll do so again once I get it all cleared.'

'I did not!' Megan laughed.

'But you will, won't you?' Rick asked.

Megan looked down into the water. It felt a long time since she'd been that adventurous young girl plunging into icy water. What had happened to her? Those long summer days full of freedom had slowly been eroded by study and, gradually, Megan's world had become an indoor one. And she loved that, of course. To be surrounded by books and sharing her love of them with others was one of the greatest privileges, but she'd lost a little of herself along the way and, as she gazed into the moat, she wondered if she could get her back again. She'd already seen a glimpse of her here at Oak Farm Cottage and it would take only the slightest of encouragements to find more.

So she nodded. 'I will!'

'You will?' Rick sounded thrilled.

'First warm day the moat's cleared, I'll be in it!' she declared and there was no going back now because she had witnesses.

She felt Rick's arm around her and felt quite unembarrassed when he kissed her cheek.

'I'll hold you to that,' he said.

'You'll be getting in with me, won't you?'

'I wouldn't miss it for the world!'

For a brief moment, Megan forgot her parents were there, she was so lost in the thought of that swim to come with Rick. But then her father cleared his throat and Rick sprang into action.

'Come and see the house!' he said quickly and everybody followed him inside for a tour. The progress that had been made recently took Megan's breath away. Not only was the roof nearly finished and the back wall in place, but the wall at the end of the property was up too.

'I might have had a bit of help,' Rick said with a shrug. 'I wanted to take my own sweet time with everything, but summer's passing by so quickly and it's important to get the place weather-tight before the autumn rains arrive.'

They all admired what he'd achieved and then he whistled for the dogs and took everyone for a look around the meadow and the wood at the end of the land. The long hedges that lined the way were now thick with ripening blackberries and the sky was full of larks.

Oak Farm Cottage had never looked lovelier. Megan kept stealing little glances at her parents and could tell that, just like her, they'd fallen under the spell of the place.

As they were heading back to the house, Megan's father pointed to the barn and Rick offered to show him inside. The dogs followed and flopped down in the shady interior.

'Give a man a shed and he's content,' her mother said with a chuckle.

'Do you want to see inside?' Megan asked.

'No, I'd rather be out in the sun.'

'Me too,' Megan said, enjoying the opportunity to chat to her mother.

'This really is a special place,' Bonnie told her.

'It is, isn't it? I love it.'

'Can you see yourself here?'

Megan tried to bite back a smile but failed completely. 'We haven't really talked about that yet.'

'You might not have talked about it, but I bet you've thought about it. Am I right?'

Megan's smile was seriously huge now because she had, indeed, allowed herself to daydream.

'This would be a very easy place to come home to,' she said in a low voice, not wanting Rick to hear because, although they had confessed their love for each other, she didn't want to assume anything or rush anything.

The two women walked back towards the house to where Rick had placed a simple wooden bench. They sat together for a while in companionable silence and Megan tried to remember the last time they'd done that and was ashamed to admit to herself that she couldn't. Life rather had a habit of getting in the way of such moments, didn't it? But Oak Farm Cottage demanded them – it was that kind of place. It would be foolish to try and rush anything here even something as practical as getting a roof in place. You had to take your time.

It was as they were sitting there together enjoying the sun and the song of the skylarks that Megan noticed her mother's face had paled. She looked anxious. No, it was more than that. She looked distraught.

'Mum, are you okay?' The way her mother was sitting clearly told Megan that she wasn't. 'What is it? Tell me!'

At first, Bonnie didn't respond. Her eyes were fixed on the ground and she looked as if she might be in pain.

'I've been getting messages,' she said at last.

Megan's whole body suddenly went cold, but she tried not to panic. 'How?'

'Via social media mostly. But recently, they've been sending them via WhatsApp too.' She brought out her phone, her hands visibly shaking as she held it in front of her. 'I don't know what to do – they're so *ugly!*'

Megan held her hand out to take the phone and she could see there were tears in her mother's eyes.

'I don't want you to see them, love.' Her voice was barely above a whisper.

'I might have seen them already,' Megan told her.

'What? How?'

'Because I've been getting messages too. For weeks now.'

'I don't understand. Is it a scam then? Who is it?'

'I'm afraid there's no way of telling who they're from.'

'How long have you been getting them?' her mother asked.

'Weeks – no – months now.'

'Oh, Megan! Why didn't you say something to us?'

'Because I'm trying to handle it and – well – you've seen the messages. If yours are anything like mine, you'll know why I didn't want to say anything. I didn't even tell Rick at first.'

Bonnie glanced down at her phone now.

'Can I see them?' Megan asked gently and her mother passed the phone to her. Megan was dreading looking and just read a few of them. It was enough. 'I think it's the same person.'

'Do you?'

She nodded. 'Does Dad know about this?'

'No. I haven't told him.'

'Why not?'

'I didn't want to worry him. They're so horrible, Megan!'

Megan nodded, totally understanding because that's how she'd felt. She hadn't wanted to let anybody else see just how awful the messages were. It was like passing on an infection to a loved one.

'I thought they'd stop! I hoped they would anyway, but they're just getting worse.'

'Have you responded to any of them?'

Bonnie sighed. 'I asked who it was and why were they doing this? But I think that's made it worse.'

'I think it probably has – it shows them there's someone actually there.'

'I didn't know what to do!' Bonnie shook her head as if in regret.

'Have you tried blocking them?' Megan asked as she returned the phone to her mother.

'Of course.'

'I tried that too. They just pop up a different way, don't they? Tristan's had some too,' Megan confessed, hating having to worry her mother even more. 'His were different, though. He got messages he thought were from me saying I needed help and he came running into the library.'

'Megan – this is serious!'

'I know. I've been to the police.'

Bonnie looked shocked by this admission. 'Darling! You should have told us.'

Megan felt the gentle touch of her mother's hand on hers and could feel tears in her eyes, threatening to fall.

'Come here!'

Suddenly, they were both hugging and crying. It was as if they'd both been bottling up their emotions for so long and could no longer hold them back.

Megan wasn't sure how long they'd sat like that crying together, but she became aware of voices and realised Rick and her father and even the dogs were there, all looking concerned.

'Megan?' Rick knelt beside her.

'What's going on?' Ralph asked gently, a hand on his wife's shoulder.

'It's the messages,' Megan managed to say as she wiped her eyes with a tissue. 'Mum's been getting them too.'

'What messages?' Ralph asked.

Megan took a deep breath and told her father what had been going on. Her mother added her own experience. Ralph looking shocked.

'Megan's got the police involved,' Bonnie told him.

'Did you know about this?' he asked Rick.

Rick nodded. 'Megan was told to keep a note of all the messages so I think you should be doing that too, Mrs Nightingale.'

'Let me see,' Ralph told his wife and, reluctantly, she handed her phone to him. His face instantly creased into a frown. 'These are horrific! Why didn't you tell me?'

It was the question everyone asked, Megan thought, and she could see her mother's eyes fill with tears again.

'We should go to the police,' Ralph said. 'Right now.'

'Oh, no – please – not today,' Bonnie begged. 'I don't want to spoil everything.'

'I think Dad's right,' Megan said gently. 'We should let them know. They might take everything more seriously now that you and Tristan are involved. You haven't had any, have you, Dad?'

He shook his head. 'Mind you, I haven't checked my social media for some time. Should I check?'

'You've probably not been targeted if the site isn't active,' Megan said.

'Right – let's get going,' Ralph said. 'I'm sorry, Rick. I hate rushing off like this.'

'Do you want me to come with you?' he asked, addressing his question to Megan.

'No. You stay here and get some work done. It's such a perfect day.'

He leant forward, kissed her cheek and whispered, 'Will you try and come back this evening?'

She gently slipped her hand into his and gave him a look that told him that she would be there.

~

Rick was torn. He wanted to accompany Megan and her parents to the police station. He'd gone with her both times previously and knew she found it a stressful experience. But he also wanted to get on with the build. He was doing well and he was also on his own today so needed to work doubly hard if he was to make good progress. Still, he allowed himself a moment, watching as Megan waved from the back seat of her parents' car.

It all still seemed like a dream that this woman had come into his life. Now here he was showing her parents around his home, sharing his dreams with them and very much hoping that their daughter was going to be a big part of them. He wondered what they thought of him. Was he the sort of person they'd envisaged for Megan? Was he smart enough? Did he read enough? He now worried that they'd judge him for not being bookish enough. No, he thought. They didn't strike him as the judgemental type.

But what if he'd never gone into the library that day? It was strange how life could be impacted so greatly by the simplest of events and he thanked his lucky stars that he'd been looking for those books on restoration. So was it Oak Farm Cottage he had to thank, he wondered, looking up at the old building that felt so much a part of him now that he couldn't imagine life without it? He felt the same way about Megan. The two were inextricably linked in his mind and in his soul.

Whistling for the dogs who'd sneaked down the track following the scent of something delectable, Rick returned to work.

As was often the way when he was at Oak Farm Cottage, the hours passed in a glorious blur as he worked and it seemed no time at all until Megan was back.

'Rick?'

He loved hearing her voice calling for him and quickly put his tools down and went to greet her. She practically ran into his arms and they hugged for a good long while before they said anything. He adored that. Speech was highly overrated, he couldn't help thinking. There were far better ways to communicate.

'Did it go all right?' he asked at last as they made their way to the bench in front of the house where Megan had sat with her mother just a few hours before.

'We actually got taken into an interview room this time,' Megan said. 'It felt different – as if we were really being listened to.'

'Good. It's about time.'

'I guess this kind of crime is fairly new,' Megan said. 'That's the impression I got at least. It's as if the police haven't quite caught up with this online world yet and all the crime that can happen there.'

'Then they jolly well need to.'

Megan nodded. 'Anyway, PC Brodie was pretty good. He seemed to genuinely care and it's great that we now have him as a point of contact. I felt they were just form-filling before.'

'Yes, I got that impression too.'

'But this guy really listened and assured us that he'd give it his full attention. He mentioned that his teenage daughter had been bullied online not so long ago so he knows how upsetting something like this can be.'

'So, with PC Brodie taking care of things, I guess you can give me your full attention,' Rick said with a grin, trying to make light of the situation and distract her from any negative thoughts.

'I suppose I can,' Megan said. 'What did you have in mind?'

'Well, it's going to be a clear night tonight. It should be good for stargazing.'

'Clear nights are always cold, aren't they?'

'Yes,' he agreed. 'We'll have to snuggle up close.'

He felt Megan's arms wrapping around him as she snuggled up next to him on the bench. Her long hair tickled his neck and the scent of her skin filled his senses.

'Like this?' she whispered.

'Yes,' he whispered back. 'Exactly like this.'

CHAPTER TWENTY-TWO

It was so dark. Megan couldn't tell what time it was and when she reached for her clock's light, she couldn't find it. Where was it? It seemed to have fallen. For a moment, her hand scrambled around until she felt something No, that wasn't it. That was her phone. The bright screen lit up the night, hurting her eyes. She hadn't realised she'd left it on. It was rare for her to do that these days. She sat up and examined it, puzzled as to why it hadn't been pinging all night. And then a thought occurred to her. Maybe the messages had stopped. Maybe PC Brodie had worked his magic already or maybe the stalker had simply got bored or moved onto terrorising somebody else. Megan allowed herself the blissful feeling of relief even though her mind was telling her it was too early to start celebrating.

That's when her phone beeped. It practically lit up like a Christmas tree, lighting up her bedroom with its evil glow as message after message burned into her retinas.

I know what you did.

The police won't help you.

They'll never find me.

I'll be with you forever, Megan.

There's no escape.

And I'm watching you even closer now.

Megan screamed.

At least, she screamed in her head because she'd actually been asleep and the messages on her phone were part of a horrible nightmare. As she slowly remembered she wasn't even at home, relief flooded through her when she realised that she was at Oak Farm Cottage, sleeping under the stars next to Rick.

Quietly, she unzipped her sleeping bag and got out. She felt hot and shaky and needed to cool down and calm down. Luckily, Rick was sound asleep and she didn't disturb him, but she watched him for a moment, his face pale in the dim light of dawn.

Crossing the grass, Megan got herself a drink of water and sat on the bench for a moment, contemplating her dream. She wasn't going to check her phone. She'd left it in her car. But she was anxious about checking it later.

It wasn't surprising that she'd had the nightmare after the recent visit to the police station. PC Brodie had been very thorough in his questioning of both Megan and her mother and it had made her remember all the nasty little details of the messages she'd received so far. It had brought tears to her mother's eyes and her father had been red in the face, his anger wholly visible.

'Can you think of anyone who might target you in this way?' PC Brodie had asked her. The only person who had come to mind in that moment was the man in the library she thought of as "The Loner". But she hadn't mentioned him because she had no evidence whatsoever. He was simply someone who was a bit socially awkward – someone who used the library just as everyone else only he did so with as little interaction as possible. She'd occasionally see him glancing up at her, but that didn't make him a stalker, did it? It was just because most of the people of Castle Clare were friendly and liked to chat that The Loner stood out. But she didn't think it was him.

Megan had lost countless hours trying to work out who would do this to her and why? What had she done to warrant such victimisation? PC Brodie had told her it could be anyone – known, unknown, relative or friend. Who could work out what really went on in the minds of others?

Feeling a little calmer now that the sun was beginning to break over the horizon to start its long climb into the summer sky, she crossed the grass towards Rick, kneeling next to him.

'Minnow?'

'Good morning!'

He brushed a hand across his face and slowly sat up, his hair flopping into his eyes, making him look so young and adorable.

'You're up!'

'Yes.'

'You okay?'

'I had a nightmare.'

His kind face was etched with instant anxiety. 'Come here,' he told her and she didn't bother trying to resist, happy to snuggle into his arms again.

For a few blissful moments, she let herself be held in his warm embrace as the dew of the grass sparkled in the morning light. If only she could stay here, she thought, safe and loved and hidden from the world.

'I have to get ready for work,' she told him reluctantly.

'Not yet.'

She threaded her fingers through his and closed her eyes. She was so easily persuaded, she thought with a smile.

Bryony was being kept pretty busy during the Castle Clare Literary Festival. After Christmas, it was the time she loved more than any other and she looked forward to every year, preparing the shop with decorations and special displays of books by the authors who were visiting Castle Clare.

She was particularly thrilled that Callie had agreed to do an event. Although she was a hugely popular children's author, Callie was absolutely terrified of readings and signings. That had never stopped Bryony from pestering her, though. Having a local author was just too good an opportunity to miss. Besides, when Callie got going answering her audience's questions, Bryony could see her visibly relax and she always admitted to having enjoyed each event she did.

'But only after it's over,' Callie would say, making Bryony laugh.

Bryony watched Callie now as she signed books for her young fans, having given a reading and a Q&A session. She really was a natural only she didn't know it. Perhaps it was her nerves that endeared her so much to her readers. Maybe children could sense her introversion – that she wasn't a polished and perfect adult, but so much more like them.

Finally, when the last child and parent had left the shop, Bryony gave Callie a big hug.

'Wow, Callie! That was brilliant!'

'Really?'

'Yes! Did you see the look on those children's faces? They *loved* you!'

'Well, they were a perfect audience. I'm very lucky!'

'They were perfect because you held their attention.'

Callie smiled and Bryony could see at once why her brother loved her so much. She was one of the sweetest, most modest people Bryony had ever met. She certainly didn't have any of those diva-ish qualities some authors had. Bryony felt lucky that she hadn't experienced too many of them. Children's authors were generally well-behaved sort of people, but you did get the odd character who put on the airs and graces and Bryony always made sure that they were never invited back to her shop no matter how big a crowd they pulled in.

'Can I get you a tea or coffee, Callie?'

'No, thank you. I'm meeting Sam. We're heading out to the coast. Don't you just love that you can do that in the summer after work?'

Bryony nodded but couldn't help thinking it very unlikely that Ben would make such a suggestion at the moment.

'Are you all right, Bryony?' Callie asked.

'Sorry?'

'Are you okay?'

'Oh, yes. Just a bit tired.'

'Of course. It's been quite a day for you, hasn't it? Well, thanks again for arranging everything. I know I'm a pain and you always have to corral me, but I do enjoy it – once it's over!'

'Same time next year?'

'Erm – let me think about it!' Callie laughed.

After Callie had left, Bryony spent a few minutes tidying around and making everything presentable so that they could start all the fun again tomorrow with another visiting author.

Finally, it was time to go and Bryony clipped Longfellow's lead on and they left the shop together. She glanced across at Josh's shop and saw that Polly was closing up for the day too, turning the sign around before coming out. Bryony paused.

'Hey, Polly. How's today been?'

Polly looked up at the sound of her sister's voice, but her face didn't break into its usual smile. Instead, her mouth visibly tightened. 'I'm running late,' she said and, locking the door quickly, she took off down the street.

Bryony frowned, wondering if she'd done something to upset her, but couldn't think of anything. Perhaps Polly was genuinely just running late.

'Come on, Longfellow,' she said. 'Let's go.'

Unfortunately, things didn't improve once she arrived home. Ben had finished early and was making dinner in the kitchen. Bryony unclipped Longfellow's lead, took her shoes off and sneaked up behind him, looping her arms around his waist and resting her head against his back.

She felt him tense up.

'Ben?' She moved away from him, but he didn't turn around so she tried again. 'Ben? What is it?'

'Nothing.'

She shook her head. 'It isn't *nothing*. You've been acting strangely for ages now.' She could feel a nervous sort of energy flowing through her. 'This isn't my Ben,' she said anxiously. 'Please talk to me. What's going on?'

She seemed to wait an age before he spoke but, finally, he turned around and looked her directly in the eye and took a deep breath.

'Please tell me you're not seeing Colin the baker!'

His voice was so quiet that she thought she'd misheard him. 'What?'

'Are you seeing him – yes or no?'

'Ben! Why would you ask such a thing?'

'Just tell me, Bry!'

'No! Of *course* I'm not seeing Colin!'

Ben didn't respond and Bryony felt completely at a loss as he turned away to look out of the kitchen window. 'Ben? Look at me. *Please!*'

Suddenly, he was on the move. 'I'm taking Longfellow for a walk.'

'I thought you were making dinner?'

'I don't want any.'

'Well, I'll come with you.'

'No. I'm going alone.'

'Ben! *Stop!*' She grabbed his arm and, this time, didn't let go until he gave her his full attention. 'What's going on? What have I done to make you think I'm seeing Colin?'

For a moment, they just stared at each other and Bryony felt as if she was falling into the great chasm she could feel widening between them.

'Ben – tell me! What have I done?'

But he didn't reply. Instead, he shook his head and left the house with Longfellow without so much as a goodbye.

Ben wasn't sure where he was going and he was pretty sure that Longfellow didn't want to walk as far as Ben felt *he* needed to. But he was glad of the little dog's silent companionship. What must the little chap think, Ben wondered? He'd only been with them a short while and Ben was anxious that the current mood in the house was having an adverse effect on him.

'You're all right, aren't you?' Ben asked as he scooped the dog up to lift him over a stile. 'Of course you are.' He kissed the dog's soft head and popped him back on the ground once they were both across. 'I'm not sure about me, though.'

Ben sighed. Why hadn't he mentioned the messages to Bryony? To be honest, he wasn't sure. Mainly because he didn't know who was sending them. He'd asked several times, but the sender only responded with more horrible revelations about Bryony and Colin.

I saw them kissing today.

I thought you'd want to know that.

She looks so happy when she's with him.

As he strode across the field, the village falling far behind him, Ben tried to put the messages out of his mind. Had Bryony been telling him the truth? What possible reason could she have for getting back with Colin? She'd always said they just hadn't been compatible. And, once she'd forgiven him for going off travelling, they'd been getting on better than ever. Since moving into their home together and bringing Longfellow into their lives, Ben had felt a sense of peace and joy that he'd never experienced before. Only now he wasn't sure that Bryony felt the same way, and what would he do if she wanted out of the relationship? Would he go away again? Travelling the world had lost its shine for him, but he wasn't sure he could stay in Castle Clare if Bryony broke up with him. And he'd certainly never be able to eat a chocolate éclair ever again.

He groaned at his droll sense of humour while aching inside.

Longfellow gave a short sharp bark and Ben looked down at his friend.

'Have you had enough?' Ben looked back at the distance they'd covered. Longfellow might be long in body, but he was short of leg. 'Want a lift?' he asked and the dog didn't protest when Ben picked him up for the return journey.

Bryony was out when they got back. She'd left a note in the kitchen for him.

Gone to Flo's. X

Deciding that it was late enough to have an early night, he went up to shower and go to bed. It was just as he was about to switch his phone off for the night that another three messages came in.

She's still lying to you, isn't she?

Don't believe her.

You always knew she'd deceive you, didn't you?

CHAPTER TWENTY-THREE

There were just two more days left of the Castle Clare Literary Festival and the library was packed for a talk by a historian who had recently been doing the rounds on TV. They could really have used a bigger venue, but the village hall was already being used for an author panel event which were always popular. Megan was delighted with the turnout for the library, but there was a part of her that felt sad for all the authors and books that weren't lucky enough to get such publicity. It seemed that publishers backed just a few chosen books each year and those titles seemed to have everything thrown at them. Not only did that seem wildly unfair to Megan but, in her opinion, they weren't always the *best* books. Very often, the books were written by celebrities – or rather they were written by ghostwriters who'd been hired for the job. It was an odd business. How could somebody bring a book out with their name on it but not have done the hard work of actually writing it? Still, if such books got people into libraries and bookshops, she guessed she shouldn't complain. She just hoped that, while buying these well publicised titles, the readers might also discover a few other gems by *real* authors.

She leaned up against the front of her desk while the speaker rounded off his talk and opened the floor for questions. Megan usually jumped in at this stage to field things, but he seemed to be handling everything well on his own so she left him to it.

She walked round to the back of her desk and reached for her handbag. She'd switched her phone off just before the talk had begun but wanted to see if Rick had messaged. Switching it on now, her screen lit up and message after message rolled in. But they weren't from Rick. They were from the stalker and Megan's eyes blurred with tears as she dared to look at them.

How is it going with the police, Megan?

Ha ha! They can't do anything to me.

I'll be messaging you forever.

We're good friends now, aren't we?

A sob left her and several heads turned round from the gathering listening to the author. Tilly – one of Megan's young volunteers – ran towards her, a look of concern etched on her face.

'Megan!' she whispered. 'What is it?'

But Megan couldn't reply. She had no voice. It wasn't as if the messages were particularly vicious or frightening as some of them had been in the past. It was just the amount of them and their taunting nature. And the endlessness of it. She had put on a brave face. She'd managed to lose herself for blissful moments with Rick. She'd also told herself that the police were involved now and that it must surely come to an end soon. But *when?*

'You're shaking! Come and sit down,' Tilly said, placing a gentle hand on her shoulder and taking charge. Megan quickly wiped her eyes, aware that people were looking at her. She was making a scene and that was the very last thing the librarian of Castle Clare ever wanted to do.

'I'm... okay,' Megan managed to say at last, but she didn't feel okay. She could feel her heart beating wildly and a nervous sort of energy was flooding through her as if she was having a panic attack. She wanted to go home and hide herself under her duvet and only come out again when PC Brodie had assured her it was safe. But that wasn't going to happen, was it? She felt utterly alone in this. Even though she had Rick and her whole family around her, supporting her, the sense of isolation and pure terror was hers to bear alone because nobody was there with her when she read each and every one of those hateful messages and nobody – except her mother who was still receiving them – could ever comprehend how it made her feel each time she picked up her phone. The stalker seemed to be everywhere, like an evil sort of fog, and Megan truly believed that she'd never be free of him.

Somehow, Tilly managed the rest of the author event by herself, thanking the author, saying goodbye to everyone and tidying up after they'd all left. She'd kindly made a cup of tea for Megan, leading her gently to the small meeting room at the back of the library. Megan felt so grateful and was even more touched when her cousin came into the room.

'Bryony?'

'Hey! How are you? Tilly told me you weren't feeling well.' Bryony pulled a chair out from the table and sat down next to her.

'I'm sorry. I don't know what happened,' Megan told her.

'You're exhausted,' Bryony said. 'That's what it is.'

'I shouldn't have looked at my phone. Not here. Not in front of people.'

'Are you still getting the messages?'

'Worse than ever. And Mum's been getting them too.'

'Oh, Megan!'

'The stalker knows the police are involved now. But how did he find out? Are they watching me? I haven't put anything online about going to the police.'

'Maybe they're bluffing?'

'Why are they doing this?' Megan asked, her voice a kind of stressed wheeze now.

'It sounds like they're the kind of person who thrives on drama.'

'I don't understand. Who wants drama in their lives? Especially other people's?'

Bryony reached across the table and held her hand. 'Who can work out what goes on in somebody else's head?'

Megan sat there for a moment, letting the peace of the room and the comfort of having Bryony there envelop her.

'Do you want me to call Rick?' Bryony asked at last.

Megan shook her head. 'No. Don't worry him. I'll be okay.'

'Well, turn your phone off, okay?'

'It's off already.'

'Good!'

Megan smiled at her cousin. 'Are you okay? You look tired.'

'I'm okay,' Bryony said, and Megan was too tired and too wrapped up in her own worries to question the truth of her cousin's statement.

Josh was delighted when he opened his front door to April. He'd left his bookshop earlier than usual as Polly had been able to do a stint and he'd taken the opportunity to make a start on the room that was going to become the nursery.

'I didn't know you were coming over,' he said.

'I hope you're pleased to see me!' she teased.

'Of course I am.'

The two of them embraced and, after Josh had closed the door, he placed a hand on April's belly.

'I still can't feel anything!'

'Just be patient. There's definitely something in there because they're letting me know about it every day.'

'Is the morning sickness still bad?'

She nodded as they walked into the living room and sat down on the sofa.

'I bet May's delighted. I mean – after what you said about moving out once it's over.'

'Actually, she's the reason I'm here now.'

'Oh?'

'You'll never guess what's happened.'

'What?'

'May's gone out with Colin tonight.'

'Colin the baker?'

'Yes!'

'I didn't know they were an item.'

'Well, they're not *yet*, but I've been encouraging it because it's obvious he adores her.'

'I had no idea!'

'Neither did she apparently. Honestly, you have to spell these things out for her. Anyway, they've gone for a meal at The Happy Hare and I wanted to make sure she could invite him back to ours if she wanted to.'

'Do you think she will?' Josh asked.

'No! Of course not! But I thought I'd give her the option.'

Josh leaned forward and kissed her. 'You are the most thoughtful twin in the world.'

'Not really. Just doing the right thing. And don't let on, but I've brought a few of my clothes over. They're in the car. I thought I might as well make a start bringing my bits and pieces here. There's quite a lot of it.'

Josh grinned. 'I can't wait to have you here full-time.' He grinned. 'Hey! I've made a start on the nursery.'

'You have?'

'Well, I've just been clearing it of my old things really.'

'Let me guess – books?'

'I'll probably pass most of them onto Sam to sell.'

'Make sure you get a cut for the baby fund,' she told him.

'Have you decided on a colour?' he asked her.

'Not so much *a* colour,' she said.

'You mean... several?'

'I mean wallpaper!'

'Really? Is that wise with a baby that grows into a toddler with – well – sticky fingers?'

April laughed. 'I know it'll be more expensive and a bit more effort, but I think it will be gorgeous. I've seen this jungly print with animals and plants and waterfalls.'

'No snakes, right?'

'No snakes – I promise. Just gorgeous creatures like butterflies and monkeys and frogs and birds.'

'No spiders, right?'

'No spiders.'

Josh nodded, mulling it over. 'And it won't be scary or too oppressive?'

'No. It's in the most gorgeous soft colours. Mostly greens and all so serene. You'll adore it, I promise.' She paused. 'I don't want magnolia walls in our child's bedroom, Josh!'

He wrapped his arms around her waist. 'I love it when you take charge like that.'

'Good! Because I have *plenty* more ideas where that came from!'

~

It had been an exhausting day, Bryony thought as she pulled up outside Campion House. Not only had she had two more events on in her bookshop as well as helping Sam out with the author panel in the village hall, but the incident with Megan had left her feeling pretty wired.

Then there was the fact that Polly had been due to come in to help with the final event in the children's bookshop, but she'd cancelled the night before. She'd said she had a migraine, but Bryony couldn't help wondering if it was something else. Ben had also been as odd as ever. Bryony had delayed getting up that morning so as to avoid him as much as possible and they hadn't really spoken when they'd inevitably met in the kitchen.

Now, she got out of the car, letting Longfellow out a moment later. She kept him on a lead as she didn't know if she could trust him in her childhood garden. It was so much bigger than the tiny one at the terrace and Flo's.

Of course, her father was in the garden. It was one of those long golden evenings of summer that he loved so much and he'd be tinkering around until dusk fully enveloped him.

'Bryony!' he cried now as he spotted her. He strode across the lawn, bending to pat Longfellow who was beginning to enjoy his visits to Campion House more now he knew he could get the better of both Hardy and Brontë, the Nightingale's pointer and springer spaniel. 'Your mum's out.'

'That's okay. It's you I wanted to talk to.'

'Oh?'

Bryony smiled. Her father always seemed mildly surprised when she wanted to talk to him rather than her mother, but the two of them had always shared a special bond and it was sometimes easier to confide in him than her mum.

'Do you want to sit down or are you up for some gardening?'

'Do you mind if we sit? I'm exhausted.'

'You do look tired.'

'It's been one of those days.'

They walked towards her father's favourite wooden bench near the vegetable patch. It was still in the sun and it felt good to feel its warming presence after being in her shop all day with only the briefest of lunch breaks when she'd walked Longfellow up to the castle.

'So what's been happening that's robbed you of that beautiful smile of yours?' her father asked.

Bryony wasn't sure where to begin and found herself fidgeting awkwardly.

'Megan's got a problem with a stalker,' she said at last, starting at the end.

'Someone's following her?' His face was etched with concern.

'Not in person. Online. She's been receiving hundreds of messages. Probably thousands now.'

'Can't she block them?'

'She's tried. They just keep popping back up from different accounts. And it's really nasty stuff, Dad. She had a bit of a breakdown today. I've never seen her so shaken.'

'She should get the police involved.'

'She has, but they haven't been able to do anything yet.'

'Poor Megan.'

'It's awful to think there are people out there who do things like this – especially to someone as kind as Megan. It's not fair!'

'And is that what's got you so upset?' her father asked.

'That and some other things.'

And then she told him a little of what was going on – Ben's cruel accusation and Polly's strange behaviour towards her.

'What's happening, Dad? Just a few weeks ago, I was so happy! Everything was wonderful and...'

'What?'

'I was going to say everyone loved me, but that sounds vain and smug, doesn't it?'

'No, of course not. I'm afraid you're like me, Bryony – sensitive to everybody else's moods. You've always felt things deeply and carried emotions longer than most.'

'Like when Ben left.'

'Yes.'

Bryony swallowed. 'I'm afraid he's going to leave again.'

'Has he talked about going travelling?'

'No. He's not really talking to me at all other than accusing me of seeing Colin.'

'I don't understand – why would he suspect that?'

'I have no idea!'

Frank got up for a moment and Bryony watched as he bent to pull a weed from a nearby flower bed. It was a good indication that he was thinking everything over.

'Well,' he said at last as he returned to the bench, 'maybe you should stop buying raspberry tarts and chocolate éclairs for a while.'

Bryony gave a little smile. 'I don't suppose that would be a bad idea.'

'You know, I find that this sort of thing – that *anything* really – has a way of sorting itself out over time.'

Bryony pouted. 'And what do you do in the meantime?'

Her father sighed. 'You live. You look for the good things. You cuddle a dog.' He nodded down at Longfellow. 'You cook a fresh meal. You tend a garden.'

'Oh, Dad! You and your garden.'

'A garden is the best healer in the world. Aren't you finding that? At Flo's?'

Bryony thought about the summer evenings she'd spent with Flo and Sonny at Cuckoo Cottage.

'Yes.'

'Gardening is one of those things where you're totally immersed – your hands are in the soil or you're tending a delicate plant that demands all your attention. The world shrinks down to that little square metre you're tending. It's a feeling like no other. It's life in its purest form.'

'You should write a book.'

He laughed. 'Maybe. But there are probably enough books in the world.'

Bryony gasped. 'I never thought I'd hear you say that!'

He leaned in a little closer. 'You'll find that your ideas change as you get older.'

'Do they?'

He smiled and it was such a warm and heartfelt smile that Bryony couldn't help but feel comforted by it. Even if the whole world turned against her – every friend and every sibling – she knew that she'd always have the love of her father.

'Why don't you pop in and see your grandma while you're here?' he said. 'She's having a pretty good day and I know she'd love to see you and Longfellow.'

Bryony kissed her father's cheek. 'Okay.'

'And Bryony?' he said as she got up to leave. 'It'll be okay. Ben. Polly. They love you.'

Bryony felt the sudden sting of tears at his words. She only hoped that he was right.

Polly couldn't help feeling relieved that Archie was at a friend's house tonight. He'd been picked up from school and wouldn't be back for a couple of hours. She needed some time alone. She felt frazzled and fragile and there was only one cure for that – a good long walk.

'Come on, Dickens!' she called having changed into a pair of jogging bottoms and trainers.

Dickens was thrilled to be outside. A neighbour had taken him for a walk at lunchtime with her own spaniel, Horace, but the evening walk with his mistress was the one when all the rabbits came out to play and he could have a good chase.

Polly watched him now, nose to the ground as he picked up scents that made his plumy tail wag like a flag in a hurricane.

She'd turned her phone off. She'd had more messages that day via two of the social media sites she was on. She'd decided to come off one of them, but refused to give the other up because she had so many good friends there. Or did she? She had spent hours trying to work out if it was one of her online friends who was sending her these messages. The latest ones had sounded so intimate.

I care about you, Polly.

I think you should know the truth.

It must be someone she knew to talk like that, but why do it anonymously? And so often? It was like they were trying to elicit a response from her.

Polly felt exhausted with it all. She still hadn't told Jago about the messages or questioned him. Just the thought of asking him if he'd been seeing Bryony made her feel ill. Then, seeing Bryony yesterday outside the shop, Polly hadn't known how to respond.

What was happening to her? She felt that everything she'd been building so carefully since she and Archie had started their new life with Jago was slipping away from her and she didn't know what to do.

CHAPTER TWENTY-FOUR

Nobody in the Nightingale family would ever admit it, but they were all secretly glad when the Castle Clare Literary Festival finally came to an end. Chairs were stacked in the village hall and boxes now empty of their books were saved for Frank Nightingale's compost heap.

Megan didn't have the heart to take down the bunting in the library and she knew that it would be kept up in town for a good while longer, fluttering until you had to finally admit that summer was over and it was time for another school year to begin. It was one of the tell-tale signs of the passage of time in the little market town.

But the weather still proclaimed that it was the heart of summer and, as Megan drove out to Melton Green, she gloried in the feel of the warm air through the open window of the car.

Rick was washing under the outside tap and Megan had to stop for a moment to make sure the scene before her was real. It looked so old-fashioned, so natural – so beautiful.

'Hey!' he called as he spotted her, the spell broken but wonderfully so because she now got to be a part of it.

They met in front of the house with Truffle and Blewit joining in.

'You've finished for the day?' she asked as they kissed.

'Definitely. I thought we could go for a walk.'

'I'd love to,' she said.

Hand in hand, with the dogs gambolling ahead, they walked down the drover's lane, the early evening sun filtering through the leaves of the trees which turned the place into a green tunnel. Megan took a deep breath. She loved it here. It was a haven and a heaven. It also helped that there was patchy mobile reception out here so the rest of the world truly was left behind.

As they left the shady track and walked out into the sun-bleached fields, they stopped by a hedgerow to pick a handful of blackberries, ripe and juicy. A heron flew high overhead, its shape prehistoric – like something out of the dinosaur picture books that were ever popular with the younger readers in the library.

'I had a bit of a wobble this week,' Megan confessed to Rick as they picked more of the fruit that glistened in the hedge.

Rick reached out and touched her face, his hand warm and comforting. He then pulled her into a gentle hug. It was enough to tip her over the edge again and, before she knew it, she was crying. She hadn't meant to. She thought she had got it out of her system but, standing there in the golden field, she realised how vulnerable she still felt even with no phone reception and with the arms of the man she loved wrapped around her.

And Rick did the most wonderful thing – he let her cry. He didn't tell her it was going to be okay and that it was all going to be over soon because he couldn't make such promises, nor did he tell her to stop crying because nobody was worth her precious tears. He simply held her tightly and kissed her sweetly until the tears were finally over.

Sunday lunch at Campion House seemed to come round much too quickly for Bryony that week. She did think about cancelling, but her mother would not be pleased, she knew that, and could root out a non-genuine excuse at fifty paces – or the six miles between their properties. Nothing less than an important university deadline or a health emergency was classed as a good enough excuse to miss Sunday lunch with the family. But Bryony was dreading it. For one thing, she'd have to go there with Ben because he was too polite and conscientious to pull out, and they'd have to pretend that everything was hunky-dory between them. Then she'd have to face Polly without actually knowing what she'd done to deserve her cold shoulder.

Ben had taken Longfellow out first thing that morning and then scooted over to Flo's to help with some chores. He'd barely spoken to her and the monosyllabic treatment continued in the car on the way over to Campion House. Bryony was on the verge of telling him to pack his bags and take off to wherever it was he wanted to go if he was this unhappy with his life and still suspected her of being unfaithful to him. If she couldn't persuade him she loved him more than anything then she wasn't sure what she could do.

She glanced at him as he drove. He looked so sad and withdrawn. His phone was beeping. It had been beeping a lot recently, she'd noticed.

'Who's that? Shall I check?'

'No!' he cried. 'Leave it.'

She pressed herself into the back of the car seat, feeling utterly miserable. Was he messaging somebody about her? Or was he seeing somebody else? If he sincerely thought she was seeing Colin, perhaps he'd decided to see someone else too. So why was he joining her family for Sunday lunch? She sighed. Nothing made any sense anymore.

Polly and Jago's drive from their home to Campion House was almost as icy as Bryony and Ben's. The atmosphere between them was only slightly lightened by Archie's babble about his new friend at school who could do sums in his head and spoke French and Spanish.

'He's a triliquid,' Archie declared.

'Tri*lingual*, Arch,' Jago corrected.

Archie giggled. 'He sometimes answers the teacher in French, but she tells him off. Can I learn French?'

'You will at your next school,' Polly told him.

'No – now?'

'Haven't you got enough with your normal schoolwork and learning the guitar?' Polly asked.

He shrugged. 'It sounds cool.'

'Well, maybe ask your friend for lessons. What's his name?'

'Pierre.'

'Of course!' Jago said with a laugh.

'We just call him Pie because "Pierre" looks so weird, doesn't it?' Archie confessed and then he went on to recite all the French words he'd learned from Pierre so far. Polly was thankful for his enthusiasm because it masked the dreadful silence that hung between her and Jago.

Slowly, couple by couple, Campion House began to fill. The dining room doors into the garden had been opened and a warm breeze ruffled the white linen tablecloth. Jewel-coloured vases of flowers marched down its centre and there were two jugs of elderflower cordial waiting to be poured, pretty with ice cubes and lemon slices.

Bryony distracted herself by helping in the kitchen, taking plates of food through as they were passed to her by her mother. Sam and Callie helped too. Josh was talking to Grandpa, and Polly was chatting to April. Ben, Jago and Archie were playing with the dogs, and her father was guiding Grandma to the table. There was only one person missing.

'Mum – where's Lara?' Bryony asked.

'In her room, I think.'

'Is she okay?'

Her mother wiped her hands on a tea towel. 'She's been a bit quiet lately, to be honest.'

Bryony frowned at that. Lara had never been the quiet sort. If she was quiet, something was definitely wrong.

'Shall I go up and see her?'

'Would you, darling? And let her know we're serving.'

Bryony left the kitchen and went upstairs. It always felt a little strange being back in this part of the house – like going back in time to her childhood – and it was a comfort to know that all their old bedrooms were still there if they ever needed them. Except Sam's. He'd given his parents his blessing when they'd asked if they could turn his childhood bedroom into a gym. Bryony grinned as she peeped into it now. She still couldn't imagine her mum on the rowing machine.

Walking down the landing, Bryony paused outside Lara's door. It was closed.

'Lara?' she called, knocking gently.

'Come in.'

Bryony opened the door and walked inside. Her sister was sitting on her bed, a copy of *Vanity Fair* beside her. The bookmark inside looked to be hovering around page one. Bryony sat down beside her.

'You okay?'

Lara shrugged. 'I guess.'

'Mum says you've been quiet.'

'Yeah?'

'And that's not like you.' Bryony watched her sister. She looked tired and there was something about her that didn't look right. 'Are you okay? You're not unwell, are you?'

'No. I'm fine.'

'You sure? Is it uni? Are you worried about your final year?'

'Only about getting through the reading list,' Lara confessed.

'Ah! The dreaded Thackeray!'

'I've got Shakespeare's history plays too.'

'I never could get my head around all those Henrys,' Bryony said with a laugh. 'But it might be a good excuse to watch the Tom Hiddleston adaptations again?'

That made Lara smile.

'You see?' Bryony went on. 'Whatever the problem is, Tom Hiddleston is the answer.' She got up off the bed. 'Ready for lunch?'

Lara got up and Bryony saw her glancing at her phone on the bedside table. Maybe that was the problem she thought.

'Waiting to hear from someone?' she asked.

'No!'

Bryony frowned. The word came out almost defensively and she wanted to question Lara about it, but their mother was calling them from downstairs. It was time for Sunday lunch.

The chat around the table was mostly about the literary festival. What had been the greatest success? Who would they invite again? Had there been any divas?

'There was that moment when the royal biographer refused to answer a question,' Josh said.

'What was the question?' Frank asked.

'I'm afraid I didn't hear it. I was helping an old lady who'd dropped her handbag.'

'Ever the gentleman!' Eleanor said to her son with a proud smile.

'Anyway, he got all pompous. Quite red in the face! I had to step in with the "Just time for one more question" trick.'

'Don't invite *him* back!' Polly said.

'Well, Callie answered *all* the questions her audience had for her,' Bryony said, causing Callie to blush to the roots of her fair hair. 'Even the embarrassing ones.'

'Oh, what were the embarrassing ones?' Archie demanded.

'Yes – do tell,' Grandpa Joe agreed.

Callie covered' her face with her hands.

'First of all,' Bryony began, 'Isla Knight asked if she could go to the toilet and then Jimmy Bainbridge politely put his hand up and surprised everyone by asking Callie if writers went to the toilet!'

Laughter rippled around the table.

'What did you say?' Jago asked Callie.

'I said only after a good morning's writing.'

Everybody laughed again.

'Callie is the best speaker ever!' Bryony declared.

'We'll not put her on the blacklist then,' Josh said. 'Unlike the pompous biographer.'

April looked concerned by this. 'Do you really have a black list?'

Josh shifted a little in his seat. 'Well, not written down as such. It's more of a mental list, right?' He addressed the question to Sam.

'Right! I think we know who we want to invite back and who we'd rather not work with again.'

'Just as you do,' Josh told April. 'Remember that woman? What was her name? She made you paint that Welsh dresser three times because she couldn't make her mind up about the colour.'

'Oh, yes! She was a nightmare to work with!'

'And, as self-employed business people, we get to make that call, don't we?' Josh said.

'As long as you're able to still make a living by turning away the occasional bit of work,' April agreed.

'It'll be up to Lara next year, won't it?' Sam said. 'We'll be relying on you to make all the major decisions.'

'I think she'll be more than ready,' Josh said.

Everybody turned Lara now, but she didn't respond. In fact, Bryony noticed for the first time that she had barely touched her food.

'Lara?' she said gently.

Eleanor looked concerned too. 'Lara darling? Are you okay?'

Without warning, Lara burst into tears.

Eleanor was on her feet in an instant and by her daughter's side. 'Lara! What is it?'

Lara's face was bright red now as she continued to cry. Eleanor wrapped her arms around her and Bryony could see that there were tears in her mother's eyes too.

'Darling – tell us,' she said gently.

'I've been getting messages,' Lara managed in a half-choke.

'What sort of messages?' Frank asked his daughter.

'Horrible messages saying the worst things.'

'What sort of things?' Frank asked as Eleanor passed her a tissue.

Lara dried her eyes, but her tears were still coming. 'Threatening me. Saying awful things that aren't true.'

Lara lifted her head and looked straight at Bryony.

'It isn't true, Bry. I swear it isn't.'

'What isn't true?'

Lara gave a huge sniff. 'About me and Ben.'

Bryony's mouth dropped open. 'What do you mean?'

'This person – they accused me of seeing Ben behind your back. But I'm not! Tell her I'm not, Ben!'

Bryony turned to look at Ben. Like Lara, his face was quite red.

'Of course it's not true!' Eleanor said. 'Who would say such a thing?'

'I don't know,' she said through her tears. 'The messages are all anonymous.'

'How many have you had?' Bryony asked.

'I don't know. I deleted some of the early ones, but they just kept coming.'

'Ben?' Eleanor looked at him now and Bryony saw him swallow hard. 'Do you know anything about this? Is there a reason someone's been targeting Lara?'

He shook his head. 'I've been getting them too.'

'What?' Josh said.

'Were the messages about me?' Lara asked.

'No. They were about Bryony.'

Bryony felt floored by this revelation. 'You didn't tell me.'

'I know.'

'What did they say?' Bryony dared to ask.

He sighed. 'They told me you were seeing Colin.'

'Ben!'

Lara had stopped crying now and sounded more serious than upset. 'How many messages have you had?' she asked Ben.

'Too many to count.'

'Me too.'

'Who's doing this?' Grandpa Joe demanded of no one in particular while Grandma Nell just looked confused.

'They don't say,' Ben said.

'Didn't you block them?' Jago asked.

'Of course,' Ben said. 'But they kept coming back from different accounts.'

'Same,' Lara said.

Bryony gasped as realisation dawned.

'Do you know who it might be?' Lara asked.

'Sort of.'

Everyone looked at Bryony who hurried to explain. 'Well, I don't *actually* know. But it sounds like this could be linked to Megan.

'Megan's sending the messages?' Eleanor asked, her face aghast.

'No, of course not, Mum! She's been getting them for months now. Really nasty ones – they sound like yours, Lara. I think it's the same person. Her mum's been getting them too.'

'Have they been to the police?' April asked.

'Yes. But nothing's been done yet. They've been asked to keep records of every message.'

'How do you know it's the same person?' Lara asked.

'It's got to be, hasn't it? You've not had them before, have you? How long have you been getting them?'

'Since the festival began,' Lara said.

'I've been getting them for a few weeks,' Ben said.

A shocked silence fell over the table while everyone took this in, and then a small voice spoke.

'I've been getting them too,' Polly said.

'Polly!' Jago cried, turning to her.

'I didn't know what to do!'

'Why didn't you tell me?'

She shook her head. 'They said you were seeing Bryony.'

'Oh my god!' Bryony shook her head.

Sam, who'd been watching silently up until now, spoke for the first time. 'Wait a minute – so this person – and we think it's the same person – accused Lara of seeing Ben, told Ben that Bryony was seeing Colin, and said Jago was seeing Bryony?'

'Who'd do such a thing?' Callie asked.

'Has anybody else had any messages?' Frank asked, looking as baffled as everyone else at what was happening.

'I got some,' Archie said. 'But I think they were just from Pie in Spanish.'

'His new friend at school,' Jago explained.

'Why would someone say all these things, though?' Callie asked.

'It sounds like somebody just out to make trouble,' Grandpa Joe said.

'Who's making trouble?' Grandma Nell asked.

'We're trying to find out, Grandma,' Sam told her.

'Can I see your phone?' Bryony asked Polly.

Polly took the phone out of her pocket, unlocked it and passed it to her sister. Bryony scrolled through the most recent messages. A moment later, she looked up from the screen.

'They don't name names.'

'What do you mean?'

'Look, Poll – Jago isn't mentioned once. The messages just say 'He' – like this one: 'He's cheating on you.''

'Let me see,' Jago said and Bryony passed the phone down the table to him.

'They're just messing with you. Playing on a person's insecurities

– pushing you in a direction they want you to go in and leaving you to fill in the details.'

Polly took her phone off Jago and looked back through the messages. Ben was doing the same now.

'You're right, Bry,' Ben said. 'They've not named names.'

'You did their work for them,' Bryony said, feeling the hot sting of tears in her eyes. 'You just assumed, didn't you?'

Ben shook his head. 'Bry!'

Everyone started talking at once, passing phones between one another and asking questions.

Eleanor left Lara's side and went to the head of the table.

'I think we all need to take a moment, don't you?' She looked directly at Bryony who nodded back and quickly left the table.

'Bry! Wait!'

Ben was behind her, but she didn't stop for him. She just had to get out of Campion House as quickly as she could.

CHAPTER TWENTY-FIVE

For the first time in the history of Sunday lunches at Campion House, dessert wasn't eaten and the family didn't go for a walk together. Grandpa Joe and Josh took Hardy and Brontë out while April kept Grandma Nell company in the front room. Lara was in her room again and everybody else had left.

'Well, that wasn't what I'd bargained for!' Frank said as he and Eleanor cleared the kitchen together.

'Poor Bryony. The look on her face!'

'They'll sort themselves out. They've been through worse together.'

'And Polly too!'

'We'll get this reported to the police right away. If this has been going on with Megan and Bonnie as well, and if it's all linked, they should know sooner rather than later.'

'I can't believe nobody told us,' Eleanor said.

'Bryony did mention that Ben and Polly had been acting strangely,' Frank confessed to her now.

'You didn't tell me that.'

'I didn't think anything of it, to be fair. I thought it would all work itself out.'

'You have to tell me these things, Frank!'

He put down the bread plate he was holding and put his arms around her. 'I'm sorry.'

'And Lara! Who's doing this? Do you think it's all connected?'

'It's a bit too much of a coincidence not to be, don't you think?'

'I don't know how these things work. But it does seem like someone's coming after the family.'

'I'm not so sure about that,' Frank said. 'That makes it sound personal and I think it's probably random – they've chosen the Nightingales, yes, but only as we're all linked together on these social media sites. It's a way of causing maximum mayhem.'

'What sort of person would even *think* to do something like that? It's vile!'

'Are you sure you've not had any messages?'

Eleanor shook her head. 'Mind you, I hardly go online these days. It's all so time-consuming and ugly, isn't it?'

'You know how I feel about it all. I have my one online gardening group and that's quite enough.'

She nodded in agreement. 'I'd better check on Lara.'

'Why not take her up a bowl of that trifle? It seems a pity nobody's had any yet.'

'That's a good idea.'

'And I might have some myself.'

They smiled at one another. They might not be able to sort out all the problems around them at that particular moment, but they could definitely make things taste just a little bit sweeter.

Polly did her best not to cry for the entire journey home, but it was hard to hold the tears back.

'I'm sorry,' she whispered.

'It's okay,' Jago whispered back.

As soon as they arrived back at Lilac Row from Campion House, Archie had gone up to his room and Dickens had been let out in the garden, Polly broke down.

'I can't believe I listened to a total stranger!'

Jago gently took her in his arms. 'It's not your fault.'

'But I didn't even try talking to you.'

'Yeah, that was a mistake!' he said with a small laugh.

'I'm so sorry!'

He hugged her close. 'These parasites just make trouble – they play on our insecurities and...'

'What?'

'Dare I say it? You've been pretty insecure lately. Well, emotional, I should say. Fragile, perhaps.'

Polly pulled back from him and looked into his eyes which were so full of love and empathy.

'I have?'

'A little,' he said diplomatically, stroking her hair away from her face.

'I'm so mad at myself. To think I let someone control me like that.'

Jago might have called her fragile, but she could now feel that fragility turning into fury because she'd allowed somebody to create chaos between her and Jago, planting fear and doubt in her mind. She'd lashed out, driving a wedge between them and hurting the man she loved.

'We'll sort it out,' Jago told her. 'We'll get together with Ben and Bryony and Lara, and make sure the police have all the information. If they can link it to Megan and her mother, there might be a chance that they can actually do something about it now.'

'I hope so.'

They hugged again.

'And, just for the record, as much as I like Bryony because she's your sister, there's only one woman in this world for me – and that's you, Polly Nightingale!'

They kissed and it was such a warm and tender moment between them that Polly didn't feel she deserved it.

'I'll have to apologise to Bryony,' she said after a moment. 'She must hate me!'

'She doesn't hate you.'

'Maybe I should ring her?'

'Not now,' Jago said. 'I think she'll be talking things through with Ben, don't you?'

Polly nodded. 'Poor Bryony. She's really been through it, hasn't she?'

'She'll be okay,' Jago said gently. 'Now, I somehow managed to miss out on dessert today. What are we going to do about that?'

'There's some chocolate cheesecake in the fridge,' Polly told him.

'That,' he said, kissing the tip of her nose, 'is the right answer!'

When they got home, Ben sank onto the sofa. Bryony joined him and Longfellow jumped up onto her lap.

'I don't know what to say,' he told her without looking at her. 'I feel so ashamed. You can kick me out if you want. I won't blame you.'

'I'm not going to kick you out.'

'But I didn't even give you a chance, Bry.'

'It's okay.'

'No it's not! We should have talked about this. I don't know what happened. I just kind of clammed up, didn't I?'

'Yes. You kind of did. I thought you were planning to leave again,' Bryony confessed.

'What?' Ben looked genuinely shocked by this.

'I didn't know what to think. You weren't talking to me, Ben. So I thought you wanted to leave or that you might have found somebody else.'

Bryony watched his head lower as if he was too ashamed to be seen.

'I never meant to push you away like that. The thought of losing you – it's my worst nightmare. But I nearly did by acting the way I did!'

'You didn't. I'm still here, aren't I?'

He turned to face her at last. 'I'm so sorry.'

'I'm sorry too.'

'You? Why?'

'For you to even begin to believe I'd do something like that – I must have given you reason,' Bryony said.

'No. This isn't your fault – not at all.'

'But that time I played that awful trick on you with Colin at the dance. I still hate myself for hurting you like that.'

Ben shook his head. 'That was ages ago, Bry. We said we'd never talk about it again.'

'But I still feel bad about it.'

'And I feel bad about this,' Ben said. 'So maybe we're kind of equal now?'

Bryony felt a small smile tickling the edges of her mouth and she took Ben's hands in hers.

'Let's promise, then – no more muddles like that between us. It's not just the two of us in this family anymore,' Bryony said, gazing down at Longfellow. 'We have to trust one another.'

Ben nodded. 'Yes.'

Just then, Longfellow rolled onto his back.

'You know what that means in dog language?' Bryony said.

'No. What does it mean?' Ben asked.

'It's the ultimate expression of love and trust.'

Ben smiled, then leaned forward to kiss her and the three of them snuggled up on the sofa together – the perfect family.

CHAPTER TWENTY-SIX

It was just over two weeks after the eventful Sunday lunch at Campion House. Megan was cooking dinner for Rick at her place when her phone rang.

'You okay?' Rick asked a moment later after she'd hung up and returned to the kitchen from the living room.

She nodded. 'That was PC Brodie. He's on his way over.'

'What did he say?'

'Just that. He's coming over and will be here in about an hour.'

They had just enough time to finish their dinner when there was a knock on the door.

Megan looked at Rick. 'I'm a bit nervous,' she confessed.

'Do you want me to answer it?'

'No. I'll get it.' She got up from her chair and opened the door.

PC Brodie was in his late thirties and had sandy-coloured hair and a kind face. He gave a tight smile and nodded. 'Miss Nightingale – how are you?'

'Anxious to hear what you have to say.'

'Yes, of course.'

'Come in, please. You've not met Rick, have you?'

The two men shook hands.

'Can I get you a tea or coffee?' Rick asked him.

'No, thank you. I'll get straight to the matter if that's all right?'

'Absolutely,' Megan said.

Megan and Rick sat next to each other on the sofa and PC Brodie perched on the chair opposite them.

'We have some news for you. It's all happened much faster than I expected, although I realise that the last few months must have seemed like forever to you.'

'Yes,' Megan agreed. 'They have.'

'Well, you'll know that your family members have all been in and made reports and the information they've given us has made it possible to make links and gather evidence and I'm now in a position to tell you that an arrest has been made.'

'Really?' Rick said, glancing at Megan to gauge her response.

'His name's Paul Johnson. He's thirty-four and lives in Manchester.'

'*Manchester?*' Megan looked at Rick. 'But I always thought it was someone nearby.'

'He's been targeting people all over the country. For years, it would seem. He has quite the digital footprint and we're still finding out how many people it's affected. I've never seen anything like it before. It's taken a while for the different forces to piece it all together. My colleagues in Manchester have a huge file of previous investigations going back years, but there's never been enough hard evidence to tie everything together and cybercrime...' He paused, 'well, let's just say we've got more knowledge about it these days and it's being taken more seriously than in the past.'

'So how did the Manchester police link him to us?' Megan asked.

'Through all the connections. One name leads to another and another. You'll know that yourself through the social media sites.'

'I told you it was never personal,' Rick said, taking her hand in his.

'But it *feels* personal,' Megan said.

'Of course,' PC Brodie agreed.

'I don't understand why someone would do something like this.'

PC Brodie took a deep breath. 'Power? Control? Who knows what goes on in the mind of someone like that? But I think it's a kind of psychological warfare for personal amusement.'

'And what's going to happen now?'

'Well, it's always tough getting these cases to court and getting a custodial sentence, but we've got plenty of evidence. There was a case a little while back where a man got nine years and this case is certainly comparable.'

Megan nodded.

'Now, we can't promise you anything at this stage, but I'll do my best to make sure he's not able to communicate with you or your family again.'

'Have you let my cousins know yet?'

'No. I came to see you first, but I'll be in touch with them as soon as I can. But maybe you could let your mother know?'

'Yes, of course. I still can't believe he targeted so many of us,' Megan said. 'So where is he now?'

'He's being held in custody in Manchester.' PC Brodie stood up. 'We'll keep you informed.'

'Thank you,' Megan said, standing up.

'I'll let myself out. You have a good evening.'

'Thank you,' Rick said and, a moment later, they heard the door shut.

'Did that really just happen?'

'Yes!' Rick cried. 'He's been arrested, Min! It's over. He's never going to hurt you or your family again.'

'I must let Mum know!'

Rick nodded and Megan quickly made the call. When she came off the phone, Rick got up from the sofa.

'Was she crying like you?'

Megan sniffed as her tears fell. 'Yes!'

'Come here!' he said, putting his arms around her a moment later.

'They're tears of relief!' she assured him.

'I know!'

'But I'm so scared. What happens next? Will I have to go to court? Will I have to *see* him?'

'I don't know. But, if you do, I'll be right there with you.'

They stood in the centre of the room just holding each other and then Megan looked up at Rick's kind face.

'It's so strange – to think that it was somebody over two hundred miles away.'

'The power of technology,' Rick said. 'The *terrible* power of technology.'

'Yes,' Megan agreed. 'But there is a bright side to that, though.'

'What's that?'

'At least it wasn't anyone from Castle Clare!'

Rick smiled. 'So, it wasn't a bored Winston after all!'

'Oh, Rick!'

'Or that poor chap. What's your nickname for him?'

'The Loner,' Megan said. 'No. It wasn't him. And now I feel awful for even imagining for a second that it might have been.'

'That's what these malicious people want – they want their victims to turn on one another and point fingers. It's all about creating mayhem.'

'He certainly did that.'

Rick stroked his fingers through her hair and Megan closed her eyes, soothed by his touch.

'How about we head out to the cottage?' he whispered.

'For the night?'

'It's still warm enough for sleeping under the stars, isn't it?'

She beamed him a smile. 'I'll get my toothbrush!'

The September Castle Clare book club meeting was held on an evening that could so easily have passed for summer. The day had been perfect in bright blues and soft golds and the air was still warm as Sam greeted everyone at the open door of his bookshop.

'How was your holiday, Winston?' Sam asked as his old friend arrived, remembering he'd been looking forward to his first holiday in years.

'Ah, marvellous, Sam! Thank you for asking. Wells-next-the-Sea is a very good spot. Plenty to do although one too many chip shops,' Winston said, patting his belly.

'And how's Monty?'

'He's good. I tried to persuade him to come back home with me, but he's just joined his local golf club and said there was some kind of match on. Match? Is that the right word for golf?'

'Tournament?' Flo suggested as she came through from the back of the shop where she'd been helping to arrange the chairs with Callie.

Winston nodded. 'That could be it.'

'Sounds like he's doing well,' Sam said, remembering Winston's brother's visit to Castle Clare earlier in the year when he'd been having a hard time after his wife's death.

'He is. He'll be coming for Christmas.' Winston frowned. 'Or am I going to his? I'd better check that.'

'No Delilah this evening?' Callie asked, looking around for the Labrador.

'She ate something unsavoury on our afternoon walk so I thought it was best that she have some – er – alone time.'

'Good idea!' Sam said, mightily relieved that they'd be spared any olfactory disturbances that evening. 'Anyway, come in and take a seat. Honey's brought some blackberry and apple slices for everyone and Antonia's made flapjack.'

Winston's face beamed in delight as he practically trotted into the back of the bookshop in pursuit of baked goods.

It was a good turnout that night. Winston was joining Flo, Honey and Antonia. There was also Callie, Polly and Jago, and Megan was there for the first time and she'd brought Rick with her. Sam was delighted because he thought that the book they'd chosen for this month was very special indeed and it was lovely to be sharing the joy of it with his friends, family and neighbours.

84 Charing Cross Road by Helene Hanff was something of a classic. It was a collection of letters between an American woman, Helene Hanff, and Englishman Frank Doel of Marks & Co Booksellers in London. The twenty-year correspondence had begun in October 1949 after Ms Hanff saw an advert by Marks & Co Booksellers and wrote to enquire if they had some specialised books that she couldn't get in the US. Sam adored the slow "getting to know you" quality that letters forced and how the tone slipped wonderfully from formal to friendly. Helene had even sent food hampers for the staff to share.

Thinking about that now, Sam smiled at the thought of the glorious treats the ladies of the book club had arranged for the evening so he closed the door of the shop and went into the back room to join everyone.

Sure enough, Antonia Jessop was passing a superior eye over her rival, Honey Digger as she passed her blackberry and apple slices around.

'Not for me,' Antonia said. '*Far* too much sugar, I imagine!'

'I'd say you could do with a little sweetening,' Honey said.

Winston guffawed but it instantly turned into a cough. Luckily, Jago was on hand with a slap on the back and a glass of water.

'Flapjack, anyone?' Antonia asked, passing her plate around.

'Flapjack – such a simple standby to have in one's repertoire,' Honey said. 'It was the first thing I learned to make. When I was five, if I remember rightly.'

'So!' Sam said, clapping his hands together in an attempt to stop a potential bun fight. 'We could chat all night about holidays and the festival and – erm – flapjack, but we're here to discuss the book.'

'Were we meant to read a book?' Winston asked.

Sam frowned. 'You haven't read–'

'I'm just teasing!'

'Oh, Winston – you naughty man!' Honey said with a chuckle.

'Actually,' Sam interrupted, 'I should just introduce our new members this evening although one is known to many of us here because she runs the Castle Clare library – Megan Nightingale. And her partner, Rick Wildman.'

There was a chorus of welcomes for Megan and Rick and Sam couldn't help noticing that Rick was getting particular attention from Honey who had shoved her plate of apple and blackberry slices under his nose several times while smiling like a teenager.

'Okay, so who wants to begin?' Sam asked.

'Well, I loved it. Although it wasn't a romance, it *felt* romantic!' Honey said.

'There are more kinds of relationship than romantic ones,' Antonia pointed out.

'Yes, and that's explored in the letters between Helene and Frank, isn't it?' Sam said, steering the conversation into safer waters. 'What do we think of their friendship?'

'Friendships forged over books are always the best, I think,' Callie said.

'He's married, isn't he?' Honey asked. 'The man – Frank?'

'That's right,' Sam said.

'I wonder what his wife thought of the correspondence between him and Helene? She sent gifts to him too, didn't she?'

'Well, they were for everyone in the shop.'

'And the staff wrote to Helene too, didn't they?' Flo said.

'Oh, I loved that!' Polly said. 'Wasn't it Cecily Farr? She wrote to Helene but told her not to tell Frank that she was writing.'

'Secret letters!' Honey said with a giggle.

Sam smiled too and noticed a private look pass between Megan and Rick.

'There was a sentence that really struck me,' Sam went on, 'and I'd love to know what you all think of it. It's on page forty-three of my old edition. Helene writes that she can't get interested in things that happened to fictional people. What do we think about that? Does anyone agree with Helene?'

'If we did agree with her, I don't think there'd be much point being in a book club,' Antonia said.

'Fiction can seem more real than life,' Flo said. 'At least it can to me.'

'I agree. You get close to the characters in books because you enter not just their world but their minds,' Sam said. 'It's a very special connection.'

'It's company, isn't it?' Winston said. 'Characters can become friends. Family even. You care about them.'

Sam smiled at Winston's assertion.

'And I'd be out of a job if nobody wanted to read about fictional characters,' Callie pointed out.

There was some laughter in the group at that.

'But aren't people reading less fiction?' Honey asked. 'I read somewhere that it's a struggle to get children to read these days.'

'Well, Callie had a pretty good turnout at her festival event last month, didn't you?' Sam said.

'Yes!'

'How have you found things at the library recently?' Sam asked Megan.

'It's good. We have some very dedicated parents who make sure their children are brought up around books. I don't know what it's like elsewhere, but life in Castle Clare does tend to revolve around books, and new readers walk into the library all the time.' She smiled at Rick and Honey gasped, a hand dramatically raised to her chest as she watched the two sweethearts.

'So, did we *like* Helene?' Sam asked.

'That's a good question,' Winston said. 'She comes across as being very forthright, doesn't she?'

'She knows what she wants!' Flo added with a chuckle.

'And she's not afraid to show her emotions,' Callie said. 'There was a bit I loved. Where is it?' Callie opened her book to one of the many dog-eared pages.

Antonia gasped. 'You've bent the corner down!'

'Yes – it makes it easy to find a favourite bit,' Callie said.

'I thought with you being a writer, you'd have more respect for books!'

'But I do respect them,' Callie insisted. 'Using them, loving them, is respecting them.'

Sam grinned. Callie simply refused to be intimidated by Antonia.

'Here it is!' Callie declared. 'Helene Hanff says she marks out all the best passages in pencil.'

Antonia gasped again. 'But to write in a book! That's even *worse* than dog-earring the pages!'

'That's an interesting point,' Sam said. 'What do we all think of that? Does anyone else dog-ear their pages or write in their books?'

'They'd better not if they're library books!' Megan said and everyone laughed although Winston's laughter seemed a little nervous to Sam.

'That reminds me of a bit,' Polly said, removing a bookmark.

'See!' Antonia said pointedly to Callie. 'That's what bookmarks are for!'

'What were you looking for, Polly?' Sam asked.

'Just something Helene writes about how she loves to find notes in the margins.'

'Ah! Marginalia!' Sam said with a smile.

'Yes! And having that feeling of connection to other readers who've read a book before you.'

Everybody nodded as if understanding perfectly.

'That's beautiful!' Honey enthused.

'Although turning library pages can be fraught with danger as I discovered recently,' Antonia said pointedly to Megan.

Megan shifted uneasily in her seat.

'And secondhand books,' Flo agreed. 'Sorry, Sam, but you do find unsavoury marks in them sometimes. There's a horrible stain in my copy here – look!'

The group looked at the reddish-brown stain and wrinkled their noses.

'Why do people have to bleed over books?' Antonia asked. 'It's a disgusting habit.'

'They probably don't do it deliberately,' Sam pointed out.

Jago laughed. 'Yes, like I've got a nice bit of Graham Greene to pour this paper cut over.'

'Don't be foul!' Antonia chided.

'And there's still a lot of life left in a book with a stain or two in it,' Sam declared.

'Didn't Helene say something about only having three bookshelves and throwing books away?' Callie asked.

'That's right,' Polly said. 'I remember that bit. She said if she's never going to read a book again, she just throws it out!'

'But she professes to love books!' Antonia said.

'I suppose only when they're useful to her,' Sam said.

'It's good to have a sort-out,' Megan said. 'It keeps a collection alive.'

They talked a little more about the book – moments that they'd loved and how sad it was that Helene and Frank had never got to meet.

'It's a beautiful book, Sam,' Flo said. 'Good choice!'

'I'm glad you enjoyed it.'

'It shows us so many things about what it means to be human, doesn't it?' Flo went on. 'Like friendship and compassion.'

Honey nodded. 'And passion!'

Antonia gave her a haughty stare.

'Passion for *books*,' Honey said.

Megan smiled. 'The important thing for me is that none of us would be connecting to any of these emotions shared by Helene and Frank and the others if it wasn't for the art of letter writing. Letters are precious. They're valued. You tend to keep letters, don't you? They're not like the texts or emails that flood our world today in a tsunami of information. Letters take time to write and give the writer and the reader a real chance to connect. It makes me sad that so few of us take the time to write letters now.'

Sam nodded in agreement and again noticed the secret looks Megan and Rick were exchanging.

'Perhaps we should write letters!' Flo said. 'I used to love getting them in the post from friends, but it just doesn't happen anymore, does it?'

'My eyesight's too poor to write letters these days,' Winston complained. 'And don't get me started on the price of stamps!'

'Yes, it's become an expensive way of communicating, I'm afraid,' Sam agreed. 'But what do you think about us writing letters to each other?'

'What do you mean?' Winston asked.

'They wouldn't have to be long – they could be whatever length you like really. And we could drop them off here at the shop whenever it's convenient so you wouldn't need to worry about postage.'

'Sort of like a Secret Santa but with letters?' Flo asked.

'If you like. Or you could pick somebody in particular.'

'That's such a fun idea!' Callie said.

Suddenly, everybody was talking excitedly and the delicious nibbles were passed around again. Sam turned towards Callie.

'I hope you'll write to me.'

'I will if you promise to reply!' she said.

Sam smiled. 'I love it. We're reviving the lost art of letter writing.'

He glanced across to where Megan and Rick were sitting, noticing once again the sweet looks they were sharing and wondering if they'd join in with the letter-writing fun.

CHAPTER TWENTY-EIGHT

September mellowed into October and the leaves continued to fall from the trees, carpeting the lawns, greens and lanes of the Suffolk countryside. As Megan drove out to Oak Farm Cottage after closing the library, she thought about the eventful summer that had passed oh so quickly. She thought about the hundreds – no thousands – of terrifying messages she'd been sent and the fear she and her family had felt over the last few months. She thought about Josh and April and how they were now living together and looking forward to their baby in the spring, and she thought about that day Rick had walked into her life and the letters he'd written and the kisses they'd shared. Life could change in the space of a heartbeat and you never quite knew what it would bring but, like the seasons, it was always coming and going, ebbing and flowing.

As she drove down the track to Rick's house, parked and got out of the car, she marvelled at the progress he'd made. He'd worked so hard and the result was incredible. Most of the scaffolding had been taken down now, but there was still some up around one of the chimneys.

'Hey!' he called as he spotted her. He was coming out of the barn, some tool in his hand which Megan couldn't begin to name. His excited voice alerted Truffle and Blewit who got to her before Rick did. She bent down to fuss them and then stood back up to greet Rick with a warm kiss.

'That was nice,' he said.

'There's more where that came from!'

They kissed again.

'I've just had a call from Leo,' he said brightly.

'How is he?'

'He sounds as loved up as we are!'

'Really?'

'He met someone at an elephant sanctuary in Thailand. They were both volunteering and he sounds pretty smitten.'

'What's her name?'

Rick frowned. 'I've forgotten.'

'Oh, Rick!' Megan smiled. Things were changing again, she thought. Everybody's lives were ever evolving.

She put her arms around him as she took in the wonderful sight of Oak Farm Cottage.

'You've done it, Rick! I'm so proud of you!'

'Well, there's still a lot of work to do inside, but she's pretty much watertight for winter.'

'She looks beautiful – a real home!'

'I want to show you something.' He took her hand and led her into the house which now had its own front door. Once inside, he stopped, looking a little anxious, she thought. 'Now, I know I just said there's still a lot to do – you know – a few internal walls and ceilings and floors and such, but I kind of prioritised something else for a little while.'

'What is it?' Megan asked, not sure what might be deemed more important than walls, ceilings and floors.

Still with her hand in his, he led her into the heart of the cottage, turning right at the fireplace. Megan hadn't been inside for a while and, when she saw the room he'd been working on, her hands flew to her mouth.

'Rick!'

'You like it?'

She nodded, gazing to the left and to the right and then back. The entire room had been lined with beautiful bespoke shelving.

'You did this?'

'With a little bit of help from a friend.'

'It's wonderful! You're going to have your very own library.'

He put his arms around her and rested his head on her left shoulder.

'*We're* going to have our very own library.'

Megan turned to face him. They were very close now – their lips just a whisper away from one another.

'This place wouldn't be complete without you in it, Minnow. And *I* wouldn't be complete either.'

'I feel the same way about you. This last summer – it all feels like a dream and I don't ever want it to end.'

'It won't!' he told her.

'Even when I'm fifty?'

'Nope!'

'Or eighty?'

'You'll be even lovelier then because you'll have been loved by me for decades!'

Megan smiled. She loved that answer.

'You *will* still write me letters, won't you? Even when I'm old and grey and only have three teeth left?'

Rick laughed at the image she painted of herself. 'You want me to?'

'Of course! I love your letters so much. I'd hate them to *ever* stop.'

'Well, that's very lucky because there's one waiting for you.'

'Where?'

Rick grinned. 'Somewhere in the house – you'll have to find it!'

She giggled. 'There's one for you too! After the book club, I thought it was about time I wrote a letter to you!'

'When did you hide it?'

'Last time I was here. But that's the *only* clue you're getting!'

'But I'm *hopeless* at finding things!' he said.

'That's not true! You found this place,' she told him. 'And you found me.'

They kissed again and then he did something he'd never done before: he tickled her.

Megan shrieked.

'Give me a clue, Min!'

'No!' she cried. 'No clues!'

She tried to wriggle away from him, but he kept on tickling. Finally, she broke free and ran through the cottage and out across the lawn towards the moat, her dark hair loose and streaming out behind her as she laughed. And, in that laugh, Rick could have sworn he heard the future, and the romantic vision he'd had when he'd first viewed Oak Farm Cottage – of a life with a family – seemed to be manifesting before his very eyes.

The Book Lovers
VICTORIA CONNELLY

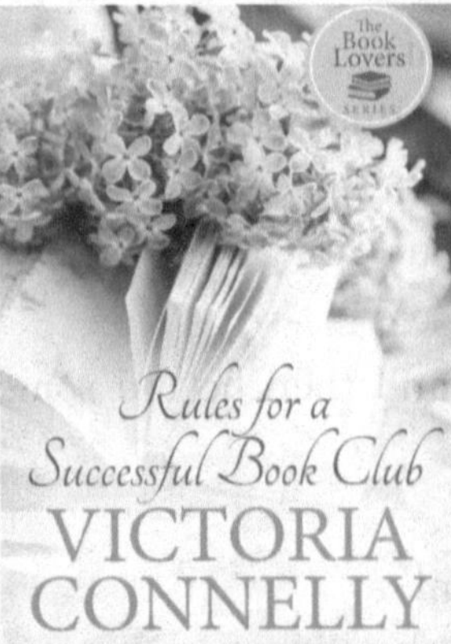
Rules for a Successful Book Club
VICTORIA CONNELLY

Natural Born Readers
VICTORIA CONNELLY

Scenes from a Country Bookshop
VICTORIA CONNELLY

Christmas with the Book Lovers
VICTORIA CONNELLY

One More Page Before I Kiss You
VICTORIA CONNELLY

AFTERWORD

I was hugely inspired by Roger Deakin's property Walnut Tree Farm at Mellis in Suffolk, and the book written by Rufus Deakin and Titus Rowlandson about its restoration – *Life at Walnut Tree Farm*. In the summer of 2023, I was lucky enough to visit on a perfect day in late summer. The meadow had been scythed and the hedgerows were thick with blackberries. I just knew I had to write about it!

If you visit Mellis, you can also walk down the old drovers' lane or 'long green' which runs alongside the property – the lane that Roger Deakin fought passionately to preserve. I also highly recommend that you listen to 'Roger Deakin – A BBC Nature Collection' on audio book. This collection includes a truly wonderful 'sound tour' of the old house and grounds.

And you can visit the library in Castle Clare (Clare in Suffolk) which is more or less as I write about it in this book. Clare is a beautiful village and well worth a visit. I sometimes confuse myself, believing that the three bookshops and Well Bread, the bakery, really do exist there, and I half expect to see my characters walking its streets.

ACKNOWLEDGEMENTS

To the wonderful librarians who answered so many of my questions: Janet Bray, Karla Greenwood and Rachel Berry.

To Roy Connelly, Jane Dixon Smith, and Catriona Robb for the brilliant support in getting this book to publication.

And to my dear readers who have been waiting very patiently for the fifth Book Lovers novel!

ABOUT THE AUTHOR

Victoria Connelly is the bestselling author of *The Rose Girls* and *The Beauty of Broken Things*.

With over a million sales, her books have been translated into a dozen languages. The first, *Flights of Angels*, was made into a film in Germany. Victoria flew to Berlin to see it being made and even played a cameo role in it.

A Weekend with Mr Darcy, the first in her popular Austen Addicts series about fans of Jane Austen has sold over 100,000 copies. She is also the author of several romantic comedies including *The Runaway Actress* which was nominated for the Romantic Novelists' Association's Best Romantic Comedy of the Year.

Victoria was brought up in Norfolk, England before moving to Yorkshire where she got married in a medieval castle. After 11 years in London, she moved to rural Suffolk where she lives in a pink thatched cottage with her artist husband, a springer spaniel and her ex-battery hens.

To hear about future releases and receive a **free ebook** sign up for her newsletter at www.victoriaconnelly.com.

ALSO BY VICTORIA CONNELLY

The House in the Clouds Series

The House in the Clouds

High Blue Sky

The Colour of Summer

The Book Lovers Series

The Book Lovers

Rules for a Successful Book Club

Natural Born Readers

Scenes from a Country Bookshop

Christmas with the Book Lovers

Other Books

Family Portrait

The Way to the Sea

The Beauty of Broken Things

One Last Summer

The Heart of the Garden

Love in an English Garden

The Rose Girls

The Secret of You

Christmas at The Cove

Christmas at the Castle

Christmas at the Cottage

The Wrong Ghost

The Christmas Collection - Volumes One and Two

A Summer to Remember

Wish You Were Here

The Runaway Actress

Molly's Millions

Flights of Angels

Irresistible You

Three Graces

A Weekend with Mr Darcy

The Perfect Hero (Dreaming of Mr Darcy)

Mr Darcy Forever

Christmas With Mr Darcy

Happy Birthday Mr Darcy

At Home with Mr Darcy

Escape to Mulberry Cottage (non-fiction)

A Year at Mulberry Cottage (non-fiction)

Summer at Mulberry Cottage (non-fiction)

Finding Old Thatch (non-fiction)

The Garden at Old Thatch (non-fiction)

Introvert Abroad

VICTORIA CONNELLY

The House in the Clouds

Two strangers, one house, and a secret to be revealed.

Artist Abigail Carey has always dreamed of a life in the country and,
when Winfield Hall comes up at auction, she's desperate to make the
place her home. The only trouble is that businessman, Edward
Townsend, has exactly the same idea.

With its position high on the Sussex Downs, Winfield is a stunning
house, but it hasn't been a home for a long time and there's a lot of
work to do to restore it to its former glory. It's going to take a lot of
time and money, so Edward and Abi decide to take a risk and share
the house, each living in their own wing.

But can these two strangers agree on a vision that suits them both?
And will free-spirited Abi ever get the rather reserved Edward to
reveal the secret he's been hiding for so long?

www.ingramcontent.com/pod-product-compliance
Lightning Source LLC
Chambersburg PA
CBHW010020200726

48283CB00015B/3209